THE
HATERS

ALSO BY ROBYN HARDING

The Drowning Woman
The Perfect Family
The Swap
The Arrangement
Her Pretty Face
The Party

THE HATERS

ROBYN HARDING

GRAND
CENTRAL

New York Boston

Grand Central Publishing
Hachette Book Group
1290 Avenue of the Americas, New York, NY 10104
grandcentralpublishing.com
@grandcentralpub

First Edition: July 2024

Grand Central Publishing is a division of Hachette Book Group, Inc. The Grand Central Publishing name and logo is a registered trademark of Hachette Book Group, Inc.

The publisher is not responsible for websites (or their content) that are not owned by the publisher.

The Hachette Speakers Bureau provides a wide range of authors for speaking events. To find out more, go to hachettespeakersbureau.com or email HachetteSpeakers@hbgusa.com.

Grand Central Publishing books may be purchased in bulk for business, educational, or promotional use. For information, please contact your local bookseller or the Hachette Book Group Special Markets Department at special.markets@hbgusa.com.

Print interior design by Taylor Navis

Library of Congress Cataloging-in-Publication Data

Names: Harding, Robyn, author.
Title: The haters / Robyn Harding.
Description: First edition. | New York : Grand Central Publishing, 2024.
Identifiers: LCCN 2023051888 | ISBN 9781538766101 (hardcover) | ISBN 9781538766125 (ebook)
Subjects: LCGFT: Novels.
Classification: LCC PR9199.4.H366 H38 2024 | DDC 813/.6--dc23/eng /20231106
LC record available at https://lccn.loc.gov/2023051888

ISBNs: 9781538766101 (hardcover), 9781538769607 (Canadian edition), 9781538766125 (ebook)

Printed in Canada

MRQ

Printing 1, 2024

*For everyone with the courage to put their work—
and themselves—out into the world.*

THE
HATERS

Orchid Carder is poised to become the First Lady of Chicago. Her husband, Michael, has just announced his campaign for mayor and he's the clear front-runner: young, passionate, brilliant, and with a photogenic and altruistic wife on his arm. But Orchid has a secret that could destroy his ambitions. And their marriage. Because Orchid was once an entirely different person: Orchid was once a monster.

Pushed to the limits through neglect, poverty, and abuse, Orchid created an empire on the meanest streets of LA. Collecting damaged girls like coins, she polished them and then used them as currency: to steal, to scam, even to kill. Her gang became a family of sorts, a collective of lost girls who wouldn't survive on their own. And then, after a devastating tragedy, Orchid found the courage to claw her way out of the muck. She reclaimed a life of goodness and decency that morphed into one of privilege and opportunity. But will the past stay buried? Or will it resurface to destroy everything she has built?

With humanity and compassion, Camryn Lane traces the rise of a girl once driven to the unthinkable, and the young women who populate a dangerous world. *Burnt Orchid* is a story of struggle, redemption, and the desperate lengths people will go to in order to protect the ones they love.

1 THE LAUNCH

I LOCK THE BATHROOM door, hike up my gunmetal-gray skirt, and peel my Spanx down to my knees. I have exactly six minutes to pee before I'm due onstage. My bladder has always been nervous, and the two glasses of champagne I've downed in quick succession may have been a mistake. But the bubbles have softened my jangly nerves, made everything feel warm and smudgy and effervescent. This is a celebration, after all. I mustn't forget that.

I've never been comfortable being the center of attention. There were fourteen people at my wedding, including Adrian and me. My master's degree in counseling was marked by take-out Thai food and a six-pack of beer. And when I had Liza, I politely refused a baby shower, so my colleagues delivered onesies, teddy bears, and swaddling blankets to my windowless office, one by one. Twelve years later, my best friend, Martha, threw me a divorce party. She knew I'd never allow it, knew I thought it was gross to fete the demise of an eighteen-year union, no matter how unhappy we both were. I'd walked into the restaurant expecting a quiet dinner with my oldest friend, only to be surprised by thirty drunk women wearing pink feather boas and tiaras that spelled out DIVORCED AF. I'd had no choice but to go along with it: to drink the sugar-rimmed Pink Señoritas, to nibble on the penis-shaped cookies (why?), to dance the night away to the female empowerment playlist Martha had curated. The failure of my marriage was the biggest celebration of my life. Until now.

Wriggling my Spanx back into position, I hurry to the sink to wash my hands. My reflection stares back at me, smoldering and dramatic. Liza did my makeup, my *glam*, as she called it. At seventeen, my daughter has turned her obsession with YouTube tutorials into a career as a makeup artist, but I don't feel like myself with these smoky eyes, the contoured hollows in my cheeks, the nude glossy lips.

"You're famous now," Liza had teased when I'd expressed my discomfort. "Time to step up your game."

"I'm hardly famous," I'd said, but I couldn't help but smile. I felt proud and emotional. My first novel, *Burnt Orchid*, has been out in the world for two days. The manuscript I poured my soul into for almost three years now sits on bookstore shelves, and it's the achievement of my life. When I'd first gotten the publishing offer, it had felt like success, like winning the lottery or, more aptly, the Olympics. After years of dedication, toil, and perfecting my craft, it was the ultimate accomplishment. But now the book is real, available for readers to buy. Or not. This is the culmination of a journey, and the very beginning.

When I return to the narrow lounge with its dim lighting, eclectic décor, and retro soundtrack, the party is in full swing. Theo approaches with a flute of champagne. "How're you holding up?" His hand is warm and intimate on the curve of my back. We've been seeing each other for almost two years, but sometimes it still feels new, a little awkward. Like now. There are people at this event who have never met my boyfriend, and I know they'll be surprised. Theo is nine years younger than I am, though it's not readily noticeable. At thirty-five, he's rugged, athletic, outdoorsy—a typical West Coast guy. He owns a company that rents Jet Skis and paddleboards in the summer, snowmobiles and skis in the winter. Theo and his staff of exuberant Gen Z'ers offer guided tours, too. He's an odd choice for a human house cat like me, but somehow, we work. Still, I know how we appear: mismatched, like a hiking boot and a fluffy slipper. My ex, Adrian, and I bickered and sniped constantly, but we looked the part.

"I'm nervous," I admit, and Theo pulls me close, kisses the side of my head.

"Drink up," he suggests, and I take a tiny sip. There's a fine line between taking the edge off and slurring.

My bestie, Martha, hurries up to me, her eyes shiny and unfocused. She has no reason to curtail her free champagne intake, and she clearly hasn't. "Okay, babe, let's do this." She squeezes my free hand. "I'll introduce you and then I'll call you up onstage for the toast."

"Thanks." I squeeze her hand back. Martha had insisted on playing emcee. She loves the spotlight, I know this about her, but she also loves me. When I told her that a publisher had offered six figures for my debut novel (just barely six figures but still!), she'd reacted with a pure, unadulterated joy that almost matched my own. "I knew you could do it!" She'd wrapped me in a hug so tight my ribs ached. There was no envy. No resentment. No doubt that I was worthy. The same could not be said for some others in my orbit.

Martha turns to Theo. "Have you got the book?"

"Got it." He presents a copy of my novel, a bookmark slipped into the first chapter.

"I'll call Camryn up for the toast," Martha continues. "After that, you take her glass and hand her the book for the reading."

"Thanks, you two." I smile at them each in turn, my eyes glistening, a thickness in my throat.

"Oh my god, stop," Martha chides. "You're so emotional."

And I am. Because this is my dream realized. After years of rejection and false starts. After paying money I didn't have for workshops and courses. After being scammed by a fake agent; neglecting my daughter so I could write; doubting my talent, questioning my tenacity, and cursing my luck, I am a published writer. An author. It's a validation my soul has craved since I was a girl.

My best friend steps onto the small stage where a musician with a guitar plays cover tunes on the weekends. Theo and I sink into a darkened corner beside it. Martha moves to the mic, taps it. *Thunk, thunk.* "Thank you all for coming." The crowd quiets in response. "We're here tonight to celebrate the launch of my dear friend Camryn's first novel, *Burnt Orchid.*"

Applause. A few exuberant hoots. I dab at a tear that threatens my smoky eye. Looking out at the crowd of well-wishers, my heart swells. All these people have come out for me. To show their support and toast my achievement. I'd reached deep into the friend archives for this event. Martha said we needed to fill the room. And I want people to buy my book, of course. There are over fifty people filling the sticky little bar I've rented for the occasion, and I appreciate every one of them.

Closest to the stage is a cluster of my colleagues: three high school counselors, a handful of teachers, some of the admin staff. They work hard for mediocre pay at a school in a rough neighborhood. It's Thursday night, and tomorrow they'll have to wrangle angry, troubled, recalcitrant teens. But they're imbibing freely, nibbling the circulating canapés, happy for an excuse to blow off steam. To celebrate a co-worker rising out of the trenches. Partway out, anyway. I'm still working three days a week. For now.

Behind my co-workers is a mishmash of friends and acquaintances. Martha's husband, Felix, nurses a beer, eyes bright as he watches his gregarious partner of eight years. I note the gaggle of stay-at-home moms from Liza's private school (Adrian's parents insist and pay the fees), their clingy outfits skimming their yoga-toned bodies. They had all but dropped me when Adrian and I divorced. No one wants a single woman at their dinner party. What if she drinks too much and flirts with the husbands? What if they flirt with her? But when they heard my publishing news, they came out of the woodwork, my exile forgotten.

My college roommate is here, now an orthopedic surgeon with three sons in high school. I spy my hairdresser and her pals; a cluster of neighbors; a crew from the gym I never have time to go to. My publisher has invited some local salespeople, and a woman in a wrap-dress who works for the distributor. A few high school friends whisper among themselves, accustomed to Martha's rambling speeches.

At the back of the room, huddled together in a tight little knot, is my writers' group. There are five of us: Rhea, Marni, Spencer, Navid, and me...although Rhea isn't here tonight. A head cold, she said, though I have my doubts. Up until now, Rhea had been the most accomplished in our circle, publishing a few short stories and winning a prestigious but obscure literary award. I know my success is hard for her, for all of them. Because it would be for me. I remember the envy, the visceral longing to be recognized. This is what they are all striving for, the end goal of their years of work. They're all smiling but I see the strain in it.

My phone vibrates in my tiny purse: a notification. It will be one of my loved ones who couldn't make it tonight: my mom or my sister on the other side of the country; or Liza, stuck at her dad's place because she's too young to attend a party at a bar. Maybe it's my agent or my editor, wishing me luck tonight. Martha is still talking, moving on to our meeting in the eighth grade, and I realize this introduction might be longer than my reading. I set my flute on a table and pull out my phone.

It's an email, sent to my author account. I'd been encouraged by my publisher to set up a website, to include a "contact me" form. It feels fortuitous to receive my first fan mail moments before I take the stage. Eagerly, I tap to open the message.

INGRID WANDRY
RE: Burnt Orchid

I just finished reading your book and I enjoyed it, for a piece of mindless garbage. But when I read your bio that says you are a high school counselor, I was disgusted. Your novel has a prominent teen storyline, and you've obviously exploited the psyches and crises of your vulnerable public school students to make a few bucks. Shame on you. I hope their parents sue you.

Humiliation burns my cheeks, makes me feel dizzy and sick. I wobble in my heels as though this woman has reached out and slapped me. Theo cups my elbow to steady me.

"What's wrong?" he asks, but I can't talk. My mouth is dry and sour. I wasn't prepared for such hatred and vitriol. The ugliness of the words has rattled me, dredged up all my self-doubt and insecurities.

"Please raise your glass," Martha says, glancing into the wings. It's my cue. "To the success of *Burnt Orchid*. And our good friend Camryn Lane."

Blindly, I stumble onto the stage.

2 THE HANGOVER

I WAKE TO A dull pounding behind my eyebrows, my throat so dry it feels burnt. Fridays are now a day off, a day for drafting my next novel, though I already know I won't get any writing done. The champagne intake I'd so carefully monitored before my speech had been all but forgotten after it. Once the crowd thinned and only the diehards remained, the evening had devolved into debauchery. The yummy mummies had insisted on shots. My old roommate had taken to the stage to perform a raunchy dance solo. I'm not normally a big drinker, but I partied like I was in college. And now my forty-four-year-old body is paying for it.

A glass of cloudy water sits on my bedside table. (Theo, I assume? I have a foggy recollection of him pouring me into an Uber, helping me into the apartment, putting me to bed.) I reach for it, my mind drifting to the antics of the night as I gulp the tepid liquid. Despite my inherent discomfort with the spotlight, I'd relished it: the dancing, the laughter, the words of love, support, and admiration. I'd felt so happy, so *worthy*. And yet there is an ugly gray feeling pressing down on me, a malaise unrelated to alcohol's depressing effects. The email.

Those hateful, accusatory words snake their way into my memory. As a high school counselor, I'm no stranger to abuse. It's my job to break up fights, mediate vendettas, soothe disgruntled students angry at the world. I've been called horrible things to my face; I can only imagine what is said behind my back. But those insults came from a place of anger. Those kids were lashing out at an authority figure. The email is different.

The name is trapped in my mind like a wasp in amber: Ingrid Wandry. She's the woman who bought my book, sat down to read it, and assessed it as "mindless garbage." She has a right to her opinion, but why did she want me to know it? Maybe it never occurred to her that most writers are highly sensitive beings, and that attacking their book is like a physical blow. Perhaps she thinks AI robots devoid of feelings have already taken over. Or did she *want* to hurt me? Sending a disparaging email directly to a writer seems so extreme, so unnecessarily mean. Who does that?

Shaking off the memory, I drag myself out of bed and into the attached bathroom. My reflection is nothing short of monstrous, the remnants of Liza's makeup smeared and garish. I wash my face, brush the fuzz off my teeth, and run a brush through my hair. Wrapping my robe around me, I move into the apartment. My place is "cozy" (in Realtor speak) but adequate for me—and Liza, every other week. It's on the third floor, at the back of a squat building, a corner unit with windows on two sides. I bought it for the light that filters in through the trees, the leaves that tickle the glass in spring and summer making me feel like I live in a tree house. It was also the only place I could afford that was within walking distance of Adrian's house. If Liza must grow up in two homes, we want them to be close together.

In the open kitchen, I find a cold pot of coffee, more evidence that Theo was here, that he spent the night, that he left early for work. Turning the machine back on, I spy my tiny purse discarded on the counter and dig my phone out of it. I have several congratulatory texts from family and friends who couldn't attend last night's celebrations, including one from my agent, Holly.

How was the party?!?!?

Holly and I have become friends over the past two years. After she signed me, we spent several months editing my manuscript, getting it ready for submission. When it sold to a big five publisher, I flew to New York to meet the team and Holly and I had lunch with my editor. That night, Holly took me to a quaint Italian restaurant in the West Village where we talked long into the night over red wine and espressos. My agent is younger than I am, she doesn't have kids, and she lives in Manhattan, the center of the economic universe. (Vancouver, in contrast, is known for its exceptionally laid-back lifestyle and high marijuana use.) But we're both divorced, both dating men with whom we have little in common (her boyfriend owns a butcher shop), and we share a dark sense of humor. Sometimes I wonder if our relationship is unprofessional— the gossip, the snarky jokes, the inappropriate conversations about Jason Momoa—but I can't deny I enjoy it.

Amazing, I text back. So hungover.

My phone rings in my hand, Holly's name on the call display.

"Hey, party animal," she teases when I answer. "How was it?"

"I had a great time," I tell her, rummaging in the freezer for a loaf of bread. Toast might help this queasy stomach. "A ton of people came out to celebrate. I felt really supported."

"How many books did you sell?" Despite our friendship, Holly is an agent, a New Yorker.

"I think about fifty? I'll check with the bookseller."

"Great. Every sale counts."

"I got an email from a reader…" I begin, closing the freezer door, but I trail off. I feel awkward, even ashamed. I know there's no truth to Ingrid Wandry's accusation, but what if Holly doubts me? What if the allegation plants a seed of suspicion?

"That's a good sign," Holly says. "It means readers are engaging with the book."

"It wasn't good," I admit, removing a slice of bread from the bag. "It was horrible. This reader accused me of stealing stories from the students I counsel."

"People are crazy." Holly dismisses it. "Unfortunately, when you put your work out into the world, not everyone is going to love it."

"This was more than not loving it. This was a serious accusation." I drop the bread into the toaster. "Do I respond? Or should I ignore it?"

"I'd say ignore it, but that's a question for your PR person."

My PR rep, Olivia Lopez, is calm, confident, and capable. She will know how to handle Ingrid Wandry appropriately, but my stomach dips at the thought of bringing this issue to her. As a debut author, I want to be *easy*. I want to bring positivity, not problems and negative feedback. I want her to spend her time promoting my book, not troubleshooting my issues.

"Right," I tell Holly. "I'll talk to Olivia."

"Don't let it bother you," Holly says. "Readers are going to love this book. And the next one."

The pressure is subtle but there. My publisher has first right of refusal on the next book I write, and Holly hopes they'll make an offer based on an outline and a few sample chapters. Unfortunately, between promoting *Burnt Orchid*, my day job, my daughter, and this hangover, I haven't made much progress.

"I'm on it," I assure her, and we say our goodbyes.

With buttered toast and reheated coffee, I sit at the small round dining table and scroll through my phone. I respond to texts from my mom, my sister, and a dear friend down with the flu. Next, I sift through emails from charities I support, clothing sales I might be interested in, petitions related to others I've signed in the past, searching for anything work-related. There is one from my publicist, Olivia, confirming a Zoom interview with a library in Cleveland. And below it is the email from Ingrid Wandry.

I open it, hoping that in the cold light of day, the message won't seem so horrible. My launch party was a heightened environment. Perhaps I'd taken Ingrid's words the wrong way? But as I reread the missive, it is just as biting, just as critical as it was last night. My cheeks feel hot and the burnt coffee churns in my stomach. Is Ingrid "crazy" as Holly suggested? Or could she have a point? Had I subconsciously usurped my students' angst for my own gains?

My character, Orchid Carder, was abused and abandoned. She went to juvenile detention for stabbing a man to death. She became a grifter, a criminal, a master manipulator. The young women in my novel are addicted to hard drugs, suffer sexual and police violence, are caught in the cycle of poverty and crime. My students have very real struggles that are not to be diminished, but they are simply not at that level.

Maple Heights Secondary School serves grades eight to twelve. It has an innovative counseling program that allows each counselor to work with the same kids for all five years. They come to me wide-eyed and nervous, and I support them through their academic, social, and behavioral progression. I've counseled my students through bullying, eating disorders, parental divorces, STDs, gender dysphoria, racism, drug use, shoplifting, and more...Had any of their experiences seeped into my work?

I hadn't told the kids that I was publishing a novel. The entire mandate of my job is to focus on their needs, not talk about myself. And even after five years with the same students, they show remarkably little interest in me as a person. But our principal, Nancy, felt the need to make an announcement.

"We have a Shakespeare in our midst!" Nancy crowed over the

intercom that morning. I knew she was talking about me even though Shakespeare was not a novelist (no one cares). "Please congratulate Ms. Lane on her new novel, *Burnt Orchid*. And tell all your parents to buy a copy."

A handful of teens (all enriched English students, but one) had stopped by the counseling suite to congratulate me, but most of the school seemed uninterested. Would any of the kids tell their parents to buy my book? And if their parents did, would they recognize their children's problems in its pages? Is it only a matter of time before they come after me with pitchforks and torches?

No, it's not. Because I've done nothing wrong. I've betrayed no trust, invaded no one's privacy. I care about these young people, and I would never exploit them, even unconsciously. In fact, I'd purposely steered my story away from any real experiences, anything remotely recognizable. Ingrid Wandry doesn't know me or my students, and she has no right to make assumptions, to judge and accuse me. She is a bitter, miserable, angry loser with no friends (a safe assumption given that her Thursday-night hobby is blasting writers for imagined offenses). I have just published my first novel. It's a huge achievement. I'm not going to let the words of a troll bring me down.

"Goodbye, Ingrid," I say into the empty apartment. With a swipe of my finger, I archive the email. Then I down my coffee and head to the shower.

3 THE SIGNING

THE BIG-BOX BOOKSTORE is bustling with weekend shoppers lazily browsing the shelves: new releases, bestsellers, Spicy Book-Tok...I meander through the displays feeling vulnerable and exposed, like I'm walking around naked among the customers. No one will recognize me, of course. But my words, my story, my heart is on the shelf, available for any of them to pick up, peruse, purchase, or dismiss. I'm scared to see *Burnt Orchid* sitting there, ignored. I'm scared to see it *not* sitting there, forgotten in a warehouse or lost on a truck somewhere. But I am here on a mission. Ignoring my discomfort, I make a beeline for customer service.

My publisher had recommended I sign local stock. This is the eighth bookstore I've visited this weekend. Yesterday, I covered the suburbs; today, I'm tackling the city. Like the neighborhood it occupies, this location is posh and upscale. In addition to books, they offer a well-curated selection of high-end home wares: blankets, pillows, framed prints, glassware...I join the queue of attractive shoppers who mostly seem to be buying scented candles or fuzzy reading socks.

"Hi." I smile brightly as I approach the young woman behind the counter. "My name's Camryn Lane. I'm here to sign copies of *Burnt Orchid.*"

She stares at me blankly, like I've just spoken to her in Romanian.

"I think my publicist called your manager," I elaborate, aware of curious eyes on us. "My book just came out on Tuesday."

"Umm..." She continues to look befuddled. "Let me call Britt. Can you stand off to the side so I can serve the customers waiting to buy things?"

I try not to feel like I'm in the naughty corner as I wait for Britt. Customers give me the side-eye as they pay, wondering if I'm someone they should know, or if I'm a strangely obedient shoplifter waiting to be scolded by the manager. All of the bookstores had been welcoming, some even excited by my presence. Here, I feel like a nuisance.

The tiny woman marching toward me in a white blouse, black trousers, and a shock of red lipstick has *frazzled manager* written all over her. But she smiles when she sees me.

"I'm Britt." Her handshake is firm. "I loved *Burnt Orchid*. Really compelling."

"Thank you so much."

"We've got you set up back here," she says, leading me away from the line of curious customers. "I hope you'll have a decent turnout."

"Turnout?"

Britt indicates a five-foot-long table stacked with copies of my book, and a bold sign on a metal stand.

AUTHOR SIGNING
CAMRYN LANE, AUTHOR OF *BURNT ORCHID*
TODAY, 2:00 TO 4:00

My heart flutters with nerves. "I didn't realize this was an actual *signing* signing. I thought I was just signing stock."

"Since you're local, we wanted you to do an in-person signing. Didn't your publicist tell you?"

"Umm...no. There must have been a miscommunication."

"We put it on our socials and took an ad out in the local paper." Britt's tone is slightly annoyed. "We'd hoped you and your publisher would share it on your channels."

"I can post something now." I force a smile, but I know it won't help. My social media presence is pathetic. Because I work with teens, I'd always eschewed the platforms, preferring to maintain my privacy. Recently, I set up author accounts on Instagram, Facebook, and Twitter. To date, I've collected about a thousand combined followers. Many live in other cities, other countries, and some, I suspect, are not even real people. The ones who do live here probably attended my launch party and bought a signed book there. There's a limit to their generosity.

"Please do," Britt retorts. "Hopefully *someone* will show up." And with that, she turns on her heel and hurries away.

I take a seat behind the table. Holding my book close to my face, I snap a selfie. My smile is bright, confident, and enthusiastic, but there is desperation in my eyes. *Come on down and get a signed copy of Burnt Orchid!* I type. *I'd really love to see you! Please!* I delete the *really* and the *please*—too needy—before posting. And then I sit, for an hour and ten minutes, hungry, thirsty, and needing to pee.

It's an interesting experiment in human behavior. Some customers look me over like I'm an exotic monkey in a cage. Others avoid eye contact lest I pounce on them and beg them to buy my book. They're not impressed by my achievement; they pity my desperation. Finally, an older white man in expensive athleisure walks up to the table, picks up a copy of *Burnt Orchid*. Hope buoys my heart.

"You wrote this?" he asks.

"I did," I say cheerily. "It's my first published novel."

"Good for you." He flips it over and reads the back blurb. "Not my cup of tea but hopefully someone will buy it." He sets the book back on the pile. "It must be humiliating for you just sitting here."

"It is," I mutter as he walks away, likely looking for a puppy to kick.

I am checking the time on my phone—twelve minutes until I can slink out of here—when I sense someone approaching. A woman is walking purposefully toward me, her face set in a scowl. She's about fifty, blond, with designer glasses and a pricey bag. I smile at her, but her expression doesn't change. In fact, it darkens, the scowl morphing into a glare. My stomach drops as a possibility hits. Could this woman be Ingrid Wandry of the nasty email?

Why hadn't I googled her? I'd been too busy (and too hungover) to bother. And it had seemed sage to erase the email, wipe the slate clean, put the ugliness behind me. But now I regret not investigating my troll, because I have no idea where Ingrid lives or what she looks like. Could she be local? Could she have seen the ad for this signing and decided to come see me? To tell me, in person, how much she hates my book? How vile I am for exploiting my students? Is she going to make an embarrassing scene, or worse? What if she's unhinged? Dangerous?

The woman is upon me now, frown firmly affixed. "Hi..." I squeak, voice tight with dread.

Her face softens, a hint of a smile. "Do you know where the bathroom is? It's kind of urgent."

At least she's not here to murder me. "I think it's over there." I point to a corner behind me, and the woman scurries away.

As I walk to my 2017 Mazda, a dent in its bumper from one of Liza's driving lessons, I feel exhausted and low. Two books. That's all I signed in two whole hours—one to a former colleague who couldn't make it to my launch party, one to an older woman who thought it would make a nice gift for her niece. Who do I think

I am, Jodi Picoult? Why would I think my signature would add value to a book? Wait a minute... *I* never thought that. This was Britt's idea. Did my publicist, Olivia, even know about this event? I wonder if these signings usually work out better for other writers, if I am the lone author on their roster who can't draw a crowd.

Climbing into the front seat of my car, I start the engine. I will go home, have a bite to eat, and then draw a bath. This negative sensation will dissipate before long, and I'll remember that it's a privilege to have a book out in the world. And while the signing was a failure, at least it made one thing clear...

Ingrid Wandry is not close enough, able enough, or angry enough to confront me in person.

BURNT ORCHID

1995

A survey had been done—by a church or a women's center or some other do-gooder organization. The outreach workers had asked one hundred women living on LA's skid row if they had ever experienced sexual violence. They all said yes. Every single one of them. Orchid and her friends had laughed at the waste of resources when the results were so utterly predictable. They also saw the irony in their circumstance, whether they used that term or not. It was sexual violence that had put so many of them there in the first place. In Orchid's case, it had been the catalyst for a series of decisions that had catapulted her from the shelter of her mother's home to this single piece of cardboard on the baking sidewalk, surrounded by the most damaged people alive.

Orchid was just fourteen when her mom's boyfriend first touched her. At first, it had seemed accidental, his hand grazing her bare thigh as she moved toward the toaster, still wearing the oversized T-shirt and boxer shorts she slept in. His expression had remained blank, innocuous, as he drank his cup of coffee, eyes scanning the sports section of the paper. Trevor was hard to read, like a dog that wags its tail while it bares its teeth. And her mother was right there, having a smoke at the kitchen table. Would he be so brazen?

The second time, there was no mistaking his intent. Orchid should have screamed or hit him, but she'd frozen, her conscious mind drifting away, her body numb to the hand fumbling inside her panties. Her fight-or-flight response was broken, she determined. Much later, she'd learn about survival mode, her psyche turning off the negative stimuli to ensure her endurance, but at the time she'd felt weak. She'd felt like a coward.

When Trevor touched her the third time, pushing her up against the wall, kissing her with his disgusting mouth, his hand forcing its way inside her, she knew it was imminent. Soon he would come to her room, while her mother was asleep or at work or passed out on the sofa after too many whiskey-and-Cokes, and he would rape her.

So she told her mom. Lorna Chambers was a brittle woman, hollow like a cave in the sea. Disappointment, disillusionment, and betrayal had carved a hole in her center where her compassion had once lived. She sucked on her cigarette, watery eyes roaming over Orchid's young body. "What the fuck are you wearing?"

It was late July. They lived in the valley without air-conditioning. Their apartment was above a chicken shop that added at least ten degrees to the internal temperature. Her mom took in Orchid's thin tank top, the shorts she'd worn since she was twelve that were undeniably too small now, and her shriveled mouth twisted with hate. It was not a question: It was an accusation.

No one spoke. The smoke curled up between them, like the ghost of something that should have been, that never would be. And then her mom tapped her cigarette on the edge of the full ashtray, touched a piece of tobacco off her tongue, and Orchid walked away.

That night, Orchid took the butcher knife from the kitchen and slept with it under her pillow. And when Trevor came, as she knew he would, she plunged it into his belly.

4 THE DEVIL

THE SEVENTEEN-YEAR-OLD GIRL seated across from me has baby-blond hair, a pretty face, and wide innocent eyes. She has excellent grades, volunteers on the yearbook committee, and played varsity volleyball until a wrist injury sidelined her last year. She is popular with her peers, charming and polite to adults, and was awarded an "all-around student" at the last year-end assembly. But I'm not fooled. I've known this girl for five years, her name is Fiona Carmichael, and she is pure evil.

When I was studying to become a counselor, there was an emphasis on understanding behavioral issues. Most challenges stem from some form of trauma: physical, emotional, or psychological. In the program, we learned that adolescents have reasons to push boundaries, to try on different personas, to rebel against expected norms. But every now and then, I encounter a bad seed. Fiona seems to come from a stable home with two loving and supportive parents. And yet this bright, attractive girl in her designer sweatshirt is poison.

"Who took the video of Abby?" I ask. I know Fiona won't tell me. There is honor among bullies. But I have seen the offending footage with my own eyes. Last term, Maple Heights implemented an online reporting tool where students can send an encrypted, anonymous message to the school regarding concerning incidents or behaviors. This "snitch tool," as we affectionately call it, is popular in the Australian school system. The administrators (three vice principals) have received reports of bullying, sexual assault, self-harm, and threats of violence. As a counselor, I have been brought in to provide intervention and support. The portal allows screenshots or images to validate the claims. That's how I learned about the video of Abby Lester.

"I don't know, Ms. Lane." Fiona's voice is childlike. "I don't really remember what happened."

"But you must know who sent the video to you?"

She looks at her hands in her lap. "It was from a fake account. I really don't know who it was from."

We are seated in my tiny office, so close together that I can smell Fiona's perfume, see the flick of her eyeliner, hear the smack of her gum. Her eyes drift over the three framed prints on my wall, muted watercolor landscapes. My décor is simple and impersonal. I keep a photo of Liza in my drawer but not on my desk. The students here don't need to know I have a daughter their age.

"But you decided to share the video on social media," I press.

"I know I shouldn't have. I just...I thought it was funny at first."

Funny. Abby Lester had taken multiple capsules of MDMA, between three and seven, according to her so-called friends. They'd been at a sleepover party in Abby's basement, three girls in attendance. She had ended up naked, vomiting, and convulsing. No one woke her parents. No one called for help. Instead, they laughed. They filmed her. And Fiona Carmichael uploaded it to Snapchat.

"I thought Abby was your friend?"

"Not really. I mean, she's okay, but I don't know her that well."

"So that excuses what you did to her?" My tone is harsher than it should be. I'm not here to punish this girl. Monica Carruthers, the vice principal, will take care of that. My job is to understand what went on, and to offer my counsel. I soften my voice. "Tell me about that night. Who was there?"

"Abby invited me, Lily, and Mysha. But some other kids sneaked in later."

"Who?"

"I don't really remember."

Yeah, right. "Was everyone taking Molly?"

"Yeah."

"Where did you get it?"

Fiona shrugs, like I knew she would. "It's all kind of fuzzy."

"Why did Abby take so many pills? Did someone pressure her?"

"No." Fiona looks up, her eyes clear and blue. "I think she was trying to impress us. Abby was kind of desperate to get in with our friend group."

Sadly, it rings true. Abby is a STEM kid, a founding member of the robotics club. Fiona and her posse are solid students, but they're more focused on their social than academic lives. And it's not the first time I've seen kids overdose trying to keep up with more experienced peers. "And no one thought to tell her to slow down? That she didn't have to impress you?"

"Like I said, we didn't really know her. It's not our fault we didn't know her tolerance levels."

Abby Lester can't remember what happened that night, her memory wiped clean by the drugs and the trauma, and I'm getting nowhere with Fiona. She knows more than she's telling, I'm sure of it, but the space between my eyebrows is starting to pound. "You can go see Ms. Carruthers now."

Fiona gets up, and I turn back to my desk. There's a bottle of Tylenol in my top drawer for these types of encounters.

"I read your book." The girl hovers in the doorway. "It was really good."

23

She's in trouble so she's trying to flatter me. And it works. I smile. "Thank you, Fiona."

"You know a lot about kids and their problems." Her perfectly shaped eyebrow arches. "That's probably why your book was so real."

Is there an accusation in her words? Or am I just defensive after that attacking email?

"My background in psychology was helpful," I say.

"And working with all of us must have helped, too. Kids tell you such private things."

"My book is fiction," I retort. "It has nothing to do with any of my students."

"Of course not." Those wide innocent eyes...

"Ms. Carruthers is waiting for you."

Before the door closes, I'm already reaching for the bottle of pills.

When I let myself into the apartment that night, there's still a dull ache in my temples. A tinkle of laughter travels from the far end of the apartment, and my heart swells. It's my week with Liza, and her presence is like a warm bath. My daughter has gone through the typical teenage phases: sullen, rebellious, angry, and superior. But over the past year, she's matured, grown into a kind and warm young woman. And she's been my biggest cheerleader through my publishing journey. In just two months, Liza will graduate, leave for college soon after, and the thought makes me want to curl into a ball and cry. But I know my daughter is going to soar. And I'm grateful I have my new career to focus on.

"Hey, Mom." She swishes into the room wearing huge gray sweatpants and a short T-shirt revealing her pierced belly button. "How was your day?"

"I need a hug." I hold out my arms and my girl steps into them. Her honey-colored hair smells like vanilla, her neck like the lavender soap she uses. She is taller than I am by three inches with her father's strong, lithe build, but her smile and her gray eyes are mine.

"What happened?" Liza asks.

I give her a playful squeeze. "You know I can't tell you what goes on at the school."

"Worth a try," she teases, stepping away.

I'm suddenly aware of a presence behind us. "Oh. Hi, Wyatt."

"Hi, Camryn."

Liza has been dating Wyatt since the end of eleventh grade. He's a nice kid, quiet but well mannered, if a little directionless. While Liza was accepted to several colleges and chose a prestigious university across the country, Wyatt is planning to take a gap year. He's very bright and got a full-ride academic scholarship to an elite private high school. He could have his choice of colleges, but he says he needs to decompress after the rigors of twelfth grade. He's planning to spend a few months on the beaches of Queensland.

"I didn't realize you were here." My tone is pointed as I turn to face my daughter. The pair was obviously in her bedroom, and that is against the rules when I'm not home. At least it is at my place. Things are very different at Adrian's house. His new wife, Tori, is a "cool mom." Her daughter, Savannah, is seventeen, and has been dating her girlfriend for about six months. They're allowed regular sleepovers, and Adrian and Tori recently brought the young couple to Hawaii where they booked them their own room. In contrast, my parenting style is delay, delay, delay. I believe there are no decisions—about sex, substances, romantic relationships—that won't benefit from more brain development.

"Relax, Mom." Liza's eye roll is subtle, good-natured even. "Wyatt just came by to go over some stats problems."

"I have to go," he says. "I've got practice." Wyatt is tall and athletic, a competitive soccer player.

"I'll walk you out," Liza offers. She prefers to kiss him goodbye in the hall, away from my prying eyes. I prefer it, too.

"I'll order sushi," I call after her. "Bye, Wyatt."

"Bye, Camryn." The door closes behind them.

5 THE RITUAL

SINCE MY NOVEL came out, I've developed an early-morning routine. I get up, move to the sunniest corner of my apartment, and do some slow, deliberate stretches. Closing my eyes, I inhale positivity, calm acceptance, and gratitude. Except I usually skip this part. More often, I stumble out of bed, pour a cup of coffee, and head to my tiny home office / converted storage closet. I turn on my laptop and check my online reviews. This can sometimes be a disheartening way to start the day, but it's become a ritual...even an addiction.

This morning, I find two new reviews on the popular review site Readem.

★★★★★
Thrilling and Heartbreaking

Burnt Orchid is amazing! It's about a woman who has it all, but the secrets of her past threaten to destroy everything. Camryn Lane has created an intriguing and conflicting character in Orchid Carder. At times, I didn't know if I should root for her or hate her, but she was always interesting. The flashbacks to Orchid's life on the streets were both terrifying and heartbreaking. She was driven to do unthinkable things...

I should devour this praise, but something has caught my eye. Beneath this glowing review, I see the next.

★

What the actual fuck?

A sick feeling clogs my throat. I know I should stop here, go back to the positive accolades. This disparaging review will upset me, shake my confidence, even impact my creativity. Today is a dedicated writing day, devoted to working on my next book idea, and I can't afford to waste any more time. So why can't I tear my eyes away from the brutal words?

My author friend Jody assures me that my skin will eventually thicken to the criticism. She's published twelve romance novels and can now read these critiques dispassionately. "They still sting," she'd said, "but it's not that bad. More like a bug bite now...Maybe a nip from a small terrier." I'm still at shark bite pain levels, and yet, like a masochist, I begin to read.

> This is not the worst book I have ever read. In fact, I found it mildly entertaining. The writing is sophomoric, and the characters are mostly clichés, but it's not terrible. What *is* terrible is the way this author exploits the very real problems of young adults for entertainment value, the young adults she supposedly helps at her job as a HIGH SCHOOL COUNSELOR! It's disgusting that Camryn Lane was so desperate for money, attention, and validation that she exposed the secrets of her vulnerable students. If she was a talented writer, she could have written a novel on any topic, but she chose to write about troubled teenagers. There's writing what you know, and then there's exploitation. If Camryn Lane doesn't face consequences (like losing her job, getting sued by the

parents of her students, or having the kids take matters into their own hands), karma will surely get her. Please consider boycotting this book and/or leaving a one-star review.

Acid burns my throat and I feel nauseous. The public nature of the forum makes the accusation even more mortifying, and others are starting to weigh in. There are already four comments below the review. Against my better judgment, I click.

Disgusting. Thanks for the heads up. I'll definitely give this one a miss.

Camryn Lane is no better than a child abuser, using and exploiting the young people in her care.

CANCEL CAMRYN LANE!

I heard this book was great. Too bad I won't be reading it now.

Returning to the review, I look at the reviewer's name for the first time. They have provided only initials.

I.W.

Ingrid Wandry. It has to be her. This woman, this total stranger, is trying to destroy me. But why? I swallow down the sob building in my chest and reach for my phone. Theo answers on the second ring. "Pacific Adventures?"

"It's me," I say, voice wobbling. "Sorry to bother you at work…"

"It's fine. Are you okay?"

His concern undoes me, and the tears burst forth. Through

jagged breaths, I tell him about the online accusations and the one-star review. "It's Ingrid Wandry," I blubber. "She's trying to ruin my book. She's trying to ruin my entire writing career!"

"Babe, you know you shouldn't read those reviews."

"How can I not?" I cry. "It's human nature. You look at Tripadvisor, don't you? You look at Yelp."

"I know, I know." His voice is gentle. "But you know you did nothing wrong. You'd never exploit your students. So you can't let the words of some angry troll bother you."

"She's so mean," I snivel. "Why does she hate me so much?"

"Jealous," he says. "You've accomplished something amazing and she's obviously an unfulfilled loser. Why else would she spend her time attacking people online?"

"I guess."

"Do you need me to come over?" Theo offers. "I can take a break."

"It's fine. I know you're busy."

"I don't mind." He lowers his voice. "I miss you."

Theo doesn't sleep over when Liza is home. Since I won't let her share her bed with Wyatt, I need to set an example. I know what Theo's suggesting, and I could not be less in the mood.

"I'll be fine," I say, a little annoyed that he can think about sex at a time like this. "I should get to work."

"Okay, babe." His voice is breezy, casual. "Chin up."

"I'll try."

I hang up, feeling just as forlorn. Theo doesn't get it. How could he? As a business owner, he's susceptible to online vitriol, but to my knowledge Theo's never received such a personal attack. Only another writer can understand this public humiliation, only someone who's been through it.

Hurriedly, I place another call.

6 THE COUNSEL

FIRST MET JANINE Kang when our daughters were in second grade. Everyone knew her; she'd been host of the city's most popular six o'clock newscast for several years. Many of the parents found her intimidating with her sleek style, her unflinching eye contact, and her measured delivery. But when Liza and Grace chose each other as besties, Janine and I were thrown together. I discovered a wise, warm, and darkly funny woman underneath the polished persona.

"Haters are part of the deal when you put yourself in the public eye," Janine assures me over peppermint tea at a homey coffee shop equidistant from our homes. While I live in a mixed-income neighborhood, a blend of low-rise apartments and modest but expensive family dwellings, Janine lives waterfront. Her home is narrow, modern, and stylish (not unlike her and her real estate developer husband), with breathtaking views of the city, the mountains, and the towering evergreens of Stanley Park. It is accessed by a private road closed off to traffic. The busy thoroughfare was shut down by a former mayor who proclaimed it a bike lane, but everyone in town considers it a gift to the multimillionaires who live along it and donated to his campaign.

"I've been putting up with email attacks and negative comments for years," Janine continues, her unique emerald ring sparkling as she picks up her tea. "Unfortunately, it comes with the territory these days. Especially for women, LGBTQ, and BIPOC journalists."

"I don't get it." My fingers are warm on my mug. "What is wrong with people these days?"

"In my case, it's usually about an imagined political agenda. We live in tense, polarized times." She sips her drink. "What happened with *Burnt Orchid*?"

My face is warm as I tell Janine about Ingrid Wandry's claims that I'm exploiting my students. "I know not everyone will love my book and that's totally fair. But the accusations this woman is making are dangerous. To my writing career and to my job as a counselor."

"You have to ignore them. It's your only option."

"Could I set the record straight, at least? Leave a comment explaining that I'm a trained professional and I would never, ever invade my students' privacy?"

"Don't engage." Janine sets her cup down. "I know it's tempting, but these people can be dangerous. Trust me."

My stomach twists. "Dangerous? How do you mean?"

Janine inhales, sits back in her chair. "Early in my career, I was working as reporter in Montreal. I started getting hateful emails from this guy who didn't like what I was saying on the air. I tried to reason with him, to make him understand that I was doing my duty as a journalist. It didn't go well."

"I'm so sorry, Janine." My voice is gentle. "What happened?"

"This guy bombarded me with misogynistic, racist emails. Up to a hundred a day," she elaborates. "Then he Photoshopped my head onto a bunch of pornographic images. He sent them to my parents, my bosses, everyone..."

"Oh my god! That's horrific."

"It got worse. He came after Grace. She was just a baby. He said he'd grab her from daycare. Said he'd *free her from my lies*. That's when I went to the police."

"Did they arrest him?"

"They did. We went to court. And he got a slap on the wrist." Her eyes fill but her voice is strong. "The judge agreed that what this man did to me was vile and abusive. But our laws don't take online stalking seriously. He got probation. And an order not to contact me."

"That's so awful." I reach for her hand. "I had no idea you went through something so traumatic."

"It was honestly the worst time in my life." She composes herself quickly, a consummate professional. "You need to be careful with the haters, Camryn. You don't know who's behind the keyboard."

A frisson runs through me at the thought. This could be worse than I even imagined. "Good advice. Thanks."

Janine reaches for her phone in her five-thousand-dollar bag. "Let me look at this review." I give her the web address and she taps at her screen, waits for it to load. Her face falls when she sees it. "Oh shit."

"What?" My stomach drops.

She turns her phone to face me, and I peer at the tiny type. There are now at least thirty one-star reviews.

When I get home, I call my publicist, my chest tight with panic. Janine had done her best to console me. "You have a strong, experienced team behind you. They'll know how to handle this." But so had she, and her online assault had turned into the stuff of nightmares.

Olivia answers on the third ring. "I'm glad you called," she says. "I wanted to apologize for the miscommunication about the in-person book signing. Britt Marsters set that up with a publicist who is no longer working here. I'm so sorry."

"It was fine," I say, the unpleasantness of the experience now a distant memory. "But there's something else. I don't know if you've looked at my online reviews lately..."

"No, I haven't. Why?"

I tell Olivia about Ingrid Wandry, about her accusations in my inbox and online. I tell my publicist that the sentiment seems to be contagious, that more reviewers have been giving the book a one-star rating.

Down the line, I hear Olivia's fingers tapping on her keyboard. "I see," she mumbles as she scans the page. "But you have a lot of positive reviews. A few one-star reviews won't have a huge impact on your overall rating."

"I'm more concerned about the false accusations."

"Let me look into it," she says calmly. "I'll check the review guidelines. We might be able to have them removed."

"It's on other sites, too." My voice wobbles. "It's everywhere."

"Okay," she says gently. "Stay offline for now. Try not to worry about it."

"Easier said than done," I mumble, feeling (and sounding) pitiful.

"I have some good news that might help," Olivia offers. "You've been invited to a book festival in Miami."

"Oh my god!" My spirits instantly lift. This will be my first-ever book festival. I've heard about the fancy hotels, the hospitality suites, the schmoozing with bestselling authors. This will also be my first time in Miami. It's all so glamorous.

"It's a new festival celebrating page-turning fiction," Olivia continues. While writers' festivals have traditionally been the purview of literary works, they've moved to include more plot-driven, commercially successful books. Lucky for me.

"It's a great lineup of authors," Olivia continues. "They want you to be on a panel. They'll provide flights and accommodations. I'll send the invitation through to you on email."

"Thank you, Olivia."

"Congratulations. We're really thrilled with the positive buzz *Burnt Orchid* is getting, and early sales numbers are strong."

I hang up, my despair nearly forgotten. The online mob will lose interest in me, move on to the next target (poor soul). All that matters is that my publisher is thrilled. The buzz is positive. Sales are strong. And I'm going to Miami.

I will cling to that.

7 DUE DILIGENCE

AND SO I make a pact with myself. I won't look at any online reviews until Olivia advises me that it is safe to do so. In fact, I will limit all social media until I feel stronger and more confident. Like any addiction, I know this will be difficult. It will require lifestyle changes, the removal of temptation and triggers, but my mental health and productivity are more important. I have an outline to write, a demanding day job, and a daughter to parent through the final months of high school. So I will remove myself from the virtual world...right after I research Ingrid Wandry.

Who is this woman and why does she spend her time attacking strangers online? It would be easy to assume that she's miserable, angry, and resentful. Perhaps she's a frustrated writer herself, jealous of those who've managed to nab a publishing deal in a difficult industry. Maybe knocking us down makes her feel validated, even powerful. Or maybe Ingrid Wandry had a painful adolescence, and the subject matter of my book triggered memories that caused her to lash out.

But I also know the human capacity for cruelty, and how anonymity increases the desire to hurt others. In my master's program, we learned about a Stanford study dating back to the sixties.

Female students were dressed in plain lab coats, some with hoods that concealed their identity, some with no hoods and name tags. They were then instructed to give other students electric shocks. Those with the hoods were twice as likely to comply. It provided a disturbing glimpse into the human psyche that did not bode well for the faceless internet age.

I dig up Ingrid's email from my archives and check the address. Ingrid.Wandry@proton.me

A quick search informs me that Proton Mail is another email service like Gmail or Hotmail, but with enhanced privacy. So it's not Ingrid's workplace. It's not surprising that trolls don't harass people from the office. I click over to Ingrid Wandry's profile on Readem.

I.W.

No photo, no cute avatar, only the blank gray silhouette of a generic reader. She has chosen to provide very little information.

Details: Female, United States
About me: Love good books. Hate bad ones.

"And you're qualified to judge?" I grumble into the silence of my cramped home office. I grab my mug of milky tea and take a sip, looking at the date she joined the forum. It was less than a month ago. Did Ingrid create an account just to roast *Burnt Orchid*? She has only rated three other books, all of them classics.

The Great Gatsby ★★★★★
Wuthering Heights ★★★★
Great Expectations ★★

The fact that Dickens only got two stars should console me, but it doesn't. Ingrid didn't provide Charles the scathing public denunciation she did me. Why would she bother? Charles is dead. She can't crush his spirit.

Picking up my phone, I go to Instagram and type in Ingrid's name. There is only one profile.

Ingrid Wandry

4	82	220
Posts	Followers	Following

I scroll down to look at her photos: One is of a gray cat, its blue eyes staring blankly into the lens; the next is a generic beach scene; and the last two images are of a blond woman in her late twenties or early thirties. In the first portrait, Ingrid appears to be on vacation, perhaps at the mystery beach. She wears a flowy, floral dress, her long pale hair blowing across her features. Behind the scrim I see a pretty, inviting smile. In the next, she's outside the glass doors of an office, drinking a large, purple smoothie. Her lips are pursed on the straw, but there's laughter in her eyes. My tormenter has a face...and not one I expected. There are no horns or warts or jagged teeth. Ingrid is an attractive young woman, warm and happy. She looks like a potential friend even.

But she's not.

I search for the name Ingrid Wandry on Facebook and Twitter, even TikTok though I'm not on the platform and might be doing it wrong.

User not found.

This doesn't strike me as odd. Until recently, I had no social media presence myself. I know plenty of people who don't view social media as a necessity. My ex, Adrian, declares the entire virtual world fake and toxic and will never partake. It's not surprising that there are other like-minded individuals out there. I try a straight-up Google search.

Did you mean:

Ingrid Wander   Ingrid Windram   Ingrid Wagner

No, I didn't.

Ingrid Wandry does not exist outside of Readem and Instagram. I return to her tiny image, stare at her warm smile, her gorgeous hair. Is this even her? Would someone so radiant be capable of spewing such ugliness? And why only about me? (And Dickens, I guess.) But I've already given her too much energy.

I vow to ignore social media going forward and turn my attention to my outline.

8 THE RELATIONSHIP

WHEN I TELL Theo about the book festival, he's excited for me. We're lounging on the sofa in my cozy living room, sipping wine. Liza is back at her dad's so Theo will spend most of the week here. We don't live together, but he does have two drawers in my dresser. It's all the commitment I can handle after eighteen years trapped in a toxic marriage. Fortunately, it works well for both of us.

"Wow. Miami," Theo says. My feet are resting in his lap, and he squeezes my toes. "I've never been."

"Me neither. We took Liza to Disney World when she was little, but we didn't go to Miami. I'm so excited."

He smiles at me, his hazel eyes warm. "You're amazing. You know that?"

"Thanks, babe." I shrug, shy under his praise, but it does feel amazing. I'm going to be flown across the continent, put up in a stylish hotel, and I get to talk about my book on a stage with other writers. It is a new and special experience for me.

Theo is still smiling at me. "Want some company?"

"In Miami?"

"Yeah." His face is alight. "I could take a few days off. We could check out Florida, maybe rent a car and go down to the Keys."

It sounds fun. And romantic. But that's not what this trip is about. "I'd love to have you with me, but it's my first writers' festival. I think I should focus on the book and my panel."

"Got it," he says, removing my feet from his lap. "More wine?"

"I'm good." I watch him move into the small kitchen and grab the bottle of red. His posture is stiff, his mouth set in a thin line. He's disappointed. Maybe even hurt.

"Why don't we go up to Whistler when I get back?" I suggest. We've gone to the ski resort town before. Theo mountain biked while I explored the village and then curled up by the fire with a book. "Or we could drive to Portland? It's fun."

"Sure." He returns and tops up his glass.

"I'll be schmoozing with other authors in Miami," I say as he sits. "It would be boring for you."

"True." He takes a big drink of wine. "Because how could I possibly carry on a conversation with a bunch of cerebral authors?"

He's being childish. I swing my feet around so they're resting on the floor. "Obviously you could, Theo, but you don't like to read."

"So I wouldn't fit in with your *literary crowd*."

"You wouldn't. But that's not a bad thing. I wouldn't fit in with your rock-climbing club. Why are you being like this?"

He takes another drink, turns to face me. "Are you ashamed of me?"

"Of course not!" And it's the truth. But I'm also aware that Theo is significantly younger than I am, that he wears shorts three hundred days a year, and that he calls people *bruh* a lot. He is adorable and kind and a successful entrepreneur, but we are very different.

"You don't treat me like your partner, Cam. You treat me like your boyfriend."

"We haven't been together that long," I say gently. "And what's wrong with being my boyfriend?"

"It's been twenty-two months," he retorts.

"And I was married for eighteen years. Twenty-two months doesn't feel that long to me."

"It does to me," he says. "And it feels like we should be making some sort of progress in this relationship."

"What do you mean, 'progress'?" I ask. "I told you when we got together that I'd never get married again. I was open about that. And even if I wanted more kids, at my age—"

"I don't need to get married or have kids." He cuts me off. "That hasn't changed. I just want to have a real relationship with you."

"This *is* real. What do you mean by 'real'?"

He runs a hand through his dark hair, a sure sign he's getting frustrated. "Maybe I could move in?"

"You already practically live here when Liza's at her dad's."

"I spend a few nights here every other week. That's not the same as living together."

"Theo..." I pause, choosing my words carefully. "I love you. And I love spending time with you. But I devoted so many years to my marriage and to motherhood, and this is *my* time. Liza's going to college soon. I have a brand-new career." I pause, reach for his hand. "I don't want a partner. I want a lover, and a companion. And a friend."

He removes his hand, folds his arms across his chest. "I don't know if that's enough for me."

I sigh, press my fingers to my forehead. "Do we have to do this right now? My book just came out. I'm trying to finish a new outline. I'm mentally exhausted."

"Obviously that's more important than our relationship." He gets up. "I'm going to sleep at my place tonight."

"Seriously?" I follow him toward the door. I knew I was dating a younger man, but I didn't realize he was *eleven*.

But he's already wrenching his road bike through the narrow hallway. Without another word, he leaves, slamming the door behind him.

BURNT ORCHID

1995

When Orchid was released from the juvenile detention center, she was eighteen: an adult. There was no one there to collect her, no home to go to, and no phone to call a friend, even if she'd had any left. Her mother now considered her a murderer, a monster; she'd chosen her dead lover over her own daughter. But there was Tash, another delinquent getting out after beating her foster sister into a coma five years ago. Tash's boyfriend, Jerome, was there to pick her up, and they offered Orchid a lift to the nearest town. Orchid didn't like or trust Tash, but she had few options.

Shortly after they left the facility, Jerome suggested they grab some vodka to celebrate. "You're free, bitches!" Tash's response was an animal whoop, while Orchid stayed silent. She thought about the pep talk she'd received from her GED teacher.

"You're smart, Orchid. Your record is sealed. You can still live a good life. A normal life. Stay on the right path, okay?"

She'd only been out of detention twenty minutes, and she was already being pulled off it.

With two bottles of Absolut, they drove to a double-wide trailer just off the highway, concealed from view by a copse of scrubby trees, their needles red with disease. The entire property emanated toxicity, from the rusted cars and broken-down appliances to the malnourished dog straining at its chain, flecks of foam flying as it barked and lunged. This would be Tash's home until she turned eighteen, Orchid learned. It belonged to her cousin Melody and Melody's boyfriend, Clyde.

Orchid followed Tash and Jerome into a haze of pungent smoke with undercurrents of stale beer and greasy hair. The pair on the plaid sofa were Tash's guardians, pale, scrawny, and indifferent to their presence. They were intent on the first-person shooter game on the TV, their hands gripping the controllers like real weapons, their bodies taut with adrenaline. And maybe meth. Across the room, a girl sat on a broken-down love seat. She was fragile and birdlike, sucking on a beer though she looked to be eleven or twelve.

"We brought vodka," Jerome announced, and led the way into the kitchen, where he filled three jars, added a splash of orange soda. Orchid took the drink and shuddered it down. She'd only tasted alcohol a few times before she was locked up for killing Trevor. But she remembered the feeling, the way the past and future went blurry and the present grew sticky, trapping her in the moment. The current scene was hardly ideal, but it was better than the fucked-up past or the unknown future, so she drank some more, trying to get to that liminal space.

Eventually, Melody's avatar was gunned down, so she left Clyde to his gaming and greeted her guests. Someone put music on. More drinks were poured. Orchid accepted the joint they passed around, noticed that the little girl partook. Her name was Lucy, and she was fourteen; not the child Orchid had first thought she was. To some people, fourteen was young, but Orchid had killed a man at that age.

Hours later, when Tash was puking in the bathroom and Melody and Clyde had gone to bed, Orchid realized she was alone. Jerome and the little bird of a girl were missing. Orchid knew this meant nothing good. But Lucy was a stranger, and this was none of Orchid's concern. She owed the girl nothing, certainly not her freedom or her fresh start. But a soft whimper traveled down the hallway, and it pulled Orchid to her feet. Without consideration, she staggered into the kitchen and fumbled through the drawers for a knife. They were small or dull, not up to the task. So she grabbed a bottle of vodka and smashed it against the counter.

With the neck of the bottle clutched in her hand, she went looking. She found them behind the second door she tried, a spare bedroom used for storing video games and workout equipment. There was a bare mattress under the detritus, and on it, Jerome pressed himself onto Lucy, her small body still and hard as stone. Orchid slipped into the room, grabbed Jerome by the hair, and pressed the bottle to his throat.

"What the fuck?" His voice was strangled.

"Did Tash tell you why I was in juvie?"

"No."

"I killed a man for trying to rape me."

"I wasn't raping her. She came on to *me*."

The glass broke the tender skin of his neck, the blood purple at first, turning red as it trickled to his collar. "Okay, okay...I'm sorry."

Lucy scurried from the room then, adjusting her clothes as she fled. Orchid planned her next move. Jerome could overpower her, turn the bottle on her, and hurt, even kill her. She needed to extricate, quickly.

"Lucy and I are leaving. Let us go or I'll tell Tash what you tried to do." She pushed off him and scrambled away from the bed.

"You fucking cunt," he growled, pressing his hand to his wound. But he didn't grab for her, he didn't come after her. His relationship with Tash meant something to him. With the bottle in her grip, Orchid sprinted from the room.

The girl was on the sofa, knees pulled to her chest, face pale but dry. She was in shock. Or else she'd already been through too much to summon tears for her recent assault.

"Come with me," Orchid commanded. "You have thirty seconds to grab your shit."

"Where are we going?"

"I don't know," Orchid said, "but I'll keep you safe."

Lucy didn't hesitate, didn't pause to consider. She flew to the kitchen, where she grabbed a plastic shopping bag and hurried around the trailer, stuffing it with clothing and trinkets. Within moments, she was back, ready.

"Let's go," she said, and Orchid saw the blind trust in the girl's dark eyes. She believed that Orchid could protect her. And Orchid would try with everything she had.

The two girls flew out the door.

9 THE FESTIVAL

Bienvenido a Miami!

It's a cheesy caption but I type it under the Instagram selfie anyway. I've been avoiding social media for the past couple of weeks, but I'm back in promo mode. I'd posted from the airport as I departed, fresh-faced and bright-eyed.

So excited to attend the Miami Festival of Books and Authors!

Now I'm pale and disheveled from the flight (six hours plus a four-hour layover in Dallas) and beaming like a madwoman, which exacerbates my crow's-feet and makes my top lip disappear. But the backdrop is stunning. I'm standing in front of my art deco hotel, just off the South Beach strip, a world away from my Pacific Northwest home. The experience is too incredible not to share. And supporting my book on social media is part of my job.

Made it! This is my first-ever festival and I can't wait to talk about BURNT ORCHID with some of my writing idols. @MiamiBooks #grateful #writerslife #Miamiglamor

At the front desk, a uniformed clerk with a Cuban accent checks me in with friendly efficiency. "Here's your key card," he says, sliding it across the sleek wood counter. "It also gives you access to the gym and our saltwater pool. The pool is amazing. You don't want to miss it. Towels are poolside."

"I'll definitely check it out," I say, collecting my card. "Thank you."

"The festival war room is down the hall to your right. They'll give you your lanyard and a schedule of events. And one more thing..." He turns to the counter behind him and gathers a small, tasteful bouquet of flowers in a round glass vase. "These came for you."

"They're lovely." I dip my face to inhale their fragrance. "Are they from the festival?"

"I don't believe so. None of the other authors received any."

For a split second, I wonder if I'm a VIP, but I know the lineup. There are hugely popular authors here with more books, more fans, and more credibility. I dig for the card among the dahlias, rosebuds, and greenery, but I already know: The flowers are from Theo.

There's been tension between us since I announced my travel plans. We've both been busy: Theo took a group of German tourists on a multiday kayak trip up Indian Arm. I've been working on my outline and immersed in the Abby Lester situation. Abby is still refusing to return to school after the mortifying video release. Her parents are worried that she might hurt herself. I've been providing all the support and resources I can, and it has been consuming. Theo and I have kept up the pretense of normalcy with regular text check-ins and social media support, but we've been avoiding each other. I'm grateful—and relieved—that he has reached out and made the first move.

Alone in my room—a sexy navy-and-white space with a private

terrace complete with clawfoot bathtub—I find the card nestled in the bouquet. It simply says:

I can't wait to see you.

The sentiment fills me with warmth. My boyfriend is a man of few words, but he's chosen perfectly. I call him, eager to tell him how much the gesture means to me. His voicemail answers.

"Hi, babe," I say brightly. "I arrived, safe and sound. Thank you so much for the beautiful flowers." There's a smile in my voice. "I know things have been tense between us lately, and I was so happy and relieved to get your bouquet. I promise we can talk about everything when I get home." I look at the flowers, so pretty, so thoughtful, and my chest fills with warmth. "I want this to work, Theo. I love you. And I can't wait to see you, either."

I hurry to the shower to freshen up.

That evening, the festival hosts a meet-and-greet for attendees on a seaside deck. We sip signature cocktails (something pink with rum) and nibble Cuban-inspired canapés. It's warm, but a sea breeze blows in, making it completely comfortable. I'm wearing a new silk dress I bought for the occasion, and despite mild jet lag I feel energized, happy, and nervous as hell.

The other authors all seem to know one another, or at least know *of* one another. I recognize some of them by face, others by their name tags. The festival is hosting bestsellers, award winners, writers I've admired since I was a kid. I'm a debut: unknown, unproven, quite possibly a one-hit wonder…and it's a mid-level hit at that (sales are "strong" but not exactly exploding). Some of the writers smile genuinely at me, others dismissively, while others ignore me altogether.

Across the crowd, I spot her. Zoe Carpenter is hard to miss, tall and curvy, with long dark hair cascading down her back. She's one of my favorite writers: fearless and insightful, with a strong, assured voice both on the page and in the many interviews and podcasts I've listened to. When Olivia told me I'd be on a panel with Zoe, my impostor syndrome kicked in with a vengeance. Zoe is talented, accomplished, even famous. And now she's moving deliberately toward me.

She holds out a manicured hand as she approaches. "Hi, I'm Zoe Carpenter."

"I know." I shake her hand. "I'm Camryn Lane. I'm such a fan."

"So am I! I absolutely loved *Burnt Orchid*."

Her compliment delights me, validates me, and makes me realize . . . maybe I do belong here after all.

"Let's go sit somewhere so I can pick your brain about your fabulous book," Zoe says. She takes my elbow and leads me toward a settee. I practically float behind her, feet just skimming the ground. My literary idol wants to chat about *my* novel, all while sipping pink cocktails. This is my personal version of heaven.

Later, when I get back to my room, I'm exhausted, tipsy, and happy. I throw myself on the bed, scrolling through my texts. There's one from Liza asking where her defrizzing hair serum is. One from Martha asking about my trip. And there's one from Theo.

Got your message. Call me.

I do.

"Hey you." The rum makes me feel flirtatious. "I miss you."

"I miss you, too." His exhale travels down the phone line. "But I didn't send you any flowers, Camryn."

10 THE PANEL

THE STAGE LIGHTS are blinding, the back of my neck sweaty despite the air-conditioned chill. I'm seated between Zoe Carpenter and a New Zealand bestseller named Timothy Rush who writes police procedurals. The audience stretches out before us, filling the rising seats. There are at least three hundred people in the theater, although I can only see the first few rows. Their presence is tangible, though, the hum of their energy and attention. They are excited to be here. They are captivated by us.

Our moderator, Analena, a compact woman in her fifties, is an author herself. A memoir, I think. She's also a book critic. Her questions are incisive and thoughtful. Zoe and Timothy are pros, their answers effortless, intelligent, and articulate. I know I'm too quiet. I know I should contribute more so the festival organizers don't wonder why they spent the money to fly me here, but I can't help but defer to their experience. Analena, however, won't let me off the hook.

"So, Camryn, what do you think about the term *women's fiction*? Is it simply a marketing term or is there something patriarchal in labeling books written by women?"

Oh god.

"Umm..." My voice is reedy. "I really don't worry too much

about labels like that. I know women read a lot, and if my publisher thinks that's the best way to market the book, then…uh, that's okay with me."

"I agree with Camryn," Zoe says, and I want to hug her. "At the end of the day, it's about appealing to readers. Historically, women often wrote under male or gender-neutral pen names to get their books read, but now the tables have turned. There are a lot of men writing under feminine or ambiguous pseudonyms hoping to appeal to the female market."

"I think the notion that men won't read fiction written by women is ridiculous," Timothy adds. "I'd say sixty-five percent of the books I read are written by women."

I sense an opening. "For me, it's about eighty percent. And most of the writers I admire are female. Like Zoe." I hastily add, "Though I'm looking forward to checking out Timothy's work."

He nods at me. "Likewise."

"Thank you." Analena smiles at us in turn. "We'll take questions from the audience now."

It's almost over. I've almost made it! And this part will be easy. The audience will have few questions for me when I'm sitting next to two such prolific writers. Plus, I have no problem talking about *Burnt Orchid*. It's like talking about my daughter or myself. The story is a part of me.

As predicted, the first few questions are directed at my compatriots. After Timothy shares a hilarious story about a snake encounter at a writers' retreat in Darwin, Analena wraps things up.

"We have time for one last question." She points toward the back of the theater, the rows obscured from my view. A volunteer with a microphone sprints up the stairs.

"My question is for Camryn Lane." The voice is feminine, disembodied.

I sit up in my seat, paste a pleasant smile on my face.

"Are you really a high school counselor?"

It's the tone, not the question itself, that makes my stomach drop. "Yeah, I am. Part-time now."

"So kids come to you to talk about their problems, and then you write about them. Don't you think that's wrong?"

Beside me, Zoe flinches, but I relish this opportunity. If I can't defend myself online, I can at least defend myself here.

"I'm a professional, trained counselor. I take my students' issues very seriously. And I would *never* write about them. In fact, in my novel, I purposely steered away from any issues I'd encountered on the job."

"But surely your students' private problems could seep into your work subconsciously. I mean, why write about teenagers at all given the risk of exposure?"

"*Burnt Orchid* is a story I've wanted to tell for years," I respond. "The teen story line is integral to the theme of catharsis."

"But if you care so much about these kids, why not just write about something else? To be safe. Couldn't you come up with another idea?"

"As I said"—my voice has taken on a defensive edge—"the teen issues in my book are entirely fictional. And they're far more serious than the ones I encounter at school."

"So you're diminishing the problems of your real-life students?"

"No. Of course I'm not. I—I'm just saying that they're different." My pulse is skittering, my words floundering.

"Why not quit your job, then?" the faceless voice says. "I guess you want to keep mining these kids for material."

"I—I'm a single mom," I stammer. "And a debut author. I don't feel secure enough to leave a job with a pension, and summers off…" Now I'm sounding privileged and pitiful at the same time. I press a hand to my throat, flustered.

Thankfully, Analena steps in. "We're out of time. Thank you all so much for coming..." She goes on to thank a number of sponsors and supporters, but I am deaf to it. All I hear is the rush of blood in my ears, my heart pounding with a mixture of anger and shame. Finally the crowd bursts into appreciative applause and we are dismissed.

Zoe catches my arm as we walk offstage. "There's one in every crowd," she assures me. "You handled it really well."

"Thanks," I mumble, emotion threatening my voice. "But I'm not so sure."

"You were frank and composed. You stood your ground. It was perfect."

Backstage, Analena apologizes to me. "I'm so sorry. People can be combative. But the rest of the event was amazing. You did a great job. All of you."

"See?" Zoe adds. "It was fine."

Timothy approaches us. "That was bloody ugly," he says. "I think we could all use a drink."

11 THE DRINK

THE THREE OF US sit at a quiet table in a darkened corner of the hotel bar. It's already ten o'clock, but it's Miami. This place is clearly a starting point for a night of fun and debauchery for many of the hotel guests. Drinks, laughter, and conversation flow. While we order three Negronis from an attractive server in a bandage dress, the mood at our table is far more subdued. It's my fault. I can't shake off the hangover of the attack.

"She was really coming for you," Timothy says, bringing his drink to his lips. "Some people love to be angry."

"Security had to be called at one of my events," Zoe contributes. "It was just after I hit the *Times* list with my second book. A woman in the audience was screaming at me. She didn't like the way I handled a sexual assault in my novel."

"I've never been confronted like that," Timothy says, his brow furrowed. "Am I just lucky? Or do you think it happens more to women?"

"People are much more comfortable attacking women and people from marginalized communities," Zoe says. "It's always been that way."

"I agree," I say, thinking about Janine's experience. "I've been getting the same kind of attacks online." I tell them about Ingrid's nasty email, her bad review.

"Been there," Zoe says. "I no longer let readers contact me directly. They have to go through my agent now."

"Did you ever respond?" I ask. "Did you ever try to reason with them?"

"You can't. They'll twist your words and use them against you." She leans closer, her dark eyes troubled. "Do you remember Chloe Winston?"

The name is familiar, but I can't place it. Zoe elaborates.

"She was big. Her fantasy novel hit all the lists about five years ago. And then she was accused of plagiarism by another writer."

"Shit," says Timothy, his big square ice cube clinking in his glass.

"Their concepts were similar, but Chloe's book was all her own. Her publisher stood by her, but this guy had a huge Twitter following."

"What happened?" I ask.

"Chloe went after him. She called him out as bitter, jealous, and entitled." She takes a sip of her cocktail. "And then the trolls destroyed her."

"What do you mean?"

"They bombarded her posts with negative comments. They left her thousands of scathing reviews. They basically killed her book. And her career."

I down the remains of my drink, hoping the alcohol will ease the flicker of anxiety in my belly.

"She couldn't take it anymore. She backed out of her two-book deal. Chloe disappeared from social media after that. I still see her for coffee on occasion. She's a brilliant writer, but she's not willing to put herself out there again."

"Shame," Timothy says.

Our server approaches carrying a single drink on her tray. "One Negroni." She sets it in front of me and addresses my companions. "Would you two like another?"

"I didn't order this," I tell her, not that it's unwelcome.

"Courtesy of the blond lady at the bar."

All four of us look toward the bar for the source of the drink.

"Oh..." our server says. "She's gone."

Timothy sees me blanch. "It was probably someone from the audience tonight who felt bad you had to deal with that nasty piece of work."

Maybe. But I'm unnerved. My mind races as Zoe and Timothy order two more drinks. When the server leaves, I speak in a thick voice. "I got a bouquet of flowers when I arrived. The card said: *I can't wait to see you.*"

"Who were they from?" Timothy asks.

"The card wasn't signed. I thought they were from my boy-friend, and he meant he couldn't wait to see me when I got home. But maybe they were from someone who couldn't wait to see me here? Onstage?"

"It's possible," Zoe says. "And the sentiment could have been sincere."

"Did you see the woman in the audience tonight?" I ask.

"The lights were shining in my eyes," Timothy says. "I couldn't see a thing past row four."

"Same," Zoe says. "Why?"

I shrug. "I looked up the woman who's been attacking me online. She's blond."

"A lot of people are blond," Zoe says gently. "Does that Ingrid woman even live in Miami?"

"I don't know where she lives," I say, pushing the drink away. "I'm going to call it a night."

"Are you sure?" Zoe asks.

"Stay," Timothy says. "We'll get you a fresh drink if you're worried about it."

"I'm just tired," I say, smiling as I stand. "Everything will seem a lot less daunting in the morning."

We say our goodbyes, our *great to meet yous*, our *see you on social medias*. Then I hurry out of the bar, alone.

12 THE CALLS

THE FIRST THING I do when I return to the room is put the flowers outside next to the outdoor bathtub. Their beauty now feels ominous, their fragrance sickly and cloying. I lock the door securely and crawl into bed, but I can't sleep. Despite the jet lag, the emotional exhaustion of the confrontation with the woman in the audience, and the alcohol, I lie in the crisp sheets, in the dark, mind swirling. This garden room, with its private walkway enveloped by lush greenery, had seemed so quaint, but it now feels too accessible. Because someone here, in Miami, could be out to get me.

Who was the woman in the audience? Were her issues with my novel sparked by Ingrid Wandry's online reviews? Did she send me the Negroni at the bar? The anonymous flowers? If she was trying to creep me out, it worked. But could she really be so incensed as to be dangerous? This is Florida. I have seen a lot of memes...

Of course, there could be an innocent explanation for these gifts. The drink was just like Timothy said, a gesture from a sympathetic audience member. And someone from home will come forward and claim the bouquet, a friend or a co-worker. Maybe it was from Janine, who knows what it feels like to deal with online haters. The words on the card aren't necessarily menacing.

At some point, I must doze off, because I'm startled awake by my phone ringing. The bedside clock reads 1:46 a.m. Panic grips my chest—is something wrong with Liza?—but I realize it's three hours earlier at home. It's not entirely unreasonable for someone to be calling me now: My daughter. Or Theo. Even Martha if she's forgotten I'm in a different time zone.

Grabbing the charger cord, I reel my phone toward me. The tiny screen displays an unfamiliar message: No Caller ID.

A wrong number. Or an automated call. Still, I answer it, just in case.

"Hello?"

There's no one there. As suspected, it's a robocall. I hang up, more than a little annoyed, and worried I won't be able to get back to sleep. But I snuggle into the high-thread-count sheets, feel myself succumbing, just as the phone rings again.

"What the hell?" I flick the lamp on this time and wrench the phone off its cord. The same No Caller ID message glows back at me.

"Hello?" I grumble. There's no response. I'm about to hang up when I hear it. Or rather, sense it. Someone is there, at the other end of the line. There is distinct yet subtle background noise. The phone must be on speaker. I hear a fridge click on, or perhaps a dishwasher is running.

"Who is this?" I ask. "How did you get my number?" My brain sifts through possibilities as I wait for a response. I don't give out my private number freely, but I'd included it on the festival paper-work. Surely, I'm not being prank-called by a festival employee or volunteer. I hear a rustle of clothing, a slight shifting. "Talk to me," I say, my tone softening. Maybe I can coax this person to open up, to explain themselves. "What do you want from me?"

I wait...thirty seconds, one minute, maybe even two...But I get nothing. Anger and frustration grip me. "I'm hanging up now,"

I snap. "And I'm blocking your number. I suggest you get a fucking life."

With trembling fingers, I tap into my recent calls. I see the No Caller ID and I select the Info button. Scrolling down, I search for Block this caller. As I'm about to press it, the phone rings again. I answer it.

"You want to play this game?" I practically scream down the line. "I can't sleep anyway. I can sit here all goddamn night."

But I can't. I have a flight in the morning. I have work to do on the plane. I hold on for a while, listening to the ambient noise, wondering who the hell is sitting there, listening to my shallow breaths, my racing heartbeat, my body betraying my anxiety. Then I hang up, quickly block the number, and try to sleep.

The morning sunshine brings with it a headache, puffy eyes, and a sense of perspective. Last night's prank phone calls seem benign, childish even, and unrelated to the flowers and the drink. In the bright morning light, those deliveries have lost their menace. Why did I think they were related to the audience member who took offense to my book? The cocktail and bouquet were kindly overtures, nothing to worry about. I have a new voicemail, from my driver, probably. The festival has secured all guests transportation to and from the airport. I dial in and the automated voice says:

"You have...*forty-six*...new messages."

I already know, all of them are silent.

13 THE REUNION

IT'S TEN THIRTY in the morning, and Theo and I are tangled up in my damp sheets. We've only been apart for a few days, but we've missed each other. I got home too late last night to see him, and by "see him" I mean have makeup sex with him. Plus, Liza was already home from Adrian's when I arrived. Now she's at school, and I'm lying with my head on Theo's strong chest, his heart beating against my cheek.

"No one's taken credit for sending the flowers?" he asks. The unexplained events in Miami are on his mind. Mine too.

I'd called the florist from a coffee shop at the airport. "If a card wasn't included with the arrangement, it's against our policy to reveal who sent it," the woman said. "It's to protect the privacy of our customers."

"You must do a great business with stalkers," I'd snapped before hanging up. Then I'd texted my friends, my family, my publishers...all the possible candidates, asking if anyone had sent me a gorgeous bouquet in Miami. They'd all responded with some form of "Ooooh a secret admirer," followed by an array of heart emojis. All except for Janine.

"Document it," she'd advised. "If you need to go to the police at some point, you'll need a record of the harassment."

I respond to Theo. "No, no one," I say.

"I'm sure someone will take credit." Theo shifts out from under me, turns onto his side. "I wish I'd sent them. I should have."

I smile at him. "It's fine. I'm just happy we made up."

"Me too." But his brow furrows. "I was thinking about those calls. How could an online troll get your cell phone number?"

I'd considered this on the flight home. I've never included my personal cell number on any of my social media accounts, even as an extra security measure. "They couldn't have. The phone calls can't be related to the book."

"It's pretty immature. Maybe it was kids from school?" Theo speculates.

"I'm dealing with some mean girls right now," I say, thinking of Fiona Carmichael and crew. "They could have gotten my number somehow. Through a parent, maybe."

"You should have dialed *69."

"Apparently it doesn't work with blocked numbers." I prop myself up on an elbow. "Janine Kang said I should document all this stuff in case I need to call the police."

"The police? For flowers and prank phone calls?"

"I know." I shrug it off. "It's nothing compared with what she went through. It's horrific what some people in the public eye have to deal with."

"It is." He leans over and kisses me. "But you're home now and nothing else bad is going to happen to you. I'll make sure of it."

"Thanks, babe. It's good to be back." I wait for him to mention moving in, the lack of progress in our relationship, but he doesn't.

"I've got to get to work," he says, climbing out of bed.

"Me too." I hurry into my robe, shy about my naked body (a downside of dating a younger man with 6 percent body fat). "I've got a call with my publicist in an hour." My tone is breezy, but I'm nervous. Olivia had initiated the conversation and I know it must be about my online reviews.

Theo pulls on his T-shirt, zips up his shorts. "Text you later."

With a peck on the lips, he's out the door.

As I get ready for my call, I send my friend Martha a voice memo via text. We often communicate through recorded messages because it's faster, it's more private, and we're a hundred years old.

"Hey, pal...Sorry I didn't get to call you when I was in Miami. Pitbull kept me out all night, and then we bumped into J.Lo. It got kind of crazy." I chuckle at my own joke. "Seriously, though...It was a weird trip. Some of it was amazing but some of it was dark. And disturbing. Anyway, I hope you're good. Let me know when we can catch up."

I've been a negligent friend, but Martha will forgive me. In fact, she may not even notice. She and Felix own a hip little café in a cool east side neighborhood. Though the coffee shop is only open eight to three, they work around the clock. Still, she always makes time for our friendship, and I owe her the same.

When Olivia calls, I'm showered, dressed, and seated at my desk, a notepad in front of me like a keen student.

"How was the Miami festival?" she asks.

"Great," I say, because I've decided not to tell her about the weirdness. She's a publicist, not a detective. And overall, the experience was positive. Even amazing. "I met some of my favorite authors, and the panel went really well."

"That's good to hear." She clears her throat, a sign our small talk is over. "I wanted to update you on the Readem situation. We were able to get them to take down some of the one-star reviews.

The most abusive ones that violated their policy against personally attacking an author, not a book."

A weight slides off my shoulders, pools at my feet. "That's fantastic. Thanks, Olivia."

"It is," she says, and I sense the but coming. "*But* the removal of these reviews seems to have spurred a backlash."

"What kind of backlash?"

"When a review is removed, Readem sends a notification email to the reviewer. People don't like to be censored. They're coming back...with a vengeance."

"Shit," I mutter, though I know it's not professional.

"The one-star reviews are coming up faster than they can be taken down. They're accusing Readem of policing free speech. And they're blaming you for reporting the reviews. Some people feel you're in a privileged position, and that you're unwilling to accept fair criticism."

"I accept it if it's fair," I say. "But I can't accept lies about the kids I work with. Could I respond to *those* reviews at least? Just the ones making false accusations."

"You don't want to go on the site. Some of the reviews are getting personal. It's not pretty."

"But you just said that reviewers aren't allowed to personally attack authors."

"The review guidelines are complicated. And Readem doesn't have the staff to monitor everything. Plus, their security is lax. There's nothing to stop people from creating sock puppet accounts to drag you."

"What does that even mean?"

"A user doesn't need to verify their email address to set up a review account, so there's nothing to stop them from creating dozens, even hundreds of fake accounts."

"So this could all be the work of one person? Or a small handful of people?" I don't know if this makes me feel better or worse.

"It's possible. It's also possible that one well-crafted review triggered a review bombing."

"So what can we do?"

"We're discussing that in-house now. But you have to trust that we will handle it. Do not try to wade into this yourself, Camryn. It could be extremely damaging."

I swallow the dread clogging my throat. "I won't."

"And don't read the negative reviews. It will only make you feel bad."

But I already feel bad. Very bad. Because my career as a writer is on a precipice. For years, I ignored the inherent craving to express myself through fiction. I told myself being a wife, a mother, and a counselor was enough. When I was married to Adrian, he'd get frustrated if I tried to take time out of our busy life to write, so I put it aside. But after the divorce, I committed to my dream. I worked hard and I made it a reality. And now it's crumbling before my eyes.

"I won't," I promise as I hang up.

And then, just for a few moments, I let myself cry.

14 THE DISCOVERY

PULL MYSELF TOGETHER, but I can't be expected to write now. My creativity has been extinguished by the toxic muck seeping into the crevices in my brain. And I'm exhausted by the emotional breakdown. I feel assaulted, battered and bruised, and yet the dark temptation to read the online vitriol tugs at me. I should get out of the apartment, fill the day with something positive and healthy.

Vancouver is one of the most scenic cities on earth, glass high-rises set against a backdrop of sparkling blue ocean and majestic mountains. It is lush and green, and this time of year there's a veritable assault of vivid spring flowers. But there is menace here, too, a dark underbelly. Illegal drugs flow through the massive port, causing an opioid epidemic that kills up to seven people each day. An affordable housing crisis has led to homelessness, tent cities, and extreme poverty. And like the rest of the world, Vancouver's mental health has suffered from the stress and isolation brought on by the pandemic. Still, the natural beauty of this place never fails to soothe me.

A walk in Pacific Spirit Park, the huge swath of woods bordering the city, would fit the bill. The health benefits of *shinrin-yoku* (Japanese for "forest bathing") are constantly cycling through my

Instagram feed: decreased anxiety, increased creativity, boosted immunity. But a woman on a solo jog was murdered in the park years ago, and no woman I know will go in alone. Even the most peaceful, beautiful places can be dangerous.

The beach is another option, but I'm bound to bump into someone I know along the popular stroll. My neighborhood has a reputation for being snobbish, but I've always found it to be warm and inclusive. In my little pocket, it's almost *too* friendly. I can't run to the shops or go for a stroll without bumping into someone I know. And I can't make pleasant small talk right now. I can't field the ubiquitous questions: *How's the book doing? How are sales?* Or my all-time favorite: *When's the movie coming out?*

I could go in to school today even though it's my day off. I could catch up on paperwork, lose myself in the hubbub and chaos of teen life. But my colleague Daniel, a support teacher, uses my office when I'm not there. Our public school is bursting at the seams, and there's a shortage of space for one-on-ones. I'd be taking the room away from kids who are struggling academically so I could faff about with admin tasks meant only to distract me.

I decide to clean the apartment, though it's practically spotless. Housework is a go-to method to allow my ideas to percolate, my stories to solidify. It's also a highly effective means of procrastination. Pulling the vacuum from the closet, I'm about to turn it on when I hear the familiar *bing* of my laptop set up in the office. A new email.

It won't be anything that can't wait until I'm done with this chore. It doesn't take long to clean 850 square feet of hardwood. But then I hear it again. And again. And again.

Bing…Bing….Bing…

Hurrying into the small office, I sit in my rolling chair and click the mouse. My email pops up on-screen. There are no new messages in my personal account. And then I look at my author account: 14 new messages. Oh no...

I open the first one, my heart lodged in my throat.

> Camryn Lane, you're a cowardly piece of shit! You can't handle readers posting the truth about the way you exploited kids in your garbage book, so you tried to rat us out! Someone's going to find you and slaughter you like the animal that you are!

I move on to the next one, naively hoping for something more positive. Nope.

> YOU SHOULD DIE, BITCH! I HOPE YOU GET CANCER!!! YOU'RE SO FUCKING UGLY, INSIDE AND OUT.

The next one reads:

> I will find out where you live, and I'll do too you what you did to those teenagers psyches. It's called rape you sick fuck! Your no better than a pedophile.

I'm desperate to reply:

> I would never exploit the kids I work with. I've done nothing wrong. Learn to spell and leave me the fuck alone!

But I can't. Both Olivia and Janine told me not to respond, not to engage, but my silence has done nothing to quell the online abuse. While lashing out might feel good and righteous, I know it wouldn't last. The endorphins would quickly leave me, and I'd feel even more jittery, vulnerable, and afraid. These trolls are all talk, I assure myself. They're not really going to come for me. And even if they wanted to, no one knows where I live. They can't find my physical location.

Can they?

On autopilot, I return to the front room, turn on the vacuum, and start to clean. The nozzle bangs into furniture, jostles plants, but I continue, moving like I'm in a trance. I know what I need to do. I will call my web designer (a friend of Theo's) and have him remove my email address from the website. I'll alert Olivia to the barrage of angry emails. But not until I have calmed down, not until I can talk without bursting into tears. Should Liza stay at her dad's, just to be safe? I drag the vacuum down the short hallway to my daughter's room.

Unlike the rest of the house, Liza's personal space is a disaster. I try not to nag her; this is a stressful time for her. Her university acceptance is conditional on her final grades not dropping, and she has a heavy course load. Not to mention the emotional turning point she's about to face: the end of school, leaving home, ending things with Wyatt...None of it will be easy. And I don't want my place to be the no-fun zone. I know that Tori and Adrian's rules are lax, that they ascribe to the parenting adage:

The kids are going to drink / have sex / smoke pot / drop acid / cook meth anyway... We'd rather they do it under our roof.

Liza accepts that I'm stricter, seems to appreciate it, even. But I don't want to be a complete ogre.

I'll just pick up the mess on the floor so I can vacuum. Liza won't be pleased. Despite the chaotic appearance, she has a "system," she says. But I gather the crumpled school papers, toss her dirty clothes into the hamper, wrap the cords around her hair appliances and drop them into a basket. When I turn on the suction, the sound of dirt rattling into the canister is satisfying, and then slightly disturbing. I'll have to have a gentle conversation about keeping a clean space before Liza moves into her dorm room.

Liza's laptop is open on the floor between the wall and the bed. She takes it to school sometimes, but not when she has to go straight to work after. She's a cashier at a veggie burger joint that has no secure storage for personal items. As I pick up the device, I can't help but notice that a text window is open. The messages are from Wyatt, gray balloons running down the side of the screen.

Where r u?

Where r u?

Where r u?

Where r u?

Where r u?

Where r u?

Where r u?

Where r u?

The texts were sent last night when Liza was out with her friends. The question itself is innocuous but the quantity is alarming. Does Wyatt have a possessive side I don't know about? Has Liza's imminent departure for college made him more needy? Even obsessive? I scroll up, searching for a preface that will give these texts some context, but there's nothing. All earlier conversations have been deleted.

There's a tight ball in my chest and I struggle to take a deep breath. My mother's intuition is screaming at me, warning me that my daughter could be involved in something messy, even dangerous. But Wyatt has never shown us a dark side, has never been anything but caring and supportive. And I'm not sure I can trust my judgment right now. I'm vulnerable and on edge. I'm rattled by all the hatred directed at me.

But the bad reviews, the emails, and the accusations will mean less than nothing if my daughter is in trouble.

Liza is far more important than my novel.

15 SECRETS

THE POLICE OFFICER sitting in the vice principal's office is in his early thirties, with dark eyes, brown skin, and strong, straight teeth. Constable Kash Gill is our school liaison officer, which means he spends several days a week at the school in a (somewhat controversial) effort to develop a positive relationship between students and the police force. He is also regularly employed to explain the harsh realities of the law to kids whose behavior flirts with the illegal.

Fiona Carmichael is seated between the cop and me, while Monica Carruthers sits behind her desk. When the vice principal invited me to this meeting, she'd said, "I'd like you to be there to support Fiona. Constable Kash is going to come down hard, and I think the seriousness of this situation is going to be upsetting for her."

Monica clearly doesn't know Fiona like I do. From what I've seen, the girl has unwavering bravado and a remarkable lack of conscience (much like her dark overlord). But I have a job to do. "Of course, I'll support her."

Constable Gill's voice is firm as he addresses the blond girl beside me. "Distributing or making available an intimate image of a person, without their consent, is an indictable offense, Fiona. You could get up to five years in prison."

"Abby took her own clothes off when she was freaking out," Fiona counters. "That's not my fault."

"She wasn't 'freaking out,'" I correct her. "She was *overdosing.*"

The girl ignores me, looks at Constable Gill with wide eyes. "Can a minor really be sent to jail for posting a video that they didn't even take?"

She's on to him. She's so savvy. But Kash is a seasoned cop. "It's rare, but minors can be tried as adults in some cases. It's also possible that Abby's parents could sue your parents in civil court."

"Abby's in intensive therapy," I add. "Her parents have had to take significant time off work. It's costing them a lot, Fiona. Emotionally and financially."

The girl is quiet, eyes in her lap. We're finally getting through to her.

"It would be in your best interest to tell us what you know about that night," Kash says gently. "Who took the video? Who supplied the drugs?"

No response.

Monica leans forward in her ergonomic chair. "Once the police and lawyers are involved, kids tend to get loose lips. And now that we have the anonymous reporting portal, someone will tell us what really happened at Abby's party."

Fiona looks up, meets the vice principal's gaze. "I doubt that."

Her words send a chill through me. Monica's eyes narrow. "What makes you say that?"

"I don't know..." The teen shrugs. "No one really likes Abby. I don't think they'd want to see someone else get into trouble for what she did to herself."

No fear, no remorse, no empathy. Fiona Carmichael is a sociopath.

"I have another appointment..." I say, tapping my watch. Fiona obviously doesn't need my support. She's the furthest thing from upset. She's controlling the entire situation.

"I think we're done here." I hear the defeat in Monica's voice as I scurry from the room.

I hadn't confronted Liza about the concerning texts from Wyatt when she got home from work last night. It was late, we were both exhausted, and despite my training and experience, I felt overwhelmed. I hope that I'm blowing the exchange out of proportion, that it's some kind of inside joke or even a technical glitch. I'm still rattled by the abusive emails I received, and that could be clouding my perception. I'm meeting Adrian at a coffee shop near the beach to discuss Wyatt's texts.

My ex is seated near the back, two paper coffee cups on the round table before him. He's scrolling through his phone, dressed in jeans and a golf shirt with his company's logo on the breast. Adrian is in property management, which sounds completely legitimate until he reveals that the property he manages belongs to his parents. His salary is a tax write-off for them. Adrian's mom still does all the books, and his dad enjoys taking care of the gardens and engaging with tenants. Adrian's job consists of placing a vacancy ad once in a blue moon and calling the occasional plumber. And yet, during our marriage, he was incapable of handling even the most basic domestic responsibilities. Martha called him a baby-man. Or was it a man-baby?

"Hey," I say, sitting down and reaching for a cup. "Thanks for the latte."

"It's green tea," he says quickly. "For Tori."

"Tori's coming?" My tone is arch.

"She's Liza's parent, too." But he sounds unconvinced himself.

On cue, Tori swoops in. "Sorry I'm late." She kisses Adrian with

75

an audible smack. Tori is tall and willowy with a blunt dark bob. She has a successful real estate staging business and dresses the part of stylish professional: cropped jacket, flowing trousers, statement jewelry. Tori runs marathons in her spare time (what spare time?). She is younger, fitter, and sexier than I am, but that's not why I don't like her. Okay, it's part of it, but there are other reasons, which, I suspect, are about to become abundantly clear.

She sits and takes a sip of her green tea. "Camryn, do you need to get yourself a coffee?"

"I'm fine. I don't have long."

"What did Wyatt's texts say exactly?" Adrian asks.

"It wasn't what they said. It was how often he said it. It was just 'where are you?' over and over again. It seemed possessive. Even obsessive."

"Liza and Wyatt spend a lot of time at our house," Tori says, placing her hand on top of Adrian's. "We've intentionally created a chill space where they can hang out and be comfortable. Just be themselves."

Unlike the North Korean prison camp that is my apartment.

"We've never seen any signs of possessiveness," Adrian says, echoing my own experience. "And Liza is a tough cookie. I don't think she'd put up with it."

Tori adds, "Wyatt is so gentle. He's so supportive. He's the gardener and Liza is the flower."

"I work with teens," I say, struggling to keep the defensiveness from my voice. "I know they can present a very different image around adults. And this is a fraught time. Liza and Wyatt are going to break up in a few months. That can trigger unhealthy, controlling behaviors."

Tori's eyes are on her tea. "They might not be breaking up."

"They're going to try the long-distance thing?" I ask. "From Australia to Toronto?"

Adrian sighs, leans back in his chair. "Liza's not sure she wants to go straight to college, Cam. She's considering deferring for a year. Maybe traveling with Wyatt and some other friends."

"Since when?" I ask.

"She's been afraid to tell you," Tori adds. "She thinks you'll try to talk her out of it."

"She thinks you'll be disappointed," Adrian says, "but we need to support her. Liza's a great kid. She should be allowed to spread her wings."

I am disappointed, but that's a "me" issue. I'm more concerned. Is Wyatt manipulating my daughter's life decisions? Influencing her plans for the future? Or is he, as Tori believes, just a gentle gardener nurturing a flower?

"How can she afford that?" I ask. "She doesn't make much at the burger shop."

Adrian flushes slightly. "My parents offered to pay. A graduation gift."

Damn my rich ex-in-laws.

"I'll talk to her," I mumble, already getting up. "I need to get back to work."

"Let me know how it goes," Adrian calls after me.

"Let us *both* know," Tori says.

"Sure." I hurry out the door.

16 THE TALK

I'M ON THE sofa, waiting for my daughter to come home so I can discuss her relationship with Wyatt, her plans to ditch college and travel Down Under, and her decision to change the course of her entire future without even discussing it with me. To ensure I'm in a sufficiently low mood, I've made a cup of tea, and I'm looking at the *Burnt Orchid* Readem page on my phone. I've kept my promise—to Olivia and to myself—not to read the bad reviews. The mere thought of the abuse and vitriol makes me feel ill. I'm simply looking at the ratings, refreshing the page regularly. Every twenty minutes or so, the rating goes down by a point. 3.30 ... 3.29 ... 3.28 ...

It hovers there for a while, and I pray it will hold. That the trolls will give up, get bored. That people who liked the book will give it five stars to counteract the damage. Readem has millions of subscribers and significant influence. I suspect this mediocre rating is impacting my sales. I've heard nothing from my publishers, no more words like: *strong, promising, on the right track*. There is a sales portal I can log into, but the tallies mean little to me without some context.

A key in the lock signals my daughter's arrival and I put down the phone.

"Hey," Liza says, dropping her heavy backpack on a kitchen bar-stool and going directly to the fridge.

"How was your day?"

"Good," she says, rummaging for a kombucha. "Some friends and I went to Martha's café after school. She says hi."

It's been ages since I've popped into my friend's coffee shop, but Liza has gone like an emissary. "How is she?"

"She was super busy." Liza opens her beverage with an effervescent hiss. "But she said she misses you."

"Me too. I'll see her soon."

"Felix came in as we were leaving," Liza says, moving around the counter and grabbing her backpack. "My friends thought he was hot, which is so gross. He's like *sixty*."

"He's forty-six," I chuckle, "but it's still gross."

"I won't even tell you what they say about Theo." My daughter rolls her eyes, heads toward her room.

"Can we talk?" My voice is tight with nerves.

"I have a ton of homework." She eyes me suspiciously. "What's going on?"

"I just want to chat." I pat the cushion next to me.

She comes over and sits beside me, but I sense her apprehension. I keep my tone light.

"How are things between you and Wyatt?"

"Fine."

"How does he feel about you going off to school in a few months?"

Liza sighs, crosses her arms. "Did you talk to Dad and Tori?"

"I did. They say you're not sure you want to go to college this year."

"I don't know..." Her words wobble. "I'm not sure I'm ready. Twelfth grade has been a lot, and four more years of school feels overwhelming right now." She plays with the strings on her hoodie.

"And it's hard to end things with Wyatt after we've been together for so long."

"If you're not ready to go to university, Liza, that's okay." My voice has slipped into counselor-mode. "As long as you're making that decision because it's right for you, not because it's what Wyatt wants."

"I know you don't like him, Mom."

"What are you talking about? Wyatt's fine."

She rolls her eyes. "That's a ringing endorsement."

"I vacuumed your room," I say, seizing on the subject. "I saw some texts that concerned me."

"You were snooping in my laptop?" She's angry. She feels her privacy was invaded.

"I picked it up. They were on the screen. Fifteen texts from Wyatt asking where you were."

For a moment, Liza looks confused; then her face crinkles with amusement. "That was a joke. I was with him when he sent those."

"I don't get it," I say flatly.

"The other night, my friends and I went to watch Wyatt's soccer game. I forgot my phone at home. He was teasing me that I'd come home to a billion texts from you. He was trying to beat your record."

"Oh." I'm too relieved to be annoyed.

"He's not some controlling jerk. Wyatt's a good guy. And I'm a strong woman. You raised me to stand up for myself."

"I know." I reach for her hand. "But strong women can get hurt too. And you're so young."

"Is this about me and Wyatt? Or is it about you and Dad?"

Adrian and I met in our second year of college. We were both studying psychology with a minor in smoking weed and drinking. I was concerned about my future, wondering what to do with such a general degree. Adrian had the family business to fall back on. He was lighthearted, carefree, enjoying the ride. I was intoxicated by him. I don't regret that we got married a few years after graduation—if we hadn't, there would be no Liza—but he wasn't the right choice for me. My ex is selfish and needy; he wanted a mother as much as a wife. And if I'd stayed with Adrian, I never would have written *Burnt Orchid*.

I touch my daughter's shiny hair, push it back behind her shoulder. "Promise me you'll put yourself first. And do what's right for you."

"I always do." There's a sparkle in her eye. "Besides, don't you have other things to worry about? Like your next book?"

She's right, I do. And now that I know my daughter is okay, I can give them my full attention.

BURNT ORCHID

1995

Orchid bought two bus tickets to LA. If she were traveling alone, she could have gone farther—south to Arizona or east to Chicago, even New York—but she'd promised to look after this thin, quiet girl and she would. Besides, LA was a huge city. If Orchid's mother was still living in the valley, if she was still alive, she wouldn't find Orchid there. Because Lorna Chambers wouldn't be looking. When Orchid killed Trevor, her mother had called her a whore, a psychopath, a murderer. She'd made it clear she no longer had a daughter.

The pair sat side by side in the second-to-last row of the Greyhound bus, Lucy's arm pressed against Orchid's, a pleasant human warmth in the air-conditioned chill. They rode in silence, Orchid watching the arid scenery of central California out the window, while Lucy stared straight ahead. Eventually, Orchid worried aloud. "We're going to need money," she said, voice camouflaged by the hum of tires on asphalt. "I don't have enough for a motel. We'll have to go to a shelter or sleep on the street."

The younger girl didn't respond, just fished in the grocery bag stuffed with clothes. "Does this help?" She extracted a small bag full of white powder. Orchid hadn't seen Lucy take it, hadn't even known it was in the trailer.

"What is it?"

Lucy shrugged, buried it back amid her clothes. "Meth, I think. That's what they usually do. It makes Clyde go crazy."

"Yeah, it helps," Orchid said. "It helps a lot." The girls exchanged a smile. They were already a team. They could both feel it. Together, they would survive.

Orchid had never bought or sold drugs, but it couldn't be hard. Some of the stupidest people she knew were adept at both. And she remembered Trevor traveling downtown to buy drugs for her mom and him. They'd snort some sort of powder and then they'd go out, not returning for days on end. She figured it would be more profitable to divvy the meth into smaller portions, but where? And how? It wasn't possible. They'd have to unload the whole bag, and with that money, they could travel farther away. Just to be safe.

She felt Lucy's head fall against her shoulder, her body still. The kid was exhausted, and she finally felt safe enough to sleep. Orchid closed her eyes, too. But she remained alert.

Two girls lost in a big-city bus station are not lost for long. The first man to approach them was a pimp, aggressive and unnerving, but they managed to shake him off. Within a few minutes, another guy sauntered over to them. He was younger, just a boy himself, despite his graying skin and dull eyes.

"You guys want to party?"

"Sure," Orchid said.

The boy offered to carry Orchid's backpack, but she declined, worried he might run off with it. Still, they followed him west for a few blocks. His name was Christian, and he was from San Diego. His stepdad had beat him up regularly, so he'd left home when he was only thirteen. He was nineteen now, making his living selling drugs, stealing from cars, selling whatever he could. "You need something fenced, I can do it," he said with pride.

Orchid glanced at Lucy pointedly. They couldn't tell Christian about the bag of meth buried in that plastic bag. He was stronger than both of them. He could easily take it from them, and then they'd have nothing to sell. Nothing but themselves. Orchid vowed they wouldn't have to do that.

Soon the barren streets became lined with tents, litter, the scent of filth and fire. A woman wailed in the distance, her words unintelligible except for FUCK and GOVERNMENT. Christian explained that a mental institution had recently closed, and the city had failed to provide the outpatient support they'd promised. All those people, mentally ill and unmedicated, had nowhere to go but to the streets.

"There's social housing, but not a lot. And it's hard to get," he said. "But not everyone down here is crazy," he added, scratching roughly at his arm, leaving red streaks on the pale skin. "Some people are hooked on drugs and booze. Some people have jobs but can't afford their rent. And then some of us just feel at home here. We don't know any different."

They joined a group clustered around a small fire in a rusted barrel. It was a cool evening, but not cold. The fire seemed mostly aesthetic, a prop that let them pretend this was a gathering of friends there by choice, not necessity. Orchid and Lucy hung back on the periphery of the crowd of mostly men but a few women, one in a wheelchair, her leg amputated at the knee. Orchid studied them all until a clear leader emerged.

He was a Black man, muscular and handsome despite missing a front tooth. He didn't speak much, but his power was evident in the reverence of those around him. Orchid leaned over to Christian and whispered, "Who's that?" She nodded subtly at the man.

"That's Mal. Don't piss him off."

She wouldn't.

Holding Lucy's arm, Orchid approached Mal. Her heart thudded like a bass drum in her chest, but somehow her voice was cool. "We have some meth we need to get rid of."

Mal looked them up and down in a purely mercenary way. What could they do for him? How could he use them? But Orchid was determined not to be anyone's pawn. She would chart her own future.

"What's your name?" he asked.

"Orchid."

"I'm Lucy."

"Follow me," Mal said. He started walking and they had no option but to scurry after him. They moved past makeshift shelters, people fixing on the sidewalk, bodies strewn on the pavement like a battlefield. They went down an alley and Orchid tried not to focus on the smells: sex, urine, feces...They paused behind a dumpster full of cardboard. It was dark and secluded, and Orchid knew how vulnerable they were. But they had no choice but to trust this man.

He lit a cigarette, the cherry glowing red like a warning light. "Let's see what you got."

Lucy fished among her clothes and offered him the bag. Mal took it, weighed its heft in his hands. Then he licked a finger, dipped it into the bag, and tapped his tongue.

"That's not meth, it's coke."

Orchid was not a user, but she knew coke was worth more money. Something hopeful flickered in her belly. "You wanna buy it?"

"Yeah," Mal said, and threw out a figure that Orchid pretended to consider. She had no idea what a bag of coke was worth, but it sounded like enough. Mal pulled a wad of bills from his pocket, counted them out by the light of his cigarette. Orchid took the money, stuffed it into her backpack.

"And I'll toss in this," Mal added, handing over a small switchblade. "You'll need it out here."

"We're not sleeping out here," Orchid said as she pocketed the knife. She had money now. She could put a roof over their heads. "Is there a motel nearby?"

"Yeah, if you like bedbugs. And the motels around here are just as dangerous as the streets." He tossed his cigarette into a filthy puddle. "Maybe more so."

Mal walked off, leaving the girls to discuss.

"It's warm out," Lucy said. "We could sleep out and save our money for food and stuff."

Orchid considered it. "Maybe for a night or two."

They would sleep on the sidewalk for nearly a year.

17 THE FUTURE

FIRST MET JODY Edwards at a writers' workshop. She was the instructor, a published author sharing her wisdom about the business with other writers. It was held at a rustic resort on one of the nearby Gulf Islands. I was there with Rhea and Navid from my writers' group. Rhea had been haughty and superior in class, suggesting that many of the issues Jody encountered as a romance writer wouldn't apply to Rhea once she published her literary masterpiece. Jody had been patient, conciliatory even, but our eyes met. We'd shared a knowing look, and a friendship was born.

Jody lives on the north shore, two bridges—and at least an hour with traffic—away from me. We meet downtown (one bridge each) about once a month, to chat about writing, the publishing industry, and books in general. When the weather is good, we walk the 10K seawall around Stanley Park. When it's pouring, we go to Jody's favorite vegan café. Today a spattering of rain falls, which we've deemed acceptable walking weather. We're both fortunate to own good waterproof gear.

"How bad is it?" I ask from within the tunnel of my hood. Jody had agreed to look at *Burnt Orchid*'s Readem page for me, to screenshot the worst offenders and give me the lay of the land without the soul-crushing specifics. I have a call to discuss the matter with my publishing team this afternoon, and I want to be informed and fortified.

"There are about thirteen hundred one-star reviews now."

"Fuck."

"Some of the reviewers are articulate. They feel you're being precious about your book. That you're trying to block a reader's right not to like it by having bad reviews removed."

"Of course readers have the right not to like my book," I mutter. "I didn't expect everyone to love it." But if I'm honest with myself, I'd never really considered people hating it. I'd worked so hard on it, poured everything I had into the pages. I'd taken for granted that people would respond positively.

Jody continues. "Others are accusing you of exploiting the kids, of writing about their personal trauma for your own benefit." She sighs. "And others are just calling you horrible names."

"Like?" She shakes her head; she doesn't want to tell me. "I can handle it," I say.

"Fat whore. Pedophile. That type of thing."

It shouldn't sting—they are generic insults from people consumed with hatred for a total stranger—but it does. It feels like an assault. A physical slap.

"Anyone who looks at the reviews will see that it's review bombing," she says, arms pumping. (Jody has one speed: fast.) "It has nothing to do with the quality of the book."

"But what about people who just look at the numbers? It was down to three stars last time I checked."

Jody winces. "I think it's dipped below that now."

"Oh god…"

"If you tweet about it, you'll probably get some author support."

"My publicist told me to stay off social. She said it could inflame things."

"True," Jody agrees. "It's all being spurred on by someone called I.W. They comment on every post, egg on the outrage."

"Her name is Ingrid Wandry," I explain. "She emailed me directly and made the same accusation."

"It's like she's trying to derail your career. But why?"

"I've been trying to figure that out," I say glumly. "Was she really that offended by my book?"

"Readem can be a scary place," Jody says. "I was extorted once. When I self-published my first romance."

"What do you mean, 'extorted'?"

"I got an anonymous email threatening to tank my book with one-star reviews if I didn't pay them ten thousand dollars."

"Oh shit. What did you do?"

"I took the book down. I didn't have a publishing house behind me. I couldn't afford lawyers or a crisis PR team. I put it up again a few years later, with a different title and a pen name."

"How can that be allowed to happen?"

"It's not allowed, but the site is hard to police."

I listen to the rain tapping on my hood, feel the hopelessness clogging my throat. There is a dark side to this business that I've been entirely unaware of. "Why does this Ingrid Wandry hate me so much?"

"It's hard to know what triggers people these days."

"I know there are trolls and keyboard warriors out there who love to do battle. But this feels so personal."

"Maybe it is," Jody suggests. "Could it be someone from high school? Or a former student you counseled? Maybe someone you met in a writers' workshop?"

"I don't remember anyone called Ingrid," I say. "It's not a very common name. And even if it's a fake, I can't think of anyone who hates me enough to do this."

"She's probably just a stranger with too much time on her hands. She wrote an angry review that got traction with the one-star brigade, and now she's getting a high off it."

I nod, force an agreeable smile.

"Smudge your office with sage," my friend suggests, because she's into such things. "Chase out the bad energy."

"It's worth a try," I respond, even though I probably won't do it. And while I feel low and fragile, at least I can talk knowledgeably about my online reviews now. I change the subject. "What's new in the romance world?"

Jody tells me about a new book she's working on, and a savvy marketing plan for her backlist. I try to focus, but I'm not there. My mind is stuck in the muck of my own issues. And the impending call to discuss my publishing future.

The Zoom call includes my agent, Holly; my PR rep, Olivia; and my editor, Nadine. Nadine Sommers is a vice president and director at the publishing imprint. She's in her early fifties, sleek, savvy, and intimidating as hell. But I'm lucky to have her. When I submitted *Burnt Orchid*, it was good, but Nadine made it better. She made it publishable. She made it something I can be proud of.

"Hi, Camryn," Nadine begins from the top left corner of my screen. "Nice to see you."

"You too." I address the other faces in the small boxes. "Hi, everyone. Thanks for coordinating this meeting."

There is a chorus of greetings, and then Nadine continues. "Olivia is going to give us an update on the issues with *Burnt Orchid*."

My publicist clears her throat. "We've been in contact with Readem several times. They're aware of the review bombing and they're taking steps to control it. But these issues can take time. And sometimes it's impossible to remedy them."

My mouth falls open, and I scramble for the words to fill it. "Impossible? What do you mean?"

Nadine's composure never falters. "Olivia means that our interventions have had little to no impact. We think it's best if we all focus on moving forward."

"So we're just giving up on *Burnt Orchid*?" I cry.

"Sales are holding steady with our mass merchants and warehouse clubs," Olivia explains. "The Readem reviews only seem to be impacting online sales."

"But that's a lot, isn't it? I mean, online sales are a huge percentage of the market."

"We're really excited about your next project," Nadine says, the picture of composure. "We think it's best to focus on the future and let *Burnt Orchid* sort itself out."

Holly jumps in. "We're excited to move forward, too. Camryn's been working hard on an outline and some sample chapters."

"Yeah," I mumble, feeling a bit guilty. "This mess has been a little distracting, to say the least."

"But you'll have something soon, right?" says Holly, eyes boring into me.

"It's getting close."

"That's great." Nadine smiles. "Let's all agree to move forward. Thanks, everyone."

And one by one, they disappear from my screen.

18 FRIENDSHIPS

As part of my virtual cleanse, I've been putting my phone in a drawer for several hours a day. When I retrieve it—after work, after writing, or after stewing on the state of *Burnt Orchid*'s reviews *instead* of writing—I'm usually too exhausted to respond to casual messages. I've been a delinquent friend, I know that. But I've felt fragile and shaky, unnerved by the hate directed my way.

Part of being a friend is understanding that sometimes life gets in the way. My social circle gets that having a debut novel out in the world is distracting and time consuming; that coming up with a sophomore book idea is daunting and difficult. My close friends know the ugliness I've been going through. They will wait for me.

My outline is finally coming together. I've decided to resurrect a short story I'd workshopped in my writers' group. It's about a couple who find each other in their forties and build a beautiful life together. But the husband has a past love who haunts him, a woman now happily married with two children. When the woman's husband dies suddenly, he reaches out to support her. The widow, broken and lonely, is desperate for his companionship. They both know it's too soon, it's a rebound, but old feelings rekindle, and a dangerous love triangle develops.

I'm eager to dig into the characters, to explore the complex emotions at play, to delve into the what-ifs that we all face. And the best part of this concept is *no kids*. Well, the widow has children, but they're young and won't feature prominently. There's no way I can be accused of exploiting anyone. But now I need to step away and pay attention to my real life. As part of moving forward, I'm going to nurture my friendships. Starting with the most important one: Martha.

We've traded a few texts, exchanged a couple of voice memos, but we haven't had nearly the engagement we usually do. It's my fault, but if anyone can understand how busy I've been, it's Martha. Owning a café is the equivalent of two full-time jobs, and she has the social life of a Real Housewife. Felix plays guitar in a jazz band, and Martha regularly goes to his gigs. She's far too busy to miss me...except she'd told Liza that she does. On my way to surprise her at her coffee shop, I picked up a bouquet of flowers.

Martha's café is called Sophia's, which may sound confusing, but it's named after the residential street it is nestled on. The city has a few of these funky little coffee shops sprinkled between houses like Easter eggs. Each one is a destination, drawing customers from across town as well as serving the locals. At Sophia's, Martha's baking is the draw. I purposely skipped breakfast, excited to indulge in a buttery pain aux raisins.

I park on a tree-lined side street near Sophia's. It's a sunny Saturday morning, and the area is alive with cyclists, young families with strollers, and post-run joggers drenched in sweat. They spread across the outdoor tables, nibbling on my friend's pastries, sipping her fancy coffees. My stomach growls as I near the café, passing a cluster of bikes locked to a stand. A familiar tinkle of laughter stops me, and I turn toward it. It's Rhea, from my writers' group, unlocking her bike. She's with a woman I don't recognize.

"Rhea," I say before I think it through. She didn't attend my book launch party. She hasn't reached out to congratulate me on my publication. Rhea had been the most successful writer in our collective until *Burnt Orchid* sold. She might be struggling to be happy for my success. It's not an unfamiliar feeling.

She looks up and her face darkens, but she composes herself quickly, arranges her features into a placid expression. "Camryn," she says flatly, a word not a name. The greeting is not quite hostile, but it's entirely without warmth. Damn my big mouth. My ego can't take any more animosity.

"How are you?" I ask, tentatively closing the gap between us.

"Great. You?"

"Umm...busy," I say. "How's your writing going?"

"Good. Still in the writers' group. Still slogging away on my unmarketable literary fiction."

It's a dig. I once gave Rhea a manuscript note that suggested she might want to dial back the purple prose and get to the meat of her story. It was not well received. But I don't react to the comment. Instead I smile. "Say hi to everyone. I miss you guys."

"Will do." Is she seriously going to get on her bike without even asking me about *Burnt Orchid*? Even if she's jealous, that's incredibly rude.

"Book doing well?" It's the bare minimum, but it's something.

"Hard to say," I admit. "The sales numbers don't mean much to me."

"Getting a publishing deal is impressive, even if no one buys the book."

"Thanks...?"

Rhea puts her helmet on, fastens the buckle under her chin as she speaks. "We've got to go." She doesn't introduce me to her friend. "Take care."

I watch her ride off, feeling strangely guilty.

*　　*　　*

Though Martha has a staff of attractive hipsters, she spends a lot of time behind the counter. She and Felix, with their warm good looks and gregarious personalities, are a draw themselves. I spot my friend plating baked goods for eager customers, but Felix is nowhere in sight. When Martha spots me, she smiles, holds up a finger.

When there's a lull, she hurries around the counter. "Hey, stranger."

"These are for you." I hold out the cloud of pale-pink peonies. "To make up for being such a bad friend."

"You're famous now, I get it." She takes the bouquet. "I've missed you." She hugs me then, which isn't the norm for us. We adore each other, but normally we see each other with such regularity that physical affection feels unnecessary, over-the-top. When Martha pulls away, her eyes are misty.

"Are you okay?"

Her face crumples, and she shakes her head. "Let's go in the back."

The office is an overstuffed multipurpose space. At one end, the heavy antique desk is cluttered with paperwork, the surrounding walls lined with shelves holding dry ingredients. Martha grabs a tissue from the box teetering on a stack of cookbooks and blows her nose.

"I didn't mean to fall apart. I just haven't had anyone I can talk to."

Guilt sticks me in the ribs. Martha has a ton of friends, but I'm her confidante. I'm the one who should be there when things are tough. But I'm here now. "What's going on?"

"It's Felix." There's an edge to her voice now. "Something's going on with him, but I don't know what. He's cut me off, physically and emotionally. He won't talk to me. He's avoiding me."

I'm shocked. My friends have an incredibly harmonious relationship, especially considering the amount of time they spend together. "Have you asked him outright?"

"Of course I have, Cam. I've asked him if there's someone else. If he wants out of the business or the relationship. If he's sick or there's something wrong with his family. He won't say. He's completely shut down."

"Do you want me to try?" Even as I say it, I know it would be pointless. Felix and I are friendly, but we're not close. And I'm so firmly allied with Martha. If he's keeping something from her, he's not going to open up to me.

"I don't think there's much point, do you?"

"What about Theo?" I suggest. Felix and Theo have gone bouldering together at a climbing gym a couple of times, and more recently went on a kayak sojourn. They seem to have an easy male camaraderie between them. "He might be able to get something out of him."

"I doubt it," Martha says, all traces of her tears gone. "But I guess it's worth a try. I can't go on like this much longer." I see the determined set of her jaw, and I know she means it. Felix and Martha have a home together, a business, a history. A split would blow up their entire world. But my friend will not be mistreated. She won't allow it.

I reach for her arm, squeeze it. "Try not to worry. Theo will try to find out what's going on."

"I have to get back to work," she says, giving me a wan smile. "I'm sure it will all work out."

"Of course it will."

But neither of us is as confident as we sound.

19 ABBY

THE LESTER FAMILY home is the back unit of a duplex on a leafy street, a half hour drive from Maple Heights High. Abby crosses boundaries to attend our school for its French immersion program, taking two buses each morning. At least she did. She is still refusing to return. She is humiliated, emotionally fragile, and socially ostracized. That's why I'm here.

I'm sitting in the living room with Abby's mom, Rebecca, while her dad, Craig, makes tea. When I offered to bring schoolwork over for Abby, to talk in a less structured, more comfortable environment, both parents scheduled time off work. Abby is academically gifted, and it would be a shame if this trauma wreaked havoc on her post-secondary future. But the Lesters and I are far more focused on the girl's mental health than her university plans.

This home is understated but lovely. Sun streams through the south-facing bank of windows, illuminating a well-tended garden in bloom. Rebecca and Craig are both in healthcare, and they radiate warmth and compassion. I can see why this is a refuge for Abby. And my heart twists at the thought of these good people finding their daughter naked, covered in vomit, barely alive after an innocent slumber party.

"How is Abby doing?" I ask Rebecca as the kettle whistles in the background.

"The same," she says, pushing back an auburn curl that's escaped from her ponytail. She wears no makeup, but her skin is flawless. "She'll be fine for a few hours, and then she retreats. She goes into her room, and she won't come out. She won't eat. She doesn't sleep. She doesn't shower."

"Is she staying off her computer?" I know, personally, how triggering online hatred can be.

"We're trying. But she needs it for school."

"There's parental control software you can buy to block internet access."

Rebecca shakes her head, her pleasant features sad. "Like for little kids?"

"It's for anyone who needs to keep their child safe from the dangers of the online world. No matter their age."

Craig enters, a teapot, milk, and sugar on a tray. He's slim and wiry, a runner, I believe. He sets the tray next to three pottery mugs. "Doesn't Maple Heights have an anonymous reporting tool?" He sits next to his wife. "Has no one reported what happened that night?"

"Not in so many words, no. The girls who attended Abby's party have a lot of social power. Frankly, they're mean girls. And the kids are scared."

"They're heartless," Rebecca says quietly as Craig pours the tea. "No one has reached out to ask how Abby is. No one has apologized."

"What is wrong with their parents?" Craig places a steaming mug in front of me. "If Abby had ever been involved in something so awful, we'd be all over it."

"You have some legal recourse," I say, though it's not really my place. "You could sue the girls' parents."

"Abby made us promise not to go after anyone," Rebecca says. "She's terrified."

Craig adds, "Even *she* won't tell us who else was at the party."

Fiona Carmichael and her friends insist that a group of kids sneaked into Abby's slumber party after Craig and Rebecca went to sleep. But of course they would say that. The invited guests all deny culpability, preferring to blame the mystery guests. But no one will name names. Not even through the anonymous portal. I can't help but wonder if they are simply fictitious scapegoats.

"Do you think Abby would talk to me?" I ask gently. While I've been in regular contact with her parents, Abby has so far only spoken to an independent therapist. I understand her wanting to distance herself from the school, but we'd previously had a congenial relationship. Abby was one of the good ones: smart, engaged, and promising.

Craig and Rebecca share a look. "I don't know if she's ready," Rebecca says.

"I understand. I just thought it might be easier..." But I trail off as I hear footsteps on the stairs. Abby shuffles into the room then. She's got her dad's height, an unconventionally attractive face, and her mother's auburn curls. Her damage is apparent in her hunched posture, her slovenly dress, her lack of grooming. She moves directly toward the kitchen in a sort of daze, seemingly unaware of my presence. And then she glances over.

"No," she barks, pointing at me as she backs away. "Not her!"

Rebecca seems flustered. "Ms. Lane brought some schoolwork, honey."

"Get her out of here!" There are tears in the girl's eyes and something else... fear. Abby Lester is afraid of me.

I stand, shaken and flushed. "I'm sorry, Abby. I just thought maybe—"

"Stay away from me!" She's screaming now, tears running down her face. She turns to her parents. "Get her the fuck out of here! Make her leave!"

"You should go," Craig says quickly, and I agree. As Abby's parents rush to comfort her, I hurry to the door.

As I enter the school's main office, Monica Carruthers is walking out, keys in her hand. "What's wrong?" she asks. It's obvious I'm rattled and unnerved.

"I just went to see Abby Lester," I say quietly. "Can we talk in your office?"

"Of course." Monica leads us inside and closes the door. She perches on the edge of her desk, and I sink gratefully into a chair. And then I tell her about Abby's frightened outburst.

"It was such an odd reaction. And it was really upsetting."

Monica sighs, runs a hand through her graying hair. "Do you think it could have anything to do with your book?"

"My *book*? I don't understand."

Monica gets up, moves around the desk to her chair. "There's something I've been meaning to talk to you about."

"What?"

"We've received some messages through the snitch portal."

"About me? About my book? What did they say?"

"Some of the kids say they're afraid to bring their problems to you now. In case you use them in your next novel."

"Oh my god." I half laugh with disbelief. "I would never do that. I've been a counselor a long time and I understand the importance of confidentiality."

"I know." But there is a hint of doubt in her voice.

"And my next book isn't going to have kids in it." I press my hands into my thighs. "Trust me."

"I do trust you," she says. "I know you'd never purposely betray these kids."

"Or subconsciously, Monica. I was so careful. I *am* so careful. There's nothing to worry about."

"Okay." She stands, picks up her keys. "I was just heading out. Let's hope this all dies down."

Let's hope.

I follow her out of the office.

20 THE ATTACK

RED WINE DOES not agree with me. I'm only halfway through a glass and already pressure is building behind my eyes, and congestion is settling into my sinuses. Theo's bottle of Pinot Noir was the only alcohol in the apartment. I'd hoped a drink might blunt the memories of the day, soften the sharp edges of Abby's dread and the students' concerns that Monica passed on. But all it's doing is giving me a headache.

With some distance from the day's events, I'm beginning to realize Abby's reaction to my presence was not so startling. To her, I represent the school, the institution that has turned against her and offered safe haven to her enemies. I know that Abby's fear and outrage had nothing to do with my novel, no matter what Monica suspects.

Tipping the remains of the wine down the sink, I think about the anonymous messages the vice principal received about me. This isn't the first time students have made accusations about staff members through the portal. They are usually about male teachers using inappropriate language, overly familiar touch, or lingering looks on body parts. The administration takes all allegations seriously, while also factoring in potential grudges or vendettas students may have. I'm not infallible—I've been charged with taking sides in disputes, of not being attentive enough, of failing to get students the classes they want—but the kids have always been up front about these complaints. I hold no power over them. I don't dole out grades. They have no reason to hide their identities when accusing me.

A thought strikes me. Is it possible that my online trolls sent messages to my workplace? Posed as students to try to get me suspended, or even fired? The portal requires a student ID to log in, but I'm sure that could be faked. Or the site could be hacked. Has Ingrid Wandry convinced her online minions that I'm a serious threat to these kids, and now they're coming after my job?

I turn on the kettle to make a cup of herbal tea. I need to be fresh and clear-eyed in the morning. My three-page outline for the next book is finally ready to send to Holly for her feedback. I'll read it over once more before work, make any tweaks, and then, with crossed fingers, I'll send it. I am moving forward. My career as a writer is not over. It can't be.

The clock on the microwave reads 11:32 p.m. Theo should be home soon. He went to Felix's jazz show on a reconnaissance mission. The plan was to watch Felix's late set and then buy him a beer, pry some information out of him. Theo hates jazz, but he likes Felix and Martha. And he was happy to be a supportive friend to Felix…and a spy for Martha.

I'm brushing my teeth, spitting minty foam into the sink, when I hear Theo come in. Quickly, I scrub my tongue, rinse my mouth, and hurry out to greet him.

"Hey," I say, then stop short. My boyfriend's face is red and swollen, his left eye beginning to close. His shirt is torn, the knees of his jeans soiled. I rush to him, feel him vibrating with adrenaline. "What happened?"

"Felix attacked me." He moves past me, toward the freezer.

"What do you mean, he attacked you?"

Theo grabs a handful of ice. I pass him a tea towel. "I went up to him after his set, offered to buy him a fucking beer." He presses the ice pack to his face. "He said he wanted to talk to me outside. And then he fucking came at me."

"Why? I don't understand."

He moves into the living room, and I follow. Theo collapses onto the sofa, and I curl up beside him, touching him gingerly, trying to provide comfort.

"Theo accused me of having an affair with Martha," he blurts.

"What? Why would he say that?"

"I have no idea. He's fucking delusional."

"My god, Theo. I'm so sorry I sent you there. There must be something wrong with Felix. Was he drunk or on drugs? Did he have some kind of psychotic episode?"

"I have no idea." He looks at me, his left eye so damaged. "It's not true. You know that, right?"

I do know that, without a doubt in my mind. Not because I am overly trusting. I'm almost positive Adrian was sleeping with Tori when we were still together, though he denied it. And I know this relationship hasn't always been satisfying for Theo, that he's been frustrated by my lack of commitment, that he could undoubtedly find someone younger, with less baggage, who has more in common with him. But Martha would never do that to me.

She has been my most loyal friend since we were in high school. Back then, I'd had a huge unrequited crush on a guy named Tobin. He was a hockey player, with an unwavering belief that he was pro material. (He wasn't. Last I heard, he sells restaurant equipment.) In hindsight, he was a pretentious idiot, but god, he was so attractive. One night, when I was home nursing a cold, he'd tried to hook up with Martha at a party. She could have done it. I had no claim to him. But she'd turned him down flat.

"I would never do anything to hurt you," she'd said, her sincerity unwavering. I believed it then. And I believe it now.

"Of course I know that." I touch Theo's cheek gently. "Could you have a concussion? Do you need to go to the hospital?"

"I'm fine," he grumbles. "I'm going back to my place. I'll take some Tylenol and go to sleep."

"You can stay here? Or I can come with you?"

"Go talk to Martha." He gets up. "Find out what the hell is wrong with her husband."

21 THE ACCUSED

MARTHA AND FELIX rent a small bungalow on the (marginally) more affordable east side of the city. It's past the café, about a half hour drive from my apartment. As I cross town, questions race through my mind. What did Felix see that made him think Theo and Martha were having an affair? Did he spot them meeting covertly? Were they concerned about me? Or planning some sort of surprise? If Felix had explained his suspicions to Theo instead of pummeling him, surely Theo would have mentioned it. I'm completely confounded.

I speak into the silence of the car: "Hey, Siri, text Martha." After the prompts, I record the message. "Martha, Felix attacked Theo. He's okay but he's hurt. And he's angry. I'm on my way over. We need to figure out what the hell is going on with him." After a beat, I add, "I don't believe what Felix said. I know you'd never do that to me. And I hope you're okay."

About ten minutes later, I turn off a thoroughfare lined with Vietnamese restaurants, dollar stores, and day spas and drive into my friends' quaint neighborhood. Parallel-parking the car with minimal care, I get out and jog up the weathered front steps. As I ring the bell, I worry that Felix might be home. I've never considered him volatile—attacking Theo was completely out of character—but he's obviously a loose cannon. But Felix has no reason to be angry with me. In his mind, we are the victims.

The door swings open and I'm relieved to see Martha. Her eyes are red, and her face is puffy from crying, but she's safe, she's fine.

"Hey." I start to move inside, but she stands her ground.

"What the fuck are you doing here, Camryn? This is all your fault."

I step back, stunned by the accusation. And even more confused than I was before. "I don't know what you're talking about, Martha."

"You did this," she says, crying openly now. "Why?"

"Did what? I have no idea what you mean."

"You told Felix that you thought Theo and I were sleeping together."

"I did not!" I cry, outraged at the ridiculousness of the statement. "Why would I say that? I know you'd never do that to me!"

"Don't deny it, Camryn. I saw the email you sent him."

The email?

"Can I see it?"

"Why? You know what you said."

"Just show me."

Reluctantly, my friend lets me in, and I follow her through her eclectically furnished home—Midcentury Modern meets Oriental design meets IKEA—to the cluttered kitchen. Martha grabs her phone off the counter, taps the screen, and hands it to me. I read.

Hi Felix,

This email will be upsetting for you, but you need to know what's going on. I strongly suspect that Martha and Theo are sleeping together. I've found incriminating texts on Theo's phone. He tells me he's going to work, but when I call, he's not there. I've noticed the chemistry between them for a while, but I didn't want to believe it.

Please don't tell Martha I sent this message. And please don't contact me to discuss this in person. I am too upset and too betrayed. You should find your own proof and confront Martha with it. When I've confirmed my suspicions, I will end my relationship with both of them.

Sincerely,
Camryn

I feel dizzy and sick. A cold chill prickles my skin. "I didn't send this email, Martha."

"It's from your Gmail address."

"I haven't used that address in ages. I must have been hacked."

"Who would hack your email to send Felix a horrible message like this?"

I put the phone on the counter, press the heel of my palm to my forehead. "There's this woman online. She's out to get me."

"Why would some random stranger want to destroy *my* marriage?" Martha asks. "That makes no sense."

"She wants to ruin *our* friendship," I say, voice shaky. "She's been sending me abusive emails, posting cruel reviews. She's rallied a bunch of trolls to come after me. They think I exploited the kids at school in *Burnt Orchid*."

"That's crazy."

"I know. She's bent on destroying me. Your marriage is just collateral damage."

"Jesus Christ." Martha moves to an open beer bottle sitting

on the counter, takes a drink. "I don't know, Cam. It's sounds so weird."

"It is weird. And horrible. It's gotten so personal."

"How does this woman even know we're friends? Does she live in Vancouver? Does she know us?"

"I don't know." My voice breaks. "But I promise I'll find out."

She doesn't respond, just turns away, eyes full of tears. My heart cracks open and a thick ache spreads through my chest like oil. I did this. I hurt my best friend, threatened her relationship, and got my boyfriend beat up. It is all my fault.

I take a tentative step toward her. "Let me to talk to Felix. I can fix this."

"You can try." Martha's voice is both angry and skeptical as she turns back toward me. "He's in his workshop."

Felix's workshop is an area in the unfinished basement furnished with sawhorses, pieces of wood, and an array of tools. There's a battered love seat against one wall, covered with a ratty blanket. That's where Felix sits now, elbows on his knees, nursing a beer. He looks up when he hears my feet creaking on the stairs.

"What are you doing here, Camryn?"

I move toward him, notice the cut on the bridge of his nose, his bloodshot eyes. Theo must have hit him back. He looks like he's been crying, too.

"I didn't send that email to you," I say, crossing the concrete floor. "I was hacked. There's an online troll after me."

"What?" he snaps. "That doesn't make any sense." His anger and confusion are expected. Gently, I explain to him that Ingrid Wandry is trying to hurt me, that she is rallying online haters to destroy my writing career, that I suspect she also hacked into the school portal to send complaints about me that could get me fired. I tell him that Ingrid must have sent the email to him, and that her goal was to ruin my relationship with my best friend.

"Fuck," he says, swiping at his eyes. "I should have trusted Martha. But once the idea was planted, I let it fester until I didn't know what to believe anymore."

"This isn't your fault, Felix. Martha knows that now."

"I said horrible things. Ugly things. I broke something between us."

"She'll forgive you," I say, desperation clogging my throat. She has to. I can't have the demise of my friend's marriage on my conscience. I sit beside him. "I'm so sorry."

"Fuck," he says, jumping to his feet. "I hit Theo. I beat the shit out of him."

"He's okay. I'll explain everything. He'll understand."

Felix looms over me, his face a dark cloud. "Who the hell is this person, Camryn? And why do they hate you so much?"

"I don't know..."

But I'm not going to play by the rules anymore. I'm going to find out, whatever it takes.

22 DAMAGE CONTROL

THE FIRST THING I do the next morning is call in sick to work. I'm too shaky and too distracted to be there. It would be a disservice to the students if I went in. And I have important things to take care of. Like finding out who hacked into my email; who is hurting the people I care about; and who is so intent on destroying me that they will scorch the earth around me.

With a strong cup of coffee in hand, I first take steps to address the email hack. I try to log into the defunct Gmail account with my standard password, Liza123, but it doesn't work. I try again, and again, but as suspected, someone has gotten into this account and changed the password. What other messages might they have sent from me? My writer friend Jody is always online. I text to ask if she's received anything odd from this address. She responds instantly.

No, nothing. Why?

Promising to fill her in later, I try the password recovery options, but they don't work. When I set up this account, when I chose such a lazy password, I hadn't included a secondary email address or my cell phone number. Security was the last thing on my mind then.

But not now. I report the breach to Google's security, change the passwords on all my other accounts, and turn off location services on all my devices. It's all I can do. That, and pray that Ingrid, or whoever is behind this, doesn't use my account to inflict any more pain, to do any more damage.

Next, I do an analysis of my social media. When I'd first started my Instagram account, I'd only posted book photos. I'd taken an advance copy of *Burnt Orchid* with me on a scenic tour of the city, photographing it on a driftwood log at the beach; next to a neighbor's blooming rhododendron bush; against a backdrop of bright-green, prehistoric-looking ferns. My plan was to keep the account promotional, maintaining my personal privacy. No pictures of Liza or Theo. Only one of myself, peeking out from behind the book cover. But then came my book launch party...

In the post-celebration afterglow, I'd posted a photograph of Theo and me, his arm around my shoulders, mine slipped around his waist. The caption read:

Thank you for your support @pacificadventures1 I couldn't have done this without you. Love you! #burntorchid #adventuretourism #vancouver #beautifulbc

There was a picture of me standing between Martha and Felix, our eyes bleary with champagne, our smiles ecstatic.

Love you two so much! And not just because you make the best pastries and coffee in the city @cafesophia #grateful #friendsforlife #eastvan

I'd thought I was helping, maybe sending some customers their way. But I had also given Ingrid Wandry access into my world, handed her details of my private life and relationships on a silver platter. I am squarely to blame.

As I'm moving to the kitchen to refill my coffee, my phone rings. It's my journalist friend Janine. I'd texted her last night, told her I needed to talk.

"Is it the girls?" she asks as soon as I answer. She's driving and has me on speakerphone. Traffic hums in the background. "Or the haters?"

She knew without the benefit of intonation that my text meant nothing good. I tell her about Theo and Felix and Martha, trying to keep my voice level and calm. "I know it pales in comparison with what you went through," I say, and emotion seeps into my words. "But Ingrid Wandry is hurting my friends. I'm upset."

"Of course you are," Janine says. "Having a stranger meddle in your personal life is terrifying. She sounds disturbed. And possibly dangerous."

"I think so, too," I say, no longer trying to hide my fear. "I don't know what to do."

"I know a cyber-security guy," she says. "I did a story on him years ago when he was a teen hacker. He's a little odd. He lives in a basement apartment filled with action figures. He was headhunted by Google, but he's too antisocial. He's expensive, but he's a genius. He could find out who is behind this."

"How much is he?" When she gives me a ballpark, I wince. There's no way I could afford him. All of my salary is allocated to rent, groceries, utilities, and my daughter's college fund. Maybe if Nadine makes an offer on my next novel, I could spend the advance on this expert. But there are no guarantees that she will.

"Keep him in mind," Janine says. "Does this Ingrid woman have social media? You can find out a lot about a person through their posts."

Don't I know it. That's how Ingrid learned about my boyfriend and my best friends. "She only has Instagram. And she doesn't show up in any Google searches."

"Look at the background of the photos she posted," Janine says over a horn honking in the distance. "You might be able to see where she lives. Where she works or shops or exercises. See who she's tagged, or the hashtags she uses. Do some digging."

"But then what?" I ask. "How do I stop her?"

"I know a lawyer who'll send her a cease-and-desist letter for a reasonable fee. Sometimes that's all it takes."

"And if it's not?"

"You've been keeping records of all the harassment, right?"

"Yeah."

"You can call the police. Have her charged with stalking and harassment. You might be able to sue her for defamation."

"Okay." My voice is small and weak. It all sounds so daunting. So expensive.

Janine's tone shifts. "Does Liza know what's going on?"

"Just that I've received some nasty emails. I haven't told her much."

"I don't think you should burden her with this. Senior year is already so stressful. And according to Grace, there's all sorts of drama swirling around right now."

"Yeah, I'm aware." But I'm not thinking about Liza. Though my daughter may be reconsidering her college plans, she seems happy, well adjusted. I'm thinking about Abby Lester. And I'm thinking about Fiona Carmichael. Yesterday, an anonymous tip had come into the portal claiming Fiona was threatening kids who knew what had happened at Abby's party. When Vice Principal Carruthers confronted her, Fiona had denied it, of course. But it sounds like her MO.

"I want Liza to focus on school and friends and college," I say. "I don't want her worrying about me."

"You're a good mom, Cam." Her words stir up my emotions, and I'm too verklempt to respond. "Call me any time," Janine says. "And try not to worry. This too shall pass."

Yeah, it will pass. Because I'm going to end it.

23 THE TAIL

INGRID WANDRY'S SMILING face fills my computer screen. Instagram is built for the phone, but I've opened it on my laptop for better viewing. I need to see Ingrid's photos enlarged so I can look for details in the background. I click past the ocean scene and the cat to the image of my nemesis at the beach. But it won't provide any clues. She's clearly on vacation, in her flowy dress, a sun hat in her hand. People who live in seaside locales don't dress like they're in a romance novel. I live four blocks from the beach and don't own anything so gauzy.

I peer at the photo of Ingrid drinking the purple smoothie. Zooming in on the image, I notice the clear plastic cup has a label, a green circle with white lettering, but I can only see the top few millimeters. It's unfamiliar, though, not from a popular juice chain. Behind her shoulder, I notice signage peeping out, partial words. They're slightly blurred but I can make out:

INE CLINIC
6 AVE SE
WA

Clinic. Why would Ingrid take a selfie outside a doctor's appointment? I inspect her shirt—white, with a collar and a zip closure—and I realize it's a uniform. Ingrid Wandry could be a doctor, a dentist, or a nurse. It shocks me that a woman in a healing profession spends her free time attacking people online. But maybe she feels it all evens out? On the breast pocket of her top, there's an embroidered logo. The words aren't visible, but a distinct image curls into view. It's a tail. Of a dog or a cat. Ingrid works at an animal clinic. My nemesis is a veterinarian, or an assistant, or a receptionist.

WA stands for "Washington State." It also stands for "Western Australia," "West Angola," and many other locales, but I start close to home. I google: Animal clinics in Washington State.

There are hundreds, of course, and my heart flutters with panic. It will be impossible to find her. But I take a calming breath and refine the search. Ingrid posted a picture of a cat, so I try: cat veterinarian. The results are diminished to something approaching manageable. I scroll through the results, and I find one that matches the partial signage.

PURR FELINE CLINIC
2705 156 AVE SE
BELLEVUE, WA

Pulse racing, I click the link to go to their website. It's rudimentary, the landing page offering contact details and opening hours, but there is a link to a photo gallery. I scroll past the cats and the interior shots and take in the storefront. Purr is located in a nondescript unit in a strip mall in the upscale Seattle suburb. Two doors down, I note a sign for Emerald Juice Bar. When I click on their product images, I see it. The circular green logo on their clear plastic cups.

"I found you!" I say, slapping the desk with delight. I'm impressed with my investigative skills. Who needs Janine's expensive cyber detective? But the feeling of euphoria fades quickly. Because what do I do now? Call the police? I know virtual abuse is rarely taken seriously by law enforcement. Should I contact Janine's lawyer and send a cease-and-desist letter to Ingrid at the Purr address? Would it have any effect? My tormentor lives less than a three-hour drive away from me. Is there another, more effective way for me to handle this?

A key in the lock disturbs my reverie. I hurry toward it, already knowing that it's Theo. He took the day off, too. Apparently black eyes are off-putting to tourists.

"How did it go?" I ask as he enters the apartment. He and Felix had met at Sophia's to discuss last night's mêlée.

"Felix apologized," Theo mutters, moving into the kitchen. But all is clearly not forgiven. The physical pain is not the only lingering symptom. He pours himself a glass of water, takes a big drink, then turns to me. "The fact that he believed I'd sleep with Martha. And that you'd send an email like that. It pisses me off."

"This isn't Felix's fault. It's the troll's."

He puts the glass on the counter. "If you'd published your book under a pen name, none of this would have happened."

I'm instantly defensive. "So this is my fault now?"

"No, of course not." He sighs, runs a hand through his hair. "But is Felix even our friend if he's so quick to believe the worst? Of both of us?"

"He is our friend," I say, but really, he's *my* friend. Because he's married to Martha, who will always be in my life. Theo and Felix don't have the same history. Or the same loyalty.

"This is so fucked up, Cam."

"I know. I'm sorry."

"You need to find out who did this and call the police."

I should tell him that I've found her. That Ingrid Wandry is just across the border, that I could confront her face-to-face in a couple of hours, if I wanted to. But for some reason, I don't tell him. Instead, I lie.

"I'm researching all the options," I say. "Leave it with me."

24 CHLOE

CHLOE WINSTON, THE fantasy author who was mercilessly attacked by trolls, is a little younger than I am, with a full, unlined face and noticeably perfect teeth. But there's a hardness to her. She wears her damage in her eyes, in the set of her jaw. Her face is that of a survivor. And it is now filling my computer screen.

I'd reached out to Zoe Carpenter—we've kept in touch since the Miami writers' festival—to ask a favor. I wanted to speak to Chloe, to compare our experiences as writers dealing with trolls and haters. Would Chloe Winston speak with me, did Zoe think? My friend had agreed to connect with her, to explain my situation, and Chloe had agreed to a video call.

After brief introductions, Chloe cuts to the chase. "Zoe says the trolls are after you."

I tell her about the reviews, the emails, and the comments. I tell her about the flowers, the mysterious drink, and the disgusting message to Felix.

"Wow. It crossed into your real life so quickly. Did you antagonize them?"

"I was advised not to respond, so I've said nothing."

"For me, it didn't get really bad until I fought back."

Zoe had told me about Chloe's literary downfall, but I need more. "Can you tell me?" I plead gently.

She takes a fortifying breath. "A writer on Twitter accused me of plagiarizing his unpublished manuscript. He'd posted it in a few online workshops and on some lit-sharing websites. He said I must have found it online and copied it." She shakes her head. "There was no merit to it. I should have ignored it. But I was pissed. I spent years writing that book. Every goddamn word was mine, and I wanted to own it."

"What did you do?"

"I called this guy jealous and bitter and entitled on Twitter. I screenshotted the angry messages he'd sent me, and I posted them. I wanted people to see that he was a ranting, irrational jerk. But it backfired."

"That's when the trolls came after you?"

"Yeah. They accused me of stealing this guy's story. They said he'd been rejected by publishers because he was a white male. They claimed I only got a publishing deal because I'm a BIPOC woman. It was total digilantism."

"What's that?"

"Online vigilantism." Chloe takes a drink from a glass of water beside her computer. "There was one troll in particular, a guy who went by Creeper98. He was part of a collective of guys who work together to destroy people online."

"They're *organized*?"

"Yeah. There are international trolling syndicates that plan coordinated attacks to get people fired, get them to quit the internet, even drive them to kill themselves."

"God..."

"The online abuse is bad, but when it seeps into your real life, it's unbearable." Her face darkens. "I was doxed." The term is only vaguely familiar to me, but Chloe explains. "They published my home address on Twitter and Reddit, and in their online troll communities. Somehow they got my mom's address, too. People threw bottles at my house, and fruit, and dog shit. They harassed my mom when she went to get groceries. She had to go stay with my aunt for a while. Sometimes a car would sit outside my house all night, just watching me."

"That's awful, Chloe."

"I was swatted, too."

I've heard of this practice, where an anonymous caller sends the police to an address claiming there are guns inside, a hostage situation, or another serious crime in progress.

"They kicked in my door with guns drawn. I was handcuffed and taken into custody. As a Black woman, it was especially terrifying."

I can scarcely imagine her fear, the very real risk to her life.

"I handled it all wrong." She sighs, shifts in her chair. "You can't fight these people online. A reaction is what they want."

"So what should I do?" I ask, the futility of my situation pressing down on me. "I've given them nothing, but my trolls won't go away. Should I just let them ruin my career when it's barely started? Let them attack my friends and destroy my relationships?"

Chloe sighs. "Maybe you could reach out to this Ingrid woman privately? Reason with her on a personal level?"

"That goes against everything I've been told to do."

"I don't know, Camryn." She takes another sip of water. "If I could do it over again, I wouldn't fight. I'd try to make them see that there's a real person with real feelings on the receiving end of all the hatred."

"Do you think that would have worked?"

"It might have. I've done a lot of reading about this. Some trolls are psychopaths who love to inflict pain. Others are narcissists who think their actions are justified. But a lot of them are in pain themselves. They're lashing out online because they're lonely and isolated. Or they have mental health issues, or substance abuse problems. Maybe Ingrid is suffering, too?"

"That's a very compassionate point of view," I say, a remarkably un-compassionate edge to my voice. "You've lost so much because of the haters."

"I've had a lot of therapy," Chloe says. "I'm working on forgiveness. But I've been diagnosed with PTSD from the experience. Other than my father dying, it's the worst thing I've ever gone through."

I thank her for talking to me, a virtual stranger, about something so painful, and we wrap up our call. But she leaves me with one last thought.

"I still just really want to know why," Chloe says. "What did they get out of it? Are they happy they destroyed me? And why me?"

It is the question that runs through my mind when I should be sleeping, writing, spending time with my boyfriend or my daughter: Why me?

BURNT ORCHID

1996

The relationship that developed between Orchid and Mal was not sexual or romantic. It was deeper than that. Despite their outward differences, they operated on the same intellectual and spiritual plane. They recognized something in each other that didn't need to be articulated: a soul connection, though neither of them would have used such a clichéd term. The trust between them was instant, inherent. Orchid knew Mal was not a good person. He was a dealer, a killer, a ruthless, even cruel leader. But she knew he would never hurt her.

Mal became Orchid's mentor and guide to surviving, even thriving on the streets. There was a brand-new painkiller out called OxyContin, and Mal knew a dirty doctor willing to write multiple prescriptions for a kickback. Mal sent his minions to pharmacies around the city to fill the scripts and bring the pills back to Mal, who then sold them for a profit. The drug company said Oxy was gentle and non-addictive, but Mal knew different. Once his mules or dealers tried it, they could no longer be trusted not to dip into the supply. He was always on the lookout for fresh meat, for people who wouldn't sample the wares. Orchid was a legal adult, capable of having a prescription filled. And she would never double-cross him.

Lucky for Mal's business model, there was a shady pharmacist willing to fill multiple prescriptions at once. Mal introduced Orchid to Allan, a bald man whose belly strained against his white lab coat. He took the scripts and filled them for a price. Orchid would handle the drop-offs and pickups. She still looked decent and respectable. She wouldn't draw attention.

One day, as Orchid waited for Allan to count out the painkillers, she noticed a sign on the plexiglass above the counter. It read:

Los Angeles County Drug Take-Back Center
Unused, unwanted, expired medications disposed of here.

"What do you do with the expired drugs?" she asked Allan when he handed her the paper bag filled with plastic bottles.

"Someone from the county collects them and they put them in hazardous waste."

"Can I buy them?" she asked. "There are people living on the streets who need medication."

Allan didn't comment that Orchid was completely unqualified to be doling out prescription meds to the sick and poor. He just smiled. "How much you offering?"

Orchid told Mal she wanted to start her own business. "People down here are suffering. They have no insurance and no doctor. There are perfectly good antibiotics and blood pressure meds going to waste."

"Sure," he said. "But I get a cut."

"Of course." She'd never doubted it.

"And you have to keep working for me. Keep doing the pickups and deliveries."

"I can do both," she assured him.

With Lucy's help, she could. Lucy was still a child, but she was already growing steely and savvy. She was fully capable of roaming the neighborhood, finding out who had an infection, an STD, a previously diagnosed condition they could no longer afford to treat. With Allan's input, they learned which medications worked for what ailments. And they sold them: for money, for recreational drugs, for favors...

The girls worked hard, and even with a portion of their profits going to Mal and Allan, they gathered enough money to rent a studio apartment. The building was derelict and dangerous, but the unit had a private bathroom, a hot plate, and a small fridge. And it was their own. They cleaned it, painted it, and furnished it with battered furniture from Goodwill. Soon another girl moved in with them. Her name was Tracey, and Orchid put her to work helping Lucy sell the meds.

Orchid had built them a home. Now she would build her empire.

25 THE TRIP

MY MAZDA SHUDDERS down the I-5, unsteady at such high speeds. I'm feeling unsteady myself, hands damp on the wheel, breath labored in my chest. The reality of what I'm about to do is sinking in, the recklessness of this decision. I've told no one that I'm coming here. In fact, I lied to both Theo and Liza. They'd have thought I was insane, would have certainly talked me out of it. But this mission still feels like the right thing to do. I'm done sitting passively by. I'm done being a victim.

Haters cannot be beaten online. This is evidenced by Janine's and Chloe's experiences, and by all the online research I have done. Reacting, hitting back on social media is just giving them what they want. *Don't feed the trolls.* Even the most novice internet user knows the adage. Of course, confronting a virtual harasser in person is ill advised, potentially dangerous. But Chloe Winston said she wished she'd shown her abusers the real person behind the online persona. And my tormentor is female. This gives me a sense of security, and a sense of hope. Maybe I can reason with her. Connect with her woman-to-woman. Maybe I can find out why she hates me so much.

The border guard had asked the purpose of my visit.

"Just getting some cheese and some gas," I'd said pleasantly. "I might stop in at Trader Joe's."

He'd had no reason not to believe me. Thousands of Canadians cross this border each day in search of bargains. Not many admit they're on a mission to confront their cyber stalker. Or at least to observe her in her natural habitat. I'm still not sure that I will approach Ingrid. I plan to surveil her, check out the situation, and listen to my instincts. If she seems violent or aggressive, I will abort. But she works with cats. She wears romantic sundresses. How dangerous can she be?

I'd called my daughter as I left the city, the car rattling past vast farms growing blueberries and cranberries, raising dairy cattle. Liza has a free period on Friday mornings, so I knew she'd be tucked up in her bed, in the small basement bedroom at Adrian's, likely scrolling through her phone. She answered after the first ring.

"Hey, honey. Just checking in. Are you coming home tonight, or tomorrow?"

"Tonight," she said. "I have to study, and Savannah is having a bunch of her nerdy friends over."

Liza gets along with her stepsister, but they travel in very different social orbits.

"Great," I said. I'm always happy when my girl comes home. "Will Wyatt be coming over to study with you?" My tone was breezy, casual, but clearly also irritating.

"Wyatt is hanging out with his friends tonight," she'd snapped. "And no, we haven't decided what we're going to do in the fall. Can you just let us work it out, please?"

I was tempted to tell her that the clock was ticking, that she had to apply for a deferral or the tuition fees Adrian and I paid would be lost. But I wasn't up for a fight. "Okay. Sorry."

"Where are you going?" Liza asked. She could hear the vehicle rattling.

"Groceries," I lied. I'd gone the day before. "I'll stock the fridge up for you."

"It sounds like you're on the freeway."

"Nope. Just a bumpy patch of road here. I'll see you tonight."

I'd felt bad lying to my daughter, but Janine is right. The less Liza knows about this mess the better.

Fooling Theo was more challenging. He's been on edge since Felix punched him in the face, since he learned my computer was hacked, since we confirmed that someone is trying to mess up my life. My boyfriend has always been attentive—texting regularly when he's not on the water or in the mountains—but now it's bordering on obsessive. He's worried about me. And if I go MIA on a day off, he'll panic. I told him I was attending a professional development course on the outskirts of the city, that my phone would be on silent. It seemed to satisfy him.

My GPS tells me to get onto the 405, and I veer east toward my destination. I'm flying past residential neighborhoods, tech campuses, and colleges, interspersed with scrubby patches of forest. It's unfamiliar territory. I've been to Seattle several times over the years—Adrian liked to come down to watch the Mariners play, and we'd taken Liza to the Museum of Pop Culture and to Pike Place Market—but I've never visited the suburbs. I've never had reason to. Until now.

As I roll into the city, I'm greeted by gleaming luxury hotels, sleek office towers, and the high-end shopping center that dominates the main drag. This upscale community is home to wealthy tech employees and those who work in the various service industries. My GPS guides me through the old part of town, down a quaint street with outdoor dining and flowers in planters, and across a busy thoroughfare. A few minutes later, I hear: *Your destination will be on your right.* And I pull into the parking lot of Purr Feline Clinic.

Suddenly, my bravado deserts me. I'd planned to go into the clinic and pretend I have a sick cat at home. I would inquire about costs and medications, and then I'd casually ask if Ingrid was available. She'd be shocked to see me there, but she wouldn't react, not in her workplace. I'd offer to buy her a smoothie on her break, to talk things through. It would be safer to meet her in a public space, near her work, where she'd be on her best behavior. But now, I find, I can't get out of my car.

I'm still sitting there, more than an hour later, when Ingrid exits. At the sight of my nemesis in the flesh, my heartbeat skitters, and I sink lower into my seat. Ingrid is in her uniform, blond hair pulled back in a ponytail, a backpack slung over her shoulder. I glance at the dashboard clock. Her shift must end at three. She is moving toward a small SUV, a Honda CR-V, and now she's climbing in. I have missed my chance to intercept her, to finally put an end to this harassment. As her car reverses out of the parking spot, my stomach clenches. I can't turn around and drive all the way home. I've come too far to chicken out now. Starting my car, I pull out of the lot behind her.

I follow her blue vehicle back through town, up a steep hill, and into a residential neighborhood. We move past luxurious two-story homes, some with views of the distant lake, and continue on for several blocks. The houses become more modest, bungalows mostly and some eighties-style ranch homes. Ingrid parks in front of a tidy house with gray siding, a red door, and neat flower beds. I stop my car a few houses away, adrenaline surging through my bloodstream, pulse pounding in my ears. Ingrid gets out of her vehicle, gathers her backpack, and moves toward her house.

It's unwise to approach her here, on this quiet street, with no one in sight. If she is mentally ill, consumed with rage, she could be dangerous. And then a gray cat, the one from her Instagram photo, scampers toward her. Ingrid kneels to scratch it under the chin. It's now or never. I climb out of my car.

"Wait!" I call.

26 THE CONFRONTATION

INGRID RISES, AND the cat scampers away. Her expression is troubled as she turns to face me. "Can I help you?" She sounds hostile and suspicious. She doesn't recognize me yet. I move closer.

"I'm sorry to show up here, unannounced. I'm not angry. I'm not upset. I just want to talk to you."

"Who *are* you?"

"It's me," I say, but her expression is blank. I know my author picture is more flattering than reality, but I don't look *that* different. "I'm Camryn Lane."

"I don't know you."

"I'm the author of *Burnt Orchid*."

"Uh...good for you." She backs away, like she's scared. Of *me*. Like I'm the one who's unhinged and dangerous.

"You've been harassing me online, Ingrid." I keep my voice calm. "And I'd like to know why. What have I done to make you so angry?"

"My name isn't Ingrid." She walks briskly toward her house. "And I have no idea what you're talking about. Please leave me alone."

And I believe her. Her anxiety is real. Have I somehow gotten this all wrong? Have I been catfished, fooled into believing an innocent stranger has been harassing me while the real perpetrator slides under the radar? The woman I thought was Ingrid is climbing her steps now, eager to get away from me. "Wait. Please." My voice cracks with emotion, and it causes her to pause. "Someone is using your image online. They've made it look like your name is Ingrid Wandry, the woman who's been trolling me."

She moves to the railing, looks down at me from her front porch. "Where did you see my photos?"

"On Instagram." I take a few steps forward, so I don't have to yell. "There's a profile with the name Ingrid Wandry. But they're pictures of you. Even your cat."

She unzips her backpack and pulls out her phone. I stand by as she brings up the page. "What the hell...?"

"I'm an author," I explain, edging forward lest I spook her. "Someone's been using your face and a fake name to harass me."

"It wasn't me."

"I believe you."

Her eyes are on her phone. "These photos are from my private Instagram page. Only my followers can access them."

"So my troll is someone you know."

She looks up, her eyes guarded. "I don't know *all* my followers."

"But you probably know most of them. Can you think of anyone who might do something like this?"

"No. Of course not."

Movement in the front window catches my eye. A young man peers out at us for a moment. He is fair and slim, probably in his early twenties. There is nothing unusual about him...except for the way he ducks out of sight.

"Who was that?"

"My nephew."

"Does he follow you on Instagram? Could he know something about this?"

The possibility flits across her features. "No, he wouldn't do that." But I can tell she is not convinced. And neither am I.

"Can I talk to him please?"

"I think you'd better leave." She has closed ranks, gone into protective mode. "This has nothing to do with him or me."

I move closer, even as she draws back. "I've been mercilessly harassed for over a month. I've had abusive, misogynistic messages sent to me, even rape threats. My book has been bombarded with bad reviews." My voice is rising, desperation making it shrill. "I've had prank phone calls. My email's been hacked. Someone is trying to hurt me. Someone using *your* face."

"I—I'm sorry that's happening to you." She's flustered—confused and afraid. "But like I said, I know nothing about it."

I should be more sensitive to her unease, but frustration takes over. "You could help me!" I practically scream at her. "Why won't you help? What is wrong with you?"

"What's wrong with *me*? What's wrong with *you*?" She's angry now. "You just showed up at my house, screaming accusations. How did you even find me? Did you follow me home from work? Have you been spying on me?"

"Someone you know is harassing me. They're trying to tank my book and destroy my career. I'm angry and I'm terrified. But you'd rather protect *them* than help me. That's cruel," I spit. "And it's heartless."

Movement in the window catches my eye. The young guy is back, and he's holding his phone up. "Is he filming us?"

She glances over at him. "Looks that way."

"Stop!" I yell, waving my arm at the boy in the window. "You don't have permission to film me."

"You're screaming at me on my property!" Not-Ingrid yells back. "You're making insane accusations! Get out of here before I call the police."

"Please," I try, one last time. "I've come a long way to talk to you."

But the woman ignores me, and she looks ready to dial her phone. It hits me then how this could look to a cop. An American cop. I turn and hurry back to my car.

The drive home is a blur, my mind replaying the ugly confrontation, swimming with unanswered questions. Ingrid Wandry doesn't exist. The face I'd considered my nemesis has never heard of me. At the border, I lie to the guard, tell her I met a friend for lunch, stopped at Target but didn't buy anything. When I pull up to my building, I scarcely remember how I got there. I parallel-park the car on the street. I have an allocated spot in the underground lot, but I feel too unnerved, too vulnerable to go into a dark, secluded space right now.

My feet are heavy as I make my way to the front door of my building. I'm eager to see my daughter, to order some sushi and then have a hot bath. The late-spring sun is still high, though it's nearly eight o'clock now. Families are gathering outside the gelato shop kitty-corner to my building, children hopped up on sugar squealing with joy. It's a beatific scene, but a prickle of fear runs up my neck. I have the distinct sensation that I'm being watched.

I pause to survey the people on the streets, but no one is looking my way, so I turn to the row of parked cars. My eyes rove down the line of vehicles, and as they land on a silver Volkswagen Golf, it suddenly animates. With a roar of the engine, the car jerks out of its parking spot. There is something panicked and guilty in its departure. And its speed is concerning, with so many kids in the area. I move back to the sidewalk for a better view. As the car stops at a traffic light, I see the driver. It's a boy, tall and broad but only a teen. He's wearing a cap, but it looks a lot like Wyatt.

When I enter the apartment, Liza is sitting at the breakfast bar, a chemistry textbook laid out before her. Beside her is a half bottle of kombucha and a bowl of trail mix. She looks up. "Hey."

"Was Wyatt here?

"No. I know you don't like him to come over when you're not here."

"This isn't about that." I move into the kitchen, lean my forearms on the counter in front of her. "I won't be mad. You just need to tell me the truth."

"Mom, he wasn't here."

"Does he have a car? A small silver Golf?"

"No."

"Do his parents?"

"I don't know what his parents drive. They're never home when I'm there. God, Mom. What's going on with you?"

"Nothing. I just thought I saw him drive off."

"Well, you didn't."

"Okay." I press my fingers into my eye sockets until I see stars. I'm physically and emotionally exhausted. It's entirely possible I'm hallucinating.

"Why don't you relax? All this book stuff is getting to you."

"I'll try," I say. "I'm sorry."

"Go have a bath. I'll bring you a kombucha."

Obediently, I stumble toward the bathroom.

27 THE RABBIT HOLE

THE CONFRONTATION HAD gone so wrong. So, so, so wrong. But it had also provided much-needed clarity. My troll is not the woman I thought she was. She may not be a woman at all. From my conversations with Janine and Chloe, and the online research I've done, it seems that the majority of trolls are young white men. Most of them are harmless, doing it for "lulz," but a handful of them exhibit alarming traits: psychopathy, Machiavellianism, narcissism, and sadism. It's the dark tetrad of personality I learned about in grad school. And it's terrifying.

As I fell down the rabbit hole of online hate, I discovered more horrifying facts than I could have imagined. There are trolls who specifically target victims of rape or sexual assault, and RIP trolls who frequent the memorial pages of the deceased, especially victims of suicide. They make cruel comments, victim-blame, tell horrible lies—anything to elicit an emotional reaction from friends, family, and loved ones. Some trolls like to go after people on the autism spectrum or who have mental illness, hoping for a bigger response. Outrage, fear, and hurt are fuel for these trolls. They get a high from it.

And then I learned about the predator trolls who seek to destroy a specific person: a random stranger with views they disagree with; a high-profile individual they feel is misusing their platform; or the victim of a personal vendetta. These trolls work alone or in teams to destroy a person's online reputation, to damage their mental health, to cause distress and emotional pain. In severe cases, the abuse may creep into real life.

Like mine.

I'm on the sofa, my laptop open on my lap. A cup of mint tea warms my hands as I stare at the home screen, formulate my strategy. The woman in Bellevue is the key to finding out who is harassing me. While I don't know her name, I know where she works. Setting the tea down, I bring up the Purr Feline Clinic website. As with my last visit, I find little useful information, so I go to their Facebook page. It's an active page, posting cat health tips, cute images, and photos and bios of their staff. The woman I encountered is about halfway down the page, her smile warm and compassionate. Her name is Megan Prince and she's a veterinary technician. Her bio says she has a bachelor of applied science degree from Whatcom Community College. She and her partner love to cycle and kayak. The gray cat's name is Gervais.

Next, I look up Megan Prince on Facebook. There are several profiles with that name, but none of them are her. Of course, it couldn't be that easy. I search for her Instagram page and finally find it: @megantheeprince_ss. It is indeed private, but the profile picture is definitely her. There is no way for me to see who follows her, to see if I recognize anyone, or to check if we have mutual followers. But one of those 207 people is using Megan's identity to harass me.

Fuck.

I go back to the clinic's Facebook page and peruse Megan's

colleagues. Surely she hangs out with some of the people she works with. There is another technician, Carolyn, who looks like friend material, and her profile page is public. Sifting through photos of a bachelorette party, a destination wedding, a Taylor Swift concert, I search for Megan. Finally, I spot her at a company barbecue, a red plastic cup in hand, arm around Carolyn and one of the veterinarians. Searching the background of the photo, I don't see anyone familiar. I don't see anyone from my past or present.

Just as I'm starting to feel like a stalker, an alert sounds on my phone. I'm meeting Navid from my old writing group for a happy-hour drink. I'd almost forgotten. Downing the lukewarm tea, I set my laptop aside and hurry to change.

Navid is a retired professor, in his early sixties with a salt-and-pepper beard and a shiny bald head. He is warm and kind, married to a lovely guy and father to a grown son. This gentle, soft-spoken man writes positively brutal horror fiction. He has secured an agent—a Herculean feat in its own right—but has yet to publish a book. I want this evening to be fun, light, a distraction from the negative side of my publishing experience. Unfortunately, Navid has other ideas.

"I'm sorry for all the shit you're going through online," he says when Aperol spritzes and a plate of calamari are in front of us.

"How did you know?"

"Rhea sent a link to your Readem page to the writing group."

"Of course she did."

"She's so jealous." He chuckles. "Last time I saw her, her skin had a greenish tinge."

"She must love that I'm being bombarded with bad reviews."

"She does." Navid sips his drink. "She hides it, of course.

Pretends to be sympathetic, even concerned for your safety. But she's delighting in your misery."

"Rhea wouldn't...?" I trail off, the words too horrible to articulate. But Navid picks up the dropped thread.

"No," he says quickly, but I see the possibility travel through his mind. "Rhea's not a monster," he continues. "I mean, she's not a very nice person, either, but I don't think she's capable of the cruel things you're experiencing."

I feel less confident. I remember the way Rhea looked at me outside Sophia's café, her eyes filled with derision, even hate.

"None of those accusations are true," I say, dipping a squid ring in tzatziki. "I didn't steal any stories from the kids I work with. I would never do that."

"Of course not. No one who knows you would believe that."

But the people who don't know me might. And that's the entire internet.

Two hours later, I return to my empty apartment. It's not even eight; Liza is still out with friends, so I grab a bag of kettle chips and settle onto the sofa to wait for her. I turn on the TV, watch a few minutes of a show about people falling in love through a wall, but I'm exhausted. Rehashing the trolling with Navid was emotionally draining. Before long, I'm asleep on the sofa.

The sound of my phone wakes me from a hazy slumber. The apartment is dark now, except for the blue light of the TV. I fumble for my device in the clutter on the coffee table, in between the couch cushions. I have no idea what time it is, but I suspect the call is from Liza, asking to extend her curfew (Adrian lets her stay out as late as she wants, but at my house, I want her home by midnight). It could be Theo calling, checking in after he took a bachelor party on a Jet Ski trip to nearby Bowen Island.

Finally, I find the phone under the bag of chips and check the screen.

10:45 PM

No Caller ID.

Not again. I already blocked the last prank caller. This is someone new.

I answer and listen to the silence.

Finally, I find the phone under the bag of chips and check the screen.

10:45 PM

No Caller ID.

Not again. I already blocked the last prank caller. This is someone new.

I answer and listen to the silence.

28 ONWARD

THE SKIN BENEATH Theo's eye has turned a sickly shade of yellow now, a sign that the damage is starting to heal. My partner's psyche is slower to mend. He's still angry about the incident, surly and uncommunicative when I suggest we accept Martha's dinner invitation, to break bread, to move on. I know we can't avoid my best friends indefinitely, but I'm not going to force the issue with my partner. And I have other things on my mind.

"I got more prank phone calls," I tell him as we sip coffees in the public market, not far from Theo's shop. The vast warehouse space is relatively quiet, but it's early, and it's a weekday. Soon the market will be overrun with locals and tourists alike, lured by the photogenic towers of fruit, the handmade pasta and sausages, the fresh fish. It is still bearable this time of year. During the summer, Granville Island market is not a place for the faint of heart.

"It has to be kids," Theo says. "You blocked one phone number, so now they're using another kid's phone."

"Probably." Something has been weighing on my mind, a thought I have yet to articulate. "I think I saw Wyatt hanging around outside our apartment when I came home the other night."

"Did you talk to him?"

"He was in a car, and he took off when I spotted him. But Liza said he wasn't there."

"She's probably lying," Theo says, breaking off a piece of donut. "You were out, and they saw an opportunity for some alone time. You remember what it's like to be that age."

Not as well as Theo does. "I guess. But Liza doesn't lie to me."

"All kids that age lie."

I'm about to argue the point, but then I remember that my daughter may be taking a gap year that she failed to mention to me. "What if Liza didn't know Wyatt was outside, either?"

"What do you mean?"

"I found some concerning texts from him on Liza's computer." I fill him in on Wyatt's "where are you" messages and my daughter's explanation. "I talked it through with Adrian and Tori. They're not concerned."

"But you think Wyatt might be obsessed with Liza?"

"It could have been triggered by her leaving for college. But now she's considering traveling to Australia with him, and I'm afraid he manipulated her into it." My voice is thin, and my eyes are damp. Theo puts his hand over mine.

"Liza is a smart girl. And you've done a great job raising her."

"Do you think I'm too strict?"

"You're pretty strict by today's standards. But then Adrian and Tori's house is like a nightclub in Ibiza, so it balances out."

I smile at him, grateful for his support and sense of humor.

"Liza is strong like you are. And Wyatt seems like a good kid." He pauses for a moment. "You're exhausted, Cam. You're feeling vulnerable and attacked. It could be coloring your perception of the situation."

I nod, my throat full of emotion. He's right. I'm tightly wound, on the edge, and I'm not sure I can trust my own judgment right now.

"Take the day to relax," Theo says. "Maybe I can come over after work and cook for you and Liza?"

It's such a kind gesture, but I feel like I should spend some quality time alone with my daughter. I tell him so, gently and appreciatively.

"I get it," he says, downing the remains of his coffee. "She's not going to open up about Wyatt if I'm around."

He walks me back to my car in a parking shed, the rafters full of cooing pigeons. When he leans in to kiss me goodbye, I wrap my arms around his strong shoulders.

"Thanks for your support," I mumble into his neck.

"Of course," he says. "I'm always here for you...except right now because there are eleven Japanese people waiting for me to take them windsurfing."

I chuckle and release him. Then I duck into my car, wary of pigeon droppings.

When I get home, there's an email from my agent.

Hi Camryn,

I really like your new outline. It's original and intriguing. The third act feels a little rushed, like it needs one more action beat. Could you flesh it out before we send it to Nadine? Let me know if you'd like to get on the phone to brainstorm.

I'd like to send this asap.

Onward!

Holly is ever positive, embracing the future, focusing on the next project. Because it's her job to be. And she has other clients.

If my career is over, Holly will be fine. I won't be. Because writing is more than a paycheck to me. It's my passion and my calling, my greatest achievement after Liza. With my daughter leaving home, with my role as a mother changing, I *need* to be a writer. Rightly or wrongly, it feels like my identity.

I respond and tell her I'll make the changes asap. And I will. But instead of focusing on the outline now, I grab my phone and bring up Megan Prince's Instagram page. It's still set to private—she's not about to open up access after a shrieking stranger showed up on her front lawn—but I realize I can send her a message. It will appear as a request that she can accept or deny, but it's worth a try.

And so, with a deep breath, I summon the words. I am a writer, after all. I can make Megan Prince understand the fear and anxiety that drove me to show up at her doorstep. I can convince her to help me find my tormentor. And I can tell her that I'm sorry.

Hi Megan, I want to apologize for showing up at your house the other day. I realize now that I made a huge error in judgment. I scared you, and I'm sorry for that, because I know that feeling all too well. I've been living in fear for the past few weeks due to the relentless harassment I've received online and in real life. Someone is scaring me, Megan. Someone you know. I'm begging you to help me identify them so I can find out why they're attacking me. I won't press charges or harm them. I just want it to stop. Thank you, Camryn Lane

I don't know if she'll ever read it. Or if it will persuade her. But it's worth a try. I press send and turn back to my outline.

29 THE REPLACEMENT

"ABBY LESTER IS coming back to school," Monica says, filling the doorway to my office. "Just part-time for now, but it's a start."

"That's great." And it is, but I'm taken by surprise. As Abby's school counselor, I should have been aware of this. I've been corresponding with her parents, sending homework to her, ensuring she still has a chance at graduating on time. I'm the one the Lesters should have notified under normal protocols.

"It is great…" Monica trails off, squeezing into my cramped space. The guest chair must be shifted in order to close the door, and I reach across to help her move it. When the door clicks shut, the vice principal takes a seat across from me.

"The family has requested that Abby be assigned a different counselor."

My stomach twists. "Why?"

Monica sighs. "Abby won't tell them why, but Rebecca and Craig want to abide by their daughter's wishes. And given her fragile state, we think it's wise."

"Of… of course. We need to do what's best for Abby."

"Ramona has agreed to take over." Ramona is the counselor for the prior year's students. "She'll ease Abby back into her classes and support her emotionally. But you still have a role to play here."

"I do?" I feel rejected, set adrift, like I just watched my prom date leave with another girl.

"I'd like you to talk to Fiona and the other girls about Abby's return. Make sure they'll be kind to her. And sensitive to the situation."

It's like asking an orca to hug a seal. "I'll do my best," I promise.

"Thanks." Monica's knees bump against my desk as she stands. "Don't take it personally, Camryn. Abby's traumatized and there might be some transference going on."

"Could Ramona ask Abby why she doesn't want to work with me?"

"I don't think that's really a priority right now. Do you?"

"No." I feel subtly scolded for my self-interest. "It's not."

I sit and watch the vice principal struggle to get out of my office.

After lunch, I summon Fiona Carmichael and her two sidekicks to the counseling suite. Lily Mathers is a willowy girl with the blankly hostile gaze of a runway model, while Mysha Naz is the alternative member of the trio, with a septum piercing and intense eye makeup. There isn't room in my office for all four of us, so I take them to a chain coffee shop a few blocks from the school. The less formal environment will set the tone for a warm, productive conversation about kindness, decency, and compassion.

When we're seated at a round table, and the girls have sugary, whipped cream concoctions before them, I broach the subject. "Abby's coming back to school soon."

"That's good," Fiona says, her smile so convincing. "I'm glad she's getting over it."

"Me too," echoes Lily. Despite excellent grades, the girl seems incapable of original thoughts or opinions when surrounded by her cohort.

"She has a long road ahead of her," I say. "She suffered something very traumatic. I hope I can count on you all to be kind and supportive."

"Of course," Mysha says, whipped cream on her top lip. "We'll be super supportive."

"Totally," Fiona says, and Lily murmurs her affirmation.

And I actually believe them. They are only girls themselves, capable of learning from past behaviors, of developing empathy and understanding. "Thanks, girls. Your kindness and encouragement will really help with her recovery. Hopefully she can put that night behind her and get back on track."

Fiona sips her frothy drink. "Will you be helping her, Ms. Lane?"

"Of course. The whole school community needs to pull together to be there for her."

"But are you still Abby's counselor?" There is the slightest arch of amusement to one eyebrow, a subtle glimmer in her eye.

She knows. But how? Monica just told me that the Lesters had asked another counselor to replace me. How could Fiona Carmichael know this? Unless...

"Have you been talking to Abby?" My tone is more accusatory than I intended.

"A bit. I just wanted to check in. Make sure she's okay."

"Do Abby's parents know you've been in contact with her?"

She shrugs. "I don't know what Abby tells her parents."

"Can we go now, Ms. Lane?" It's Mysha. "I've got history next, and I can't miss."

"Okay," I say, suddenly flustered. "I appreciate you all being so mature about this. And supporting Abby's return to school."

Under the screech of chairs on the floor, they mumble their agreement. But I clock the subtle glances darting among them, the secrets unspoken.

Fiona and Mysha lead the way back to school, with Lily and me a few paces behind. It's my job to support every student in the grade, to be a sounding board, a support system. So I ask, "How are you, Lily? Everything going okay with your classes?"

"Yeah..." She sounds unsure, but I realize that's how she always sounds.

"Good. If you need anything, I'm available."

"'Kay."

We walk in silence for nearly a block before the tall girl speaks again. "Why is Abby coming back to Maple Heights?" she asks, her voice hushed. "Why doesn't she go to a different school?"

I've been wondering the same thing. "I guess her parents think the continuity is important with her classes. And her friends are at Maple Heights."

"She doesn't have friends here." Lily's voice is just above a whisper. "She should go to a different school."

"Why?" I match her volume. "Do you know something, Lily?"

We're approaching the school now, and Fiona turns, beckons for Lily to catch up.

"Come see me," I say quickly. "Say it's for your courses."

But Lily doesn't answer. She hurries to join the pack.

30 THE REUNION

MARTHA AND I sit at the bar in a ridiculously popular nouveau Italian joint in the Olympic Village, a carafe of white wine between us. The place buzzes with energy, tables of six, eight, even ten all celebrating something, if only the end of the week. This raucous space may not have been the best choice for the conversation my friend and I need to have, but the wine is cold and the thin-crust pizza we've ordered will be delicious. And thanks to Martha's natural flirtiness, we've been comped a side of meatballs.

I used to abstain from evening plans when Liza was with me, but in the last couple of years, her social life has eclipsed mine. I'd turn down a dinner offer only to sit home alone while Liza had sushi with Wyatt or went to a movie with a group of pals or studied at a coffee shop with other students. Now I find it easier to accept invitations from girlfriends during the weeks Liza lives with me. This way, I don't have to deal with excluding Theo. And Liza is heading back to her dad's tonight, anyway. It's perfect timing for an evening with my oldest friend.

"I'm so glad we're doing this," Martha says. "It's been way too long."

"It has," I agree. "And I'm sorry everything has been so insane lately."

"It's okay." Martha pats my forearm. "Any idea who might have hacked you?"

"No, but I've narrowed it down." I have kept my recent trip to myself, but Martha is my closest friend. I tell her about examining the background of Ingrid Wandry's photos and learning she lives in nearby Bellevue. I tell her that I drove south to confront her, that I realized I'd been catfished, that the woman in the photos is really Megan Prince. I tell Martha how it all turned so ugly.

"Jesus, Cam." Martha takes a drink as she processes my story. "That sounds really risky."

"I know. But after the hack, I couldn't sit by and let her hurt my friends."

"This woman could have been dangerous. She could have been armed."

"I thought maybe I could reason with her, woman-to-woman."

"She could have called the cops," Martha continues. "And then what would have happened?"

My friend is protective, I understand that, but I'm starting to feel scolded. I move the conversation forward. "At least I learned that Megan Prince is not my troll. But it's someone she knows, or at least someone who can access the photos on her private Instagram account. But she won't give me access to it."

"I guess not after you showed up on her doorstep," Martha mutters into her glass of wine.

She's judging me, but Martha doesn't get it. How could she? Only people like Chloe Winston and Janine Kang know what it feels like to be trolled.

"Anyway," I say pointedly, "I looked up the vet clinic's website. Some of Megan's colleagues have public Facebook pages, and I found Megan at a barbecue. I searched the background for anyone I might know, but I came up empty."

"Promise me you'll be careful, Cam."

"I won't do anything reckless again," I assure her. "And please don't tell Theo or Liza."

"I'd never tell Liza," Martha says quickly. "And there's no chance of me telling Theo, since he's still refusing to talk to us." There's a snarky edge to her voice that makes me bristle.

"Well...Felix did punch him in the face."

"Only because *you* told him we were having an affair."

"Except I didn't."

"I know." Martha sighs and sets her wine down. "I'm sorry if I'm being churlish. The whole thing has been tough on us. It brought up trust issues in our marriage that I had no idea existed."

"I was surprised Felix would believe that you'd cheat on him," I say.

"So was I."

"I never doubted you." My voice is gentle. "Or Theo."

"Well, Felix doesn't know Theo that well." Martha picks up her glass. "And they've never really hit it off."

"They haven't?" This is news to me. "Theo's always liked Felix."

Martha shifts in her seat, clearly uncomfortable. "It's not that Felix doesn't like him...There's a big age gap. And they have different interests."

"They both love the outdoors. They've gone bouldering and kayaking together."

"Forget it." Martha refills my wineglass. "It doesn't matter."

"You're my best friend. And Theo's my boyfriend. It matters to me."

She swivels to face me. "Do you really want me to be honest?"

"I do."

"Felix gets a bad vibe off Theo. He always has."

My stomach churns. "What do you mean, 'a bad vibe'?"

"He says he can't put his finger on it, but...he doesn't like him. Or trust him."

I'm stunned by my friend's words. Are we referring to the same Theo? At times, I've been concerned that we're not a good fit, that our age difference and disparate life goals might cause a problem, but I've never once worried that he isn't a kind, genuine person. I look up at Martha, at her troubled face. "What do *you* think of Theo?"

"I think he's fine. Maybe...just not..."

"Just not what?"

"Just not...right for you."

"I've been with him for two years, Martha. He wants us to move in together. Why didn't you say something before I got invested in him?"

"I didn't think you were serious about him, Cam. He's so young. And then I didn't want to upset you. But when all this shit happened with the email, it stirred up some stuff for Felix. And for me."

The attractive bartender interrupts us. "Here's your margherita pizza," he says brightly, oblivious of the tension. "And the meatballs will be right up. More wine?"

"No," I say, just as Martha says, "Yes."

"I guess not," Martha says, and the bartender retreats.

The pizza smells amazing, but it sits ignored between us.

"Theo's fine," Martha says. "But we were friends before he came into the picture. And we'll be friends after. That's all I'm saying."

A wave of intense weariness washes over me, of sadness and confusion. My closest friends don't support my relationship. It is new and disturbing information, and it's all too much, on top of the mess surrounding my book, my daughter's graduation, and her imminent departure for college, or Australia. I wave to the bartender and dig out my credit card.

"Camryn, don't," Martha says.

But I'm suddenly on the verge of tears. "It's fine," I mutter as I tap my card on the machine. "I just need to go home."

"Can I come with? So we can talk properly?"

"I'd like to be alone, Martha."

She gets off her stool. "But we're okay, right? We can't fall out over this."

I give her a quick hug. "We're okay," I say.

But I'm not sure. I'm not sure of anything anymore.

The silence of my apartment is a refuge after the boisterous restaurant. I'd walked away from the enticing pizza, but I have no appetite. I bypass the kitchen and head straight to my bedroom, stripping off my clothes and slipping into an oversized T-shirt. Exhaustion (or hunger? Or a glass of wine on an empty stomach?) is making me feel woozy, a little light-headed, but I'm usually diligent about removing my makeup at night. I enter the attached bathroom, just as my phone pings with a text.

I'd plugged it in next to my bed, so I hurry toward it. I'm hoping it will be Martha, apologizing for her harsh words against Theo. She'll admit she's still smarting from the affair accusation, from the physical fight between our partners. She'll tell me that she never doubted that Theo was decent and good.

The text is from an unfamiliar number. I open the lock screen and read the words.

Here you go pedophile

And then, a horrifying image. It's a young girl, maybe eight or nine, wearing lingerie, posed in a distinctly sexual manner. My stomach lurches into my throat and I toss the device on the bed in horror.

Ping.

Ping.

Ping.
Ping.
Ping.
Over and over again, that little exploited girl comes into my messages. I feel sick to my stomach, panicked, assaulted. Grabbing the phone, I turn it off and throw it back onto the bedspread.

And then I collapse on the carpet, in tears.

BURNT ORCHID

1998

S tar was a petite girl, with acne-scarred skin and pretty brown eyes. She stood in the doorway of Orchid's single room, hands fidgeting with a gold-plated butterfly pendant around her neck.

"I'm sick." Her voice was childlike, even younger than her sixteen years. "They said you could help me."

"Maybe." Orchid surveyed the girl from her tattered armchair, like a don or a queen. There was pain in the way Star held her slight body, anxiety in the twisting of her features. Orchid recognized it, remembered it. "What's wrong with you?"

"It's private," Star said, glancing behind her. There was noise in the hallway, there always was: deals for drugs, sex, stolen goods, often devolving into arguments and violence.

"Come in." Orchid waved a magnanimous hand.

Star stepped into the room and closed the door behind her. She moved to the middle of the hardwood floor, taking in her surroundings, eyeing the other tenants. Lucy sat slightly behind Orchid: her protégée, her henchman. Orchid had kept the promise she'd made years ago to keep the girl safe. Her reward was Lucy's devotion. Her servitude. Tracey, the other girl Orchid had collected, was sprawled on the sofa, sucking on a bottle of cheap liquor. Orchid had thought she could be useful, and for a time, she was. But Tracey was proving to be too damaged, too addicted, nothing but a liability. And yet Orchid didn't have the heart to turn her out. Not yet, anyway.

Star hovered. Orchid didn't offer her a seat. "Tell me..."

Star's face flushed as she described her symptoms. "I think I might have cancer."

Giggles in stereo met her admission, but Orchid silenced them with a wave. "It's not cancer. You've got the clap. I can sell you some antibiotics. You'll be fine."

"I don't have any money."

"You can pay me back in other ways."

Her childlike face darkened, but she nodded. She'd only been on the streets for a few months. She only knew one way to survive.

"You can run some errands for me," Orchid said, and she saw the relief on Star's features. "Do some deliveries. Some odd jobs."

The girl brightened slightly. "Sell drugs?"

"Sometimes, but not like you think. There's a whole economy down here. There's power in getting people what they need."

"What about men? Do I have to...?" Star fumbled for the words, but they weren't necessary. Orchid knew.

"Not if you don't want to. I can keep you busy. I can pay you. But you will have to do things that are hard. Maybe harder than sex work."

"Nothing's harder than that," Star spat. "I will do anything else. *Anything.*"

Orchid saw the power in this tiny girl, the will to survive. She smiled.

"Welcome to the family, Star."

31 THE REPORT

THE NEXT MORNING my eyes are red and sandy, and my teeth feel loose, my jaw bruised. Stress has always caused me to grind my teeth, much to my dentist's alarm. When I was trapped in my toxic marriage, I'd worn a mouth guard at night to save my molars. I stopped when we divorced. I thought the habit was gone along with my husband. (And I didn't want Theo to see me in such an unsexy appliance.) But the problem, and the tension, are back.

I don't want to turn my phone on. I know that my service provider will try to resend the texts that I missed while it was turned off, and I can't stomach that disturbing image again. But my phone is a lifeline to my daughter, my boyfriend, and Martha, whom I'm still hoping will send an olive branch. So I turn it on and block the mysterious number. I'm too frightened to try calling it, too afraid of who might answer, what they might say. I keep the texts, though. Because I now know what I need to do.

In the kitchen I make coffee—extra strong—hoping it will clear my fuzzy head. As it brews, I get my laptop and set it on the coffee table. When the coffee is ready, I pour a cup and move to the sofa. I drink nearly half the mug, waiting for the caffeine to hit my bloodstream, to give me the energy and the courage. And then I log on.

I'd kept my promise to Olivia not to read the online hatred and vitriol, to rely on Jody's sanitized translations. But I'm ready for the abuse now. The trolls can call me ugly, fat, and old. They can say I'm a terrible writer, that I don't deserve to be published, that I only got a book deal because I'm a woman. They can tell me to kill myself, that they hope I get raped or tortured. I've steeled myself for it. Because I need to find out who is doing this to me, so I can call the police and make it stop.

The one-star reviews, as expected, are heinous. But the last one was posted several days ago. My jaw relaxes slightly. My publicist was right. If you don't feed them, the trolls will shrivel up and die, lose interest, move on to more combustible targets. My eyes drift over the write-ups, words like *predator* and *pedophile* seeping into my consciousness. But there are no clues to the identity of the authors. And there are no outright threats that I can take to the police.

There are good reviews, too, and I try to summon gratitude for the support, for the fact that there are still people who are enjoying my work, who don't believe the horrible accusations. I'd wanted to share *Burnt Orchid* with the world, to offer people an escape from their real lives, had hoped they'd develop compassion and understanding for those living in harsher worlds, forced to make difficult choices. It's comforting to know that in some cases, I've achieved the desired effect.

And then I see a word—a name, in fact—that stops my scrolling cold. Adrian Fogler. My ex-husband.

> I was married to the author for several years, and she is a sick woman. She loved telling me personal stories about the kids she worked with. I'm not surprised she'd write about them.

I'm shocked and appalled, but I know the review wasn't written by Adrian. Like most people who don't read voraciously, he's never heard of Readem. And he would never do this to me. For all the issues we had in our marriage, we share a child. We still care about each other. He'd never attack me this way.

I've seen enough. Picking up my phone, I call the police non-emergency line, and after a series of questions and an interminable hold time, I'm patched through to a female officer.

"I need to report a case of criminal harassment," I say, keeping my voice strong and steady. "I've received threatening emails, prank phone calls, and disturbing texts. I've had a barrage of online hatred on a book review site. I've kept all the evidence."

"Okay," the female officer says, clearly taking notes. "Can you tell me your relationship to the person who's been harassing you?"

"I don't know who it is. But it's someone who knows me."

"How can you be sure they know you?"

I tell her about the calls and texts to my private number, about the hacked email sent to my friends, and about the reviewer impersonating my ex-husband. I leave out my trip to Bellevue, of course. While I don't think my visit was technically illegal, it would certainly be frowned upon. And I've been scolded enough in the past weeks.

"So this is mostly related to people not liking a book you wrote?"

The officer is diminishing it, making me sound sensitive and precious. "No, that's not what it's about," I snap. "It's about dangerous accusations of child exploitation that are completely—"

"Look," the woman says, cutting me off. "If you knew who was behind this, we could talk to them or serve them with a warning letter. But there's really nothing we can do without an offender."

"I have an email address," I say quickly, bringing Ingrid Wandry's message up on my phone. "Ingrid.Wandry@proton.me. Can you trace it?"

"Proton Mail has end-to-end encryption. It's basically untraceable.

And they're probably texting you from a burner or an anonymous texting app." She's glib, almost bored.

"Isn't it your job to investigate crimes?" I ask.

"Without a direct threat to your safety, or your family's safety, we don't have the resources to investigate something that, so far, is simply an annoyance."

"They sent me a pornographic image of a child!" I cry. "That's an assault in itself!"

She asks for specifics of the photo, which I grudgingly give her. She tells me that the image, while revolting, doesn't meet the legal definition of child porn.

"Keep a log of the harassment," she advises. "When you have a credible suspect, call back."

Without a goodbye, she hangs up.

I don't know how long I sit there, feeling stunned and powerless, but my cup of coffee is cold when I hear a key in the lock. Theo walks in, a burst of fresh air and the scent of warm pastries preceding him. "I brought breakfast," he says cheerfully. But when he sees my face, he stops short. "What's wrong?"

I hurry to him and fall into his arms. I tell him everything (everything except how I recently learned that my best friends have never liked him and think he's wrong for me). I tell him about the horrible image I received, about the nasty review using Adrian's name, and I tell him that the police can't—or won't—do anything to help me.

"It's going to be okay." He strokes my hair.

"Is it, though?" I pull back. "It's just getting worse. More personal and more invasive."

My phone pings then, and acid burns my throat. I'm too scared to look, afraid it might be something disgusting, but Theo hurries toward it, looks at the screen. "It's from Adrian."

He passes it to me, and I open the message.

Hey. Do you want to come for dinner tonight?

Adrian and I may care about each other, but we don't socialize.

Is this about the review?

What review?

I knew he didn't write it. Doesn't matter, I text.
Liza wants us all to get together, he writes back.
I know, without asking, that she will be announcing her plans for the fall. And I have a strong feeling they will not include university. Does this invitation include Theo? I wonder. He doesn't have a parental role in Liza's life, unlike super mom Tori. But he is my partner. And after Martha's dismissive words, I'm feeling defensive and loyal to him. So I text back.

Theo and I would be happy to join.

32 THE DINNER

Tori and Adrian live in a refurbished Craftsman home worth over two million dollars despite its sloping floors and structural inconsistencies. In contrast to the heritage exterior, the inside is distinctly modern. Tori's job is making houses look beautiful and inviting, and her own is no exception. Despite being overrun with teenagers "hanging out, being comfortable, and just being themselves," it is magazine-worthy. Theo has never been inside before, and I hear him whistle under his breath. I can't blame him, but I wish he wasn't so impressed.

"Hey, Theo." Adrian shakes his hand.

"Great place," Theo says, handing him the bottle of wine I'd picked up on the walk over.

Adrian kisses my cheek. "Can I get you both a drink?"

"Please," I say as we slip out of our shoes, hang our jackets on the hooks above the crisp white wainscoting of the foyer. My nerves are frayed, frazzled by the horrific image I received yesterday, and I'm never comfortable in Tori's territory. Alcohol might help a little. We follow Adrian into the soothing neutral palette of the front room.

Tori appears from the open-plan kitchen wearing white jeans and a crisp blue-and-white-striped blouse. She's holding a slim jug full of a deep red liquid. "I've made blood orange French 75s!" she crows. "This is a celebration."

Is it? But of course I stay quiet. I will support my daughter in her choices for the next chapter of her life, trust that her father and I have raised a confident, self-actualized young woman. I will swallow my doubts and concerns, wash them down with the champagne cocktail Tori hands me. It is delicious. And very strong. We nibble figs and cheese and salted nuts and make small talk about the weather and Theo's latest expedition. By the time I've finished the glass, my tensions have eased, and my face feels warm and flushed. When Tori offers to make me another, I don't decline.

On her command we move to the table, and Adrian summons the kids by bellowing "Dinner!" up and down the stairwells. Tori refuses my offer to help, and shuttles in a fragrant white bean, kale, and thyme casserole (their household is vegetarian, though Adrian insisted on meat with every meal when we were together), followed by a green salad and a loaf of crusty sourdough bread.

As we take our seats at the long teak table, Tori's daughter, Savannah, enters with her girlfriend, Marley, in tow. I've met Savannah several times and Marley once. The pair attends an exclusive leadership program at one of the public schools, and they exude the calm maturity of a head of state or perhaps a commercial pilot. We greet each other pleasantly and I introduce Marley to Theo. And then Liza enters the room, holding hands with Wyatt. His presence, their united front, is not a good sign.

"Hey," I greet them, and notice how their eyes dart away from mine.

"Cocktails, kids?" Tori offers. I can't help but look at Adrian. The kids are underage. These drinks are strong.

"This is a big night," Adrian says. "A big announcement."

Tori half fills flutes with the gin and blood orange concoction, tops them up with the champagne. As she passes them to the children, I take a sip of my own drink. The bubbles fizz in my head as I turn to my daughter. "What are we celebrating, Liza?"

"I've made a decision about the fall," she says, taking her drink and avoiding my eyes. "I'm going to take a gap year. I'm going to go traveling around Australia."

Tori holds up her flute. "To an epic adventure! And to discovering your true self!" All the glasses clink together, even mine. But I can't summon the same exuberance. Despite my vow to be supportive, I can't help worrying that my daughter was pressured into this decision. And given my heightened anxiety, and the alcohol in my system, I can't help saying so.

I address Wyatt. "You must be happy about this."

Wyatt's head snaps up from his plate of beans. "Pardon?"

"You convinced Liza not to go to university so you could be together. Well done."

"Mom, he didn't," my daughter says.

"You're *kids*, Liza. You'll break up eventually. You're just delaying the inevitable."

"Harsh," Savannah mutters, and Marley shakes her head.

"I'm not even going with Wyatt." Liza practically spits her words at me. She's furious, and rightly so. I feel my bravado wilt in the face of her rage.

"Who are you going with?"

"Sage," she says, referring to a classmate. "And some of her friends that I met, and I really like."

"So you two are breaking up, then?"

Adrian grumbles, "Christ, Camryn."

"Maybe you've had enough to drink," Theo suggests, but I silence him with a look.

"We might meet up in Queensland for a bit," Wyatt says, "if it works with our schedules." I watch as he takes a bite of bread, chews nonchalantly. I have to ask...

"Were you parked outside our apartment the other night?"

"What?" But he's lying. I can see it. Apparently, no one else can.

"Mom, I told you he wasn't," Liza snaps.

Tori's voice is calm to the point of condescension. "Camryn, let's celebrate these young people and their bravery. They're going on a trip of a lifetime. Exploring a different culture…"

"A different culture?" I scoff. "Australia is like here. But with sun and sharks."

My daughter's voice trembles with rage. "You were right, Tori." But her eyes are on me. "This isn't even about me. It's about *her*."

I look to Tori, flute held in long tapered fingers, for an explanation. "Sometimes we parent from a place of ego, Camryn. We see our child's choices as a reflection of ourselves."

"Oh, give me a fucking break."

My daughter jumps up then. "This is why I don't tell you things!" And she storms from the room.

"Liza!" Tori and Adrian call in unison. Then Tori tosses the natural linen napkin off her lap, onto the table. "I'll go." She hurries after my daughter.

My head is starting to throb, and I feel close to tears. I look at Theo, who is watching me like I'm a grenade with a shaky pin, which is not unlike how I feel. Did I really just say all that? Did I really just attack and accuse my daughter and her boyfriend?

Theo speaks. "We should probably go."

"I think that would be best," Adrian mutters.

Theo and I head for the door with my ex in tow. The appalled whispers of the remaining teens follow in my wake. We hurriedly don our coats and shoes, and Adrian opens the door to usher us out.

"I…I handled that badly," I stammer as I pass by him. "But tell Liza not to book tickets until we've had a chance to discuss this."

"I won't tell her that," Adrian says. "She's thought this through, and she's made her decision. You need to respect that."

"I'm her mother!" I cry, and I feel Theo gently tugging me out the door. "I deserve some input into my daughter's future."

"Pull yourself together, Cam," Adrian growls into my ear. "If you're not careful, you could lose your daughter completely."

And with his words, the sob buried in my chest bursts out of me. I hurry off the porch and into a light drizzle.

33 TIKTOK

THE BUZZ OF my phone wakes me up and fills me with dread. The alert used to signal positive news: Liza telling me about a good grade or winning the science fair; a call from Holly about a foreign rights sale, or interest from a film producer; Martha inviting me over for dinner or to watch Felix's jazz performance. Now it's more likely to be a prank call or something negative and ugly. But as last night's disastrous dinner floods back into my memory, I fumble to answer it. It could be Liza demanding a verbal apology (in addition to the numerous written ones I texted last night) or Adrian, brokering a summit between us. But the name I see on the screen is my writer friend Jody.

"Hey," I say, voice hoarse. Theo, sleeping next to me, stirs.

"Are you up?" she asks in response to my groggy greeting.

"Yep," I fib, glancing at my clock radio. It's 9:17 a.m., late for me, even on a weekend. Theo and I had ordered Thai food after the aborted dinner party, and I'd spent several hours trying, fruitlessly, to contact Liza, until my boyfriend convinced me to give her some space. We'd fallen into bed sometime after midnight.

"There's something you need to see." Jody's voice is grave. "It's on TikTok."

"I don't have TikTok." As an (extremely) late adopter of social media, it was the one platform I didn't even consider. I'm too old to be making videos of myself, too busy to learn the skills required to create and edit them. Also, my daughter said she'd move out if I started dancing or rapping or doing stand-up comedy...whatever people do on there.

"I'll send you a link," Jody says. "Cam...it's bad."

Fuck.

"Okay. Thanks."

I sit up and wait for the text to come in. Theo rolls over, scrubs his hands over his face. "What's wrong now?" There is frustration, even irritation in his tone, and I can't blame him. I feel the same way.

"I don't know," I mutter.

Jody's text arrives, and I click the link. It takes me to a TikTok page...Megan Prince's TikTok page. The girl I met that day was pretty in a wholesome, approachable way. She is almost unrecognizable in her dramatic makeup, or maybe she's using a filter that makes her look flawless and exceptionally attractive.

"Who's that?" Theo asks, peering over my shoulder. But I don't answer, I can't. My throat is clogged with dread and despair. Soon he's going to know everything.

Megan begins. "Have you guys heard about this book *Burnt Orchid*?" The cover of my book pops onto the screen above her head. "It's not a huge bestseller or anything," she continues, "but I guess it's kind of popular. Or at least it was. Apparently, this author, Camryn Lane, is a high school counselor. And this book..."

She points to the image above her, which I must admit is impressive since the image was added later.

"...deals with all sorts of serious teen issues. So people got upset about it. They accused her of exploiting the students she works with by using their private information and writing about their personal problems. I don't know if she did or didn't. And I want to make one thing perfectly clear..." She leans closer to the camera, enunciates each word. "*I did not accuse this woman of anything.*"

The cover of *Burnt Orchid* vanishes, and a screenshot of Ingrid Wandry's Instagram page slides expertly into its place.

Megan continues. "But someone using my photographs set up this fake Instagram account to troll Camryn Lane. Using my image, they gave her some bad reviews. A bunch of people jumped on the bandwagon. Obviously, that sucks, but I always thought that public people—like actors or authors or athletes—ignored online reviews. It's all a part of putting yourself out there, right? Not Camryn Lane."

Theo takes my hand and squeezes it. He pities me. But he doesn't know what's coming. He doesn't know what I did. Megan Prince is about to tell him everything.

"She searched the background of my Instagram photos and found out where I work. She drove from *Canada* to my office. And when I came out, she followed me home."

My heart is thudding in my ears, sweat pooling under my arms. Theo's hand slips away from mine.

"And then this happened..." Megan says, and like a Spielberg movie, the footage of my tantrum seamlessly replaces the screenshot. Megan's image shrinks so that I dominate the frame. There I am, on the front lawn, face contorted by rage and frustration. I'm screaming: "Someone you know is harassing me. They're trying to tank my book and destroy my career. I'm angry and I'm terrified! But you'd rather protect *them* than help me. That's cruel. And it's heartless!" And then I turn toward the camera. "Is he filming us?" I yell, waving my arm violently. "You don't have permission to film me!"

The image freezes on me then, flecks of spit flying from my mouth, eyes wild like a rabid animal's. And the filtered version of Megan Prince returns. "Camryn Lane did send me this *heartfelt apology ...*" Up pops my Instagram message, and I can see how phony, how self-serving it reads. "But I'm still a little upset," Megan says. And then she brings it home. "So, that's the behavior of an author who's too much of a narcissist to accept online criticism. Who thinks it's her right to lash out at someone because they don't like her work. I'd think twice before buying a copy of her book...although she could use the money for some much-needed therapy."

The cover image with a large red *X* through it pops up above my ghoulish image. And then I look at the views and my heart sinks.

402,400

"Jesus, Cam," Theo says. "What did you do?"

"It's not how it looks," I murmur, but I know what I've done. I've humiliated myself, my daughter, and my loved ones. I've destroyed my career as an author and done irreparable damage to my job as a high school counselor.

I've ruined my entire life.

34 THE PLAN

WHILE THEO MAKES coffee, I call my agent. It's Sunday, but I know Holly will answer. She's my representative, but also my friend. As the phone rings, I watch Theo banging around the kitchen. He's angry, disappointed, maybe even disgusted. I'd tried to explain my trip to Bellevue, but it had sounded over the top even in my own ears. "How could you do something so reckless?" he'd asked me, his handsome face twisted. "You have a daughter who needs you."

He made it sound like I'd parachuted into a firefight, not driven a few hours hoping to have a civilized conversation with a woman who didn't like my book. My life wasn't at risk...only my reputation. My career. My relationships. Given how it all turned out, I couldn't defend myself.

"Hey, Cam," Holly answers, and I hear the ambient sounds of a restaurant in the background. "Is everything okay?"

"No." I move into my office, and I tell her everything.

"Shit," she mutters, and I hear her chair scrape back, hear her make excuses to her companions. I envision her moving through the restaurant—going outside? Into the restroom? She instructs me to send her the TikTok link as she walks. I do, and then I wait as she watches it.

"Oh, Camryn..."

"I know."

"We'll need to wait for your PR team to weigh in, but you should draft an apology now. Have it ready to post on Monday morning after we talk. Do a version for Twitter, Instagram, and Facebook."

"Please don't make me record a TikTok."

"I don't think they'll want that, if you're not comfortable on camera." A toilet flushes in the background, revealing her choice of location. "You need to be ready with the statement. You need to show Nadine that you take this seriously and you want to repair the damage you've done."

"I will," I say. "I do."

"Apologize for overreacting. Say you respect a reader's right to have an unfavorable opinion of your work."

"But that's not why I went there," I say. "I wanted my harasser to see that there was a real person behind the public image. That she was attacking a human being with feelings and emotions. Can I at least explain?"

"That might muddy things. It might seem like you're making excuses," she says. "But that's a question for Olivia."

"Okay." My voice quivers. "I'm sorry. I never thought it would blow up like this."

She's silent for a beat, and then she sighs. "I wish Nadine had made an offer on the next book before this happened," she says, and my heart sinks.

"Me too."

"I've got to go." My agent wraps it up. "We'll set up a call with the team tomorrow."

I hang up and wander back to the kitchen. Theo slides a mug of coffee toward me.

"What did she say?"

"She told me to draft an apology statement. We'll get it approved by the publishers and post it on social media tomorrow."

Theo shakes his head. "That could be too late."

"It's just one day."

"You have to get out ahead of these things before they spiral. Remember what happened to Lance Showe?"

Lance was a friend of Theo's, another outdoor guide specializing in high-end adventure tours. He'd taken a group of businessmen from Silicon Valley on a backcountry skiing adventure. There had been some drinking, some weed, and a lot of mistakes. The crew ended up requiring a helicopter rescue. It had made the news—the cost to taxpayers, the risk to rescuers' lives. Lance and his clients had done the walk of shame past the TV cameras.

"He thought the outrage would die down on its own. He thought people would forget if he just laid low." Theo drinks his coffee. "But it snowballed on Twitter, and it almost destroyed him."

"Lance didn't have a team of PR experts to rely on, and I do, so..."

"Lance should have spoken from his heart. He should have apologized right out of the gate, admitted his mistakes, and promised to learn from them." He takes a drink of coffee. "You may have a team behind you, but no one cares about your career as much as you do."

He sounds sage, wise beyond his mid-thirties, and I let the thought percolate as Theo sets his cup in the sink. "I've got to go."

"Okay. See you tonight?"

"Depends what time I get done," he says. "It's probably easier if I crash at my place."

It's an excuse. He's angry at me. Or maybe a little afraid, since he clearly thinks I'm an unhinged lunatic with an alarming lack of self-control. But he brushes his lips against mine. It's not our usual goodbye kiss, but it's something. He's not washing his hands of me completely. At least not yet.

Alone in the apartment, I work on my apology statement until noon, when I assume my daughter will be awake. She hasn't responded to the barrage of texts and voicemail apologies I sent last night, but today is a new day. I'm hoping she's feeling less angry after a good night's sleep.

A voice picks up on the fifth ring. "Cam, she's not ready to talk, okay?" It's Adrian.

"No, it's not okay," I say. "I'm her mom. She can't shut me out of her life."

"She's not shutting you out. She just needs a break."

"I just want to apologize. I know I was wrong."

"You can apologize when she comes back to your place in a few days." He lowers his voice. "Are you okay, Cam?"

"I'm fine," I say quickly. "I'm just under a lot of stress."

"So is Liza. This was a big decision for her, and she needs our support."

Tears blur my vision at his words. My daughter is the most important thing in my world, and I've let her down. I've been so wrapped up in the online attacks, obsessed with who is behind them, worried about the impacts to my social circle and my professional life, that I dropped the ball on my most important job. Being a mom.

"Tell Liza I love her and that I'm sorry. Please, Adrian."

"I will," he assures me. "It's going to be fine, Cam. Just give her the space she needs, okay?"

"Okay," I croak through the emotion clogging my throat.

I pray that he's right.

35 DAMAGE CONTROL

MY PUBLISHING TEAM has always been warm, supportive, and upbeat in our interactions. Today the faces filling my screen are somber, features arranged in neutral masks to conceal their disappointment, their distaste, if not their full-blown disgust. I hope my hangdog expression is suitably regretful, appropriately remorseful. I hope they will forgive me.

My agent starts the conversation off. "Camryn realizes she made a significant error in judgment by visiting that woman's home. But she's willing to do whatever it takes to make it right. Like all of us, she wants to move forward and focus on her writing. She's such a talented author, and she's eager to dig into her next project."

"I am," I say, a quiver in my voice. "And I'm so sorry. The online harassment got so personal and so invasive, but I never should have confronted Megan Prince."

There are tense nods in response, conciliatory smiles that are almost pitying.

Holly continues. "Camryn and I spoke yesterday, and she's drafted a heartfelt apology. Cam, did you send it to the group?"

"We got it." Nadine answers for me. It was clearly not acceptable.

Olivia clears her throat. "We've been monitoring social media since we were made aware of the situation. We've had a crisis PR team draft a statement of apology on your behalf. If you're satisfied with it, we'd like you to post it on all your social media channels."

"Sure. Of course."

"And then you need to go dark on social media," she continues. "No posting. No responding. No commenting. Nothing."

"I'll delete my accounts," I say. "I'm happy to." It's the truth.

"Just thinking out loud here," Holly says, "but maybe there's a charitable donation Camryn could make to offset some of the negative energy out there?"

"Good idea," I say while wondering whether I can afford it.

"Megan Prince works at a cat clinic. Maybe some sort of abandoned cat charity?" Holly suggests.

"If Camryn posts about it, it could be seen as performative," Olivia says. "And we need her to stay off social media altogether."

Nadine, as always, is composed. "But by all means, make a donation if it makes you feel better, Camryn."

"Okay." I nod agreeably. "I will."

Olivia continues. "I'll send the statement through. It's been thoroughly vetted in-house but of course we want you to be comfortable with it."

"I will be," I say gamely. "I trust you. I just want to fix this."

"Great. Thanks, Camryn," Olivia says. "Let's hope this does the trick."

Nadine smiles. "Most of these things tend to blow over on their own when they're left alone."

My voice trembles with self-pity. "I hope so."

And then they say their curt goodbyes.

*   *   *

The statement comes through shortly after I've hung up. The wording is eloquent and diplomatic, but it doesn't hide the gist:

I'm an idiot who should have known better than to harass an innocent person. I'm going to disappear now and work on being less of a psycho.

No explanations. No excuses. Obediently, I post the statement on Instagram, Facebook, and Twitter. And then I delete the apps, resolve not to check them. I will do as I've been told.

The day stretches long before me. Normally, I'd write, but I'm still waiting to hear back from Nadine on my new outline. Theo and I often see each other on quiet weekdays, but he said he had paperwork to deal with. It's an excuse, I know it is. He didn't come over last night. Like so many people in my life, he is disappointed in me, appalled by my behavior, likely wondering if I'm coming apart at the seams. I understand his frustration, I do, but shouldn't my partner be firmly in my corner? Willing to stand by me no matter what?

Unbidden, Martha and Felix's concerns about Theo drift into my mind. My initial reaction had been loyalty, defensiveness, but I allow myself to consider their issues, just for a moment. Is there something untrustworthy about my boyfriend of nearly two years? Have I been blinded by his puppy-dog exuberance, his gentle spirit, and his ridiculously chiseled body? He was angry when I went to Miami without him, but only because he wanted to be with me. Any discord we've had has been due to my reluctance to fully commit. I shake my head, dislodge the doubts. I trust Theo. I love him.

Martha had texted me amid the TikTok fiasco:

I'm sorry for what I said about Theo. Just forget it. You know him better than we do and I just want you to be happy. Our friendship means the world to me.

And it does to me, too. With my family across the country, Martha has become my sister. We are close enough to have arguments and disputes, and to move past them. My response had been brief but heartfelt.

It's fine. Let's move forward. Friends forever.

So I decide to drive to Sophia's coffee shop. The warm, familial atmosphere is what I need right now. I'll bring my laptop, play around with a few chapters while I enjoy a pastry and a coffee. If it's not too busy, Martha will sit with me and we'll catch up, like old times. And if she can't, at least my presence will demonstrate my forgiveness and dedication to our relationship.

The café smells of butter and flour, coffee and cinnamon. There are only a handful of tables, and I survey the room for a vacancy. Sophia's is clearly a popular spot with the mommy crowd as clusters of women with little ones spread themselves across one corner. A smattering of college students peer at their laptop screens. And then, at a small table near the window, I spot her. Rhea, from my writing group, is handwriting in a notebook, head bent, brow furrowed in concentration.

I'm tempted to leave. Navid told me that Rhea is delighting in my online abuse; she does not wish me well. But Felix, behind the counter, has spotted me. "Hey!" He waves. I turn away from Rhea and move toward him.

"It's so good to see you," Felix says, and his delight—maybe relief?—is genuine. His face has mostly healed, and only the faintest bruising remains. "Thanks for coming by."

"You can't keep me away from your pain aux raisins," I quip. "Is Martha here?"

"Getting supplies," he says. "But she'll be back in about an hour if you can hang around? I know she'll want to see you."

I glance at my watch. "I'm not sure..."

Felix lowers his voice. "Martha was really upset the other night. Is everything okay between you two now?"

"Everything's fine," I assure him. "We're family. We can get through anything."

"What I said about Theo," he continues, his handsome face troubled. "It was ages ago. I got my back up about some stupid comment he made. I can't even remember what it was, but I blew it out of proportion. He's a good guy. And he cares about you."

"Thanks, Felix. I appreciate that." I change the subject. "Do you know that woman by the window? With the notebook?"

"Yeah, that's Rhea. She's a regular. Martha knows her a lot better than I do," Felix explains. "They took a meditation class together. Why do you ask?"

"I was in a writing group with her," I say, "before I published *Burnt Orchid.*"

"Small world. Are you going to say hi?"

"Looks like she's in the zone. I don't want to interrupt."

"Maybe when Martha gets back, the three of you can have a coffee."

"Actually"—I scrunch my features—"I can't stay. I'm going to have to get that pain aux raisins to go."

I drive home, the fragrant bun ignored in my console. Suddenly, I'm not hungry, an uneasy flutter in my belly. When I'd seen Rhea at Sophia's café before, I'd thought it was a coincidence, but it wasn't. Rhea and Martha are friends. They see each other regularly, take classes together. Why wouldn't Martha mention that to me? It seems unlikely—practically impossible—that my name has never come up, that they wouldn't realize the shared connection. Martha has kept this from me for a reason.

When I pull into the underground parking lot, I'm still obsessing. What has Rhea told Martha about me as a writer? I'm sure Rhea thinks I'm overrated, undeserving of my book deal. Navid told me she sent my bad reviews to the rest of the group; she likely shares them with my oldest friend. And what has Martha told Rhea about me personally? She knows everything...my secrets, my vulnerabilities, my hopes, and my fears. Something feels off here. Something feels like betrayal.

I make my way toward the elevator. When I pass the building's garbage bins, I toss the pastry into the trash.

36 THE RETURN

"SHE LASTED LESS than two hours," Ramona says, arms folded across her ample chest, her pleasant features stern. We're seated in Monica Carruthers's office, discussing Abby Lester's return to Maple Heights High. Clearly, it had not gone well.

"What happened?" Monica asks, hands clasped on her hardwood desk.

Ramona looks at me. "Fiona Carmichael happened."

"Christ," I mutter, dismayed but not surprised. "What did she do?"

"Unfortunately, we don't know," Ramona explains. "They were in English class together. When the teacher's back was turned, something happened. Abby ran out of the room after that."

"Something like what?" Monica asks. "Did Fiona touch her? Threaten her?"

Ramona sighs. "From what we can gather, it seems like she might have...imitated her. Convulsing."

"What is wrong with that girl?" I realize Monica is asking me, and I shake my head. There's no point articulating my satanic suspicions.

"The teacher heard the desk rattle and the kids all laughed.

Then Abby bolted." Ramona runs a hand through her cropped hair. "I think we might have lost her."

"Maybe it's for the best?" I say. "I know it's hard to let her go, but this isn't the right environment for her anymore. Fiona and her crew are too powerful in this school." My voice trembles. "Abby has suffered enough."

Monica's eyes land on me. "You okay, Cam?"

I clear my throat, pull myself together. "I haven't been sleeping well," I say, which is close to the truth. I haven't been sleeping at all. Anxiety about my daughter, my boyfriend, my best friend, and my career has kept me awake. This morning, I took pains to cover my dark circles with concealer, but I know the stress is wearing on me.

Monica seems to buy it. "I feel like I haven't done my job here," she says, her expression dark. "Fiona and her posse are about to graduate. They'll go on with their lives with no repercussions. They'll have learned nothing from this experience."

"It's not your fault." Ramona sighs. "Everything they do is sneaky and subtle, but so pernicious."

"Let me talk to Lily Mathers," I suggest. "She's the weak link in their crew. She might be the one who's been reporting online."

"Worth a try," Monica mutters. "I'll talk to the Carmichaels again, but they're as scared of their daughter as everyone else is."

"Give my best to Abby," I say as Ramona gets up. She turns, gives me a pointed look, and I remember. For whatever reason, Abby views me as the enemy, as part of the problem. She doesn't want my well wishes.

Lily Mathers wears stylish jeans, a minuscule top, her blond hair ironed straight. Her makeup rivals my daughter's in its flattering application. She sits in my office chair, playing with the silver rings on her fingers. Her fingernails are long, acrylic, electric blue.

"You were in English class with Abby this morning," I begin. "What made her run out of the room?"

She shrugs, eyes on her nails. "I didn't see what happened."

"Don't you sit right behind Fiona?"

Her blue eyes meet mine. "Fiona didn't do anything." She looks down again. "It was one of the guys."

"Which one?"

"Like I said, I didn't see."

"Is Fiona dating anyone at school?"

Lily scoffs. "She only dates guys from different schools."

"Did one of these *guys* supply the Molly for Abby's party?" I ask.

The girl exhales. "Give it up, Ms. Lane. I'm not going to tell *you* anything. No one is."

The emphasis on *you* raises my hackles. "Is this about my book? I never wrote about any of the students here, Lily. And I never will."

She shrugs a shoulder, plays with her rings.

"We're fortunate enough to have the anonymous reporting tool at this school. You can do the right thing and tell us what happened that night. We can make sure everyone gets the help and support they need."

Lily says nothing, but I can tell my words are sinking in. She is goodhearted. Unlike her ringleader, she has a conscience.

"I know Fiona is your friend, but she hurt Abby so badly. She needs to learn that there are repercussions for cruel actions."

"Fiona never pays," Lily mumbles.

"Tell us who was there that night. Tell us what happened."

"I can't," she says, looking up through her thick lashes. "If I reported what really happened that night, everything would blow up."

"It might seem that way, Lily, but I promise that it wouldn't. Everything would be fine eventually."

"You have no idea, Ms. Lane." I see the determined set of her jaw, the coldness in her eyes. She's done. "Can I go? I'm missing calculus."

I nod and watch her slip out of the cramped doorway.

I devote the afternoon to less problematic students, helping them with college applications, exam prep, and graduation requirements. Liza flits into my mind, and I can't help but feel sad that she won't be following the academic path I'd hoped she would. But I will respect her decision and her space. Our relationship is the most important thing in my life. I can't have my daughter traveling to the other side of the globe hating me.

That evening, as I'm walking to my car, I feel weary and defeated. Abby Lester has left the school. We failed her. And Fiona and her minions continue to be cruel, powerful, and unstoppable. I can only hope that life, karma, meaner kids at college will bring the girl down, but I know sometimes these personalities rise to the top. Fiona will probably become a CEO or Supreme Court judge or head of a social media platform.

My phone pings with a text and my heart buffets. It could be Liza, finally ready to forgive me. But when I look at the device, the number is unknown, untraceable.

Hurry home. I'll be waiting for you.

37 THE VISITOR

THERE IS NOTHING menacing in the words themselves. If the text was from Liza or Theo, it would be welcomed. But it's not from them...not unless one of them got a new phone number without telling me. And even if they did, neither one of them is eager to see me. I drive home through the soft gray light, a gentle spring rain smattering the windshield. The radio plays soothing yacht rock but none of this calms me. I tell myself that the anonymous text could be from a student, a harmless but mischievous kid playing a prank. Or perhaps a distant troll sent it, a person who has no way of knowing where I live. It's common knowledge that I work at a high school, so guessing what time I head home from work is not difficult. But my nervous system senses danger. And my body is jittery with fear.

As I near my building, my breath is shallow, my hands slippery on the wheel. Instead of pulling into the underground garage, I circle the block looking for street parking. But even when I find a space, I pass it by, drive around the block again. I seem incapable of pulling over, of leaving the safety of my moving vehicle. I watch the people hurrying along the sidewalk, ducking into shops and cafés, waiting for the bus, hoods drawn against the drizzle. There is no one I recognize, no one who looks frightening.

"Hey, Siri, call Theo," I say to my phone as I pass by my building.

I listen to it ring. And ring. And then his voicemail answers. I hang up without leaving a message. I know how this will sound—paranoid, even histrionic. Theo is tired of all the drama. I can feel him pulling away. Instead, I'll call Martha. But as I'm about to instruct Siri to dial, I remember Martha's friendship with Rhea. A dark feeling presses down on me at the thought of them together. Am I jealous? Insecure? Afraid Rhea could turn my oldest friend against me?

There are other people I could reach out to: Navid, Jody, Ramona from work. I have plenty of friends I could ask to meet me for a happy-hour drink. But calling them would mean admitting that I'm afraid to go home; it would mean dragging them deeper into all this nonsense. I'm embarrassed by it all, even ashamed. I could make up a lie, concoct some story to explain my need for spontaneous companionship, but the thought leaves me exhausted.

Fuck this troll. On a surge of anger, I yank the wheel, turn into the parking garage. I'm not going to allow some ridiculous text to scare me out of my own home. I'm in no real danger. No one is *coming to get me.* This isn't some nineties slasher film. I park in my spot and get out of the car.

The underground parking lot is well lit and secure, but even in the best of times, I keep my wits about me. Maybe I've seen too many scary movies or heard too many news stories of women being attacked in these deserted spaces, but I'm always alert, I always move briskly. Now, though, with my nerves frayed, my fight-or-flight activated, I grip my keys between my knuckles like a weapon, survey the barren space, ears pricked for the slightest sound. It's all quiet, safe, and deserted. At the elevator, I stab the call button, and practically dive inside when the car arrives.

But a peaceful stillness greets me as I enter my apartment. This is my respite and my refuge. I am safe here behind the locked door.

187

There is nothing to fear. Dropping my bag in the entryway, I move into the living room, flick on a lamp. It's still light out, but I want to combat the spring gloom. Then I shuffle toward my bedroom to change out of my work clothes and into my sweats.

Ping.

My phone is in my purse, still in the entryway, but I hear it. I could ignore it, but I'm trained to answer, powerless to stop myself. If it's my daughter, I must respond. Digging the device from my bag, I look at it.

> I'm outside your apartment. I'm here to shut you up once and for all.

I drop the phone like it's hot, and it clatters on the hardwood. My pulse skitters, but I pick up the device and admonish myself. No one is out there. No one is *coming to get me*, to *shut me up*. Still, I go to the window and look outside. I have a limited view of the back alley thanks to the thick flora surrounding the unit. I love the greenery and the privacy, but now I feel isolated, slightly vulnerable as I peer through the leaves. There is no way for me to see the front of the building without going down to the lobby, no way to know if someone is lingering out front.

But they're not. I'm being ridiculous. This is nothing but a prank. And even if someone were out there, I'm behind two locked doors. I'm safe.

Ping

> I'm coming

Ping

> I'm almost there. Get ready to die

Ping

Ur dead bitch

I text back.

Fuck off

But then I delete it because this might be one of my students. Instead, I write:

Grow up and leave me alone

I press send, hear the message swoosh into the ether. I'm about to turn my phone off when I hear it.

Ding-dong

It's the ringtone I set to announce that someone is at the front door of my building. Someone is out there. Someone who wants to be let in.

My heart thuds in my chest. I won't answer, obviously, so they can't get inside. This kid or prankster is trying to scare me. When I don't react, they'll get bored and go away. I wait, my mouth dry and chalky.

Ding-dong

Sweat prickles under my arms and at the back of my neck. What if they don't go away? What if they get inside the building? All the tenants have been told to be wary of strangers trying to gain access without a key fob, but it's not impossible to slip inside unnoticed. Whoever is out there has threatened my life. I can't just wait here like a sitting duck.

With a trembling digit, I dial 9-1-1, listen to the muted ring. The last time I called the police, they were condescending and dismissive, but this is different. This is an emergency. When the dispatcher answers, I try to sound composed. I fail.

"Someone is outside my building," I blurt. "I got a bunch of anonymous texts threatening to kill me and now someone is at my front door."

"Where is your building?" he asks, and his keyboard clicks as I give him my address. "And what's the person at your front door doing?"

"Th-they keep buzzing to be let in," I stammer. "But I haven't answered."

"Do you know who this person is?"

"No. I've been harassed online, but I don't know who's doing it."

"Can you describe them?"

"I can't see the front door from my apartment."

"Okay. Do you have any protection orders or peace bonds against anyone?"

He thinks this is domestic. These situations usually are. "No," I say, and my screen lights up with a waiting call. It's coming from my front door.

"They're calling again." My voice sounds choked. "They're trying to get in."

"I'll have a car come by as soon as possible. Stay in your apartment with the door locked. If this person gets into the building, call back."

"Thank you." I hang up.

Ding-dong

I stand frozen, my body rigid with terror. How long will the police take to get here? Most of the force is deployed to the high-crime neighborhoods, leaving only a few cars to patrol the city's west side. It could be five minutes, ten, twenty, or more. And then, in an instant, I realize that this is my chance. My tormentor is outside right now. I can stay safe inside the building, hidden from sight, but I can finally find out who it is.

Phone in hand, I hurry out of the apartment and scuttle down the fire escape stairs. I'm in a pair of fluffy slippers, but I won't leave the confines—the safety—of my building. At the fire door, I pause, heart hammering with fear. And something else...anticipation. I burst out into the hallway, past the mailboxes, and move toward the lobby. When I'm almost there, I stop, peek around the corner at the large glass entryway.

A man in a black jacket stands near the electronic intercom. He wears a cap over dark hair, his stubble visible though he's angled away from me, gazing out toward the street. He's not a harmless kid from the high school. He's a full-grown man, a complete stranger. What the hell does he want with me?

And then he turns, and I see that he's holding six large pizza boxes. I almost laugh with relief. It's a pizza delivery guy with the wrong door code. I watch him punch in the numbers again, and my phone obediently alerts me.

I hustle out of sight before answering. "Hello?"

"Angelo's Pizza," the man says, his deep voice efficient.

"You've got the wrong apartment," I say with a relieved sigh. "I didn't order any pizzas."

"Are you sure?" He reads my address back to me.

"There must be some mistake," I say, but a picture is forming in my mind. A prank as old as time...or as old as pizza delivery.

"Look, lady, I have six cheese pizzas ordered to your apartment and they need to be paid for."

"Fine," I grumble. I don't have the energy to fight with this man who is only trying to do his job. Moving toward the doors, I ask, "Can I pay with my phone?"

38 PEACE OFFERING

THE SIX PIZZAS sit on the passenger seat next to me, filling my car with their steamy aroma. My destination is within walking distance, but I want to deliver these pies warm. And I feel safer inside my car than out on the street. Because someone was outside my building, watching. How else could they have timed their texts to the pizza delivery? To ensure their threats prefaced the doorbell at the precise moment to cause maximum anxiety? Someone, here in Vancouver, is trying to scare the shit out of me. And they're doing an excellent job.

After I paid the delivery guy, I'd called Theo. He answered this time, sounding tired and less than enthused to hear from me.

"Do the people in the office want pizza?" I asked. "I've got six plain cheese from Angelo's. I could bring them by."

"Everyone's gone but me and Matthew. Why so many pizzas?"

I told him about the prank, about the creepy, threatening texts. I told him I was frightened enough to call the police, whom I'd sheepishly called back to report the false alarm.

"Those damn kids," Theo said. "Maybe you should quit your job?"

"I can't quit," I told him. Because my future as an author is teetering on the brink. And unlike Theo, I'm still not confident my students are behind this.

"At least change schools," Theo suggested.

"I'm fine," I said dismissively. "And now I've got dinner for the next week."

"That's a lot of pizza for one person."

One person. The words made me feel small and isolated. I waited for Theo to offer to come over, at least for a few slices, but he didn't. "I should go," he said. "Talk later." And he hung up.

Traffic thins and the streets turn narrow and leafy as I approach. With vehicles parked on both sides, only one car can pass at a time, so I pull over, let a minivan through, accept the obligatory wave of thanks with my own. Across from the house, I park in a permit zone, designated for residents. But I won't be here long enough to get a ticket. Even with a six-pizza peace offering, I won't be welcome.

Carrying the stack of boxes, I jog up the steps and ring the bell. Through the four panes of glass in the door, I can see inside the immaculate foyer, catch a glimpse of the pristine living area to my left. The house is still and quiet. I worry no one is home and then Tori comes into view. She's dressed in designer loungewear and carrying a large glass of red wine. Her face falls when she sees mine in the windowpanes.

"Liza's not here," she says when she wrenches the door open.

"That's okay," I say, shifting the boxes in my arms. "I accidentally got all these pizzas delivered. I thought you, Adrian, and the girls might like them."

"I'm the only one home."

"You could put them in the fridge for later," I suggest, arms growing tired under the weight. "There's no meat on them. And they'll just go to waste at my house."

Her response is a huff, like I'm on her doorstep with six boxes full of cat diapers. But she steps back, ushers me inside. "Come in."

With her wine in hand, she leads me through the spacious

open-plan living area to the designer kitchen at the back. It's all so clean and perfect that it almost feels sterile without Adrian and the kids' presence.

"Just put them on the counter," Tori instructs. "I'll have to make room in the fridge."

The offering has backfired. I thought the slices would be gobbled up by all the teens who love to hang out in this haven of chill acceptance, but Tori is all alone. The pizzas are a nuisance.

"Where is everyone?" I ask as I dump the boxes on the quartz countertop.

Tori takes a drink of wine. "Your daughter is off with her friends, as usual. And your ex-husband is having dinner with his parents. Since Adrian's mother *loathes* me, I decided to take a pass."

Adrian's mom, Marion, is a frosty blonde with a supercilious, almost regal air. She is domineering over her two adult children, and even holds sway over her three grandchildren. It was Marion who insisted Liza attend the prestigious private school, take violin lessons, study dance instead of playing sports. Adrian's sister, Kate, moved her family to France, an effort to wriggle out from under the maternal thumb, I suspect. But since Marion is both Adrian's mother and his boss, the aprons strings are firmly tied.

"She's not an easy mother-in-law," I sympathize. Marion and I had many conflicts over the course of my marriage to her son. We'd finally developed an uneasy sort of truce about five years before the divorce.

"She loves *you*, though," Tori says, an accusation in her tone.

"No, she doesn't," I respond. "She tolerated me, at best."

"Absence must make the heart grow fonder." She reaches for the wine bottle tucked away in the corner and refills her glass. "And Marion's *so* impressed that you published a book."

It is the kind of thing that would impress Marion Fogler . . . though I'm sure she'd prefer I'd written a literary masterpiece and not a plot-driven page turner. She's impressed by achievements, by successes, by any sort of celebrity.

"She can't stop talking about it, actually." Tori turns, her glass full. "She tells everyone she knows."

"Well, she certainly wasn't impressed with me when I was married to Adrian." I jingle my keys in my pocket. "I'm parked in a permit zone. I should go."

"She doesn't accept me," Tori continues, as if I haven't spoken. "And neither does Liza."

I suddenly realize that Tori is tipsy, bordering on drunk. Her immaculate bob is mussed, her eyes bloodshot. It's unnerving. I've never seen her anything but composed.

"Liza's fond of you," I say. They're the most diplomatic words I can summon to describe my daughter's feelings toward her stepmom, which are slightly warmer than ambivalent.

"I took her shopping for her prom dress today." Tori drinks her wine. "I spent a fucking fortune."

My cheeks flush. "Liza told me she was ordering her outfit online." I've been so distracted that this mother-daughter rite of passage has slipped through the cracks. "Can I contribute?"

Tori ignores my offer. She doesn't need or want my money. "I wanted Liza and me to make a day of it," she continues. "Dinner after, maybe a movie. But Liza had to run off to be with her little friends as soon as she got what she wanted."

"She's a kid," I say, defending my child. "I think it's pretty normal that she wants to spend time with her friends. They're graduating soon and they'll all be going their separate ways."

"Savannah's stepmom doesn't do half of what I do for Liza," she spits. "But my daughter knows to treat her with kindness and respect."

My hackles rise. "If you're not happy with your relationship with Liza, I suggest you bring it up with *your husband*."

Her head tips back in dark laughter. "Bow out, like you always do, Camryn. Because you're so much more important than the rest of us."

She's drunk and upset, but I'm pissed. "I don't think I'm more important than anyone. But I'm going through something very difficult right now that you know nothing about."

"The online trolls?" She looks almost amused. "Liza told us. And she's taking full advantage of your distraction."

"What do you mean?"

"She rerouted her entire future while you were on Instagram."

"I thought you were all for her trip to Australia? You said it was an *epic adventure*. That she'd *find herself*."

"Liza's not my kid. I don't care what she does." Her smile is cold, almost cruel. "*My* daughter's going to Cambridge."

I have never seen the façade slip like this. Tori is bitter and angry, needy and insecure. And she resents the hell out of me.

"I have to go." I hurry toward the door. Tori's voice trails after me.

"Thanks for unloading your mistake pizzas onto me."

I hurry outside, nerves jangling. Dusk is starting to settle, the thick canopy of trees hiding a pink and promising sunset. A cyclist flies past me in a blur, but otherwise the street is quiet, deserted. My hand trembles as I unlock my car. Tori's vitriol was the last thing I needed after tonight's creepy messages and the unnerving pizza delivery.

Behind me, a distinctive rustling in Tori's manicured hydrangea bushes makes me turn. It's probably some urban nocturnal creature—a raccoon or a skunk—but the figure I see crashing through the foliage is distinctly human. It appears to be a male, tall and slim, broad shoulders in a gray sweatshirt. The hood is pulled up to conceal his face, but the height, the physique, the loping gate...

It appears to be Wyatt.

"Hey!" I call out, but the figure doesn't stop. It scurries down the side of Tori and Adrian's property, disappearing into the back alley.

I should go back to the house, warn Tori that someone, quite possibly Liza's boyfriend, is creeping around outside. But Tori won't thank me for the information. In fact, she'll blame me, say my lax parenting has hindered Liza's ability to set boundaries, or something like that. And Wyatt isn't dangerous. Is he?

No, he isn't. And I can't go back in there.

I get in my car and drive home.

BURNT ORCHID

1998

Orchid led Star down the stinking alleyway, past bodies slumped in doorways and collapsed against dumpsters, the results of Mal's Oxy and a recent delivery of heroin hitting the streets. Vermin scuttled out of sight as the women moved with speed and purpose, no sign of the trepidation that filled them both. Star was new to the streets, a sapling trying to thrive in the harshest conditions. Orchid was twenty-one: seasoned, hardened, inured to much of the violence and pain in this environment. But this mission was always dangerous. If the cops caught on to Orchid's racket, she'd be put away. And not to juvie this time.

Lucy usually did these pickups. At seventeen, she was still a child in the eyes of the law, but after three years on skid row, she was tougher than a full-grown man, fiercer and more ruthless. She was quick and savvy and unlikely to get nabbed, but if she did, she'd spend a few months in youth detention, basically summer camp. And Lucy would never turn Orchid in. Her loyalty was without question. But she was aging out of the role soon and needed to be replaced. By Star, who was just fifteen.

Orchid insisted on handling the training, making the introductions. There was no room for sloppiness, no room for nerves or poor judgment. She couldn't trust Star to protect her like Lucy would. If the cops got her, she'd crack eventually. She'd turn Orchid in to save herself.

At a battered metal door, they stopped. Orchid knocked, a staccato series of five taps. She and Star stepped back and waited. The door swung open, and Allan appeared. He'd grown heavier since Orchid first met him, scowl lines etched deeper into his doughy face.

"This is Star," Orchid said. "She'll be doing pickups from now on." They exchanged nods, and then Allan thrust a white paper bag into Orchid's hands.

"What have you got?" she asked.

"Expired antibiotics, antifungals, some blood pressure meds."

"Nice."

Star took the paper bag and tucked it under her jean jacket. Orchid reached into her front pocket for a wad of crumpled bills, but Allan stopped her.

"No money," he said. "I need a favor."

"What?"

Allan peered up and down the alley. No one was there, no one conscious anyway. "I need to get rid of someone."

There was no need for explanation. "Who?"

"My wife."

Orchid glanced at his wedding ring, tarnished with the years. Allan presented as a husband, a father, a grandfather. Not exactly a happy man, but a stoic one. He didn't seem like the type to have an affair or to kill his partner out of jealousy or hatred. But Allan was filling Oxy scripts and selling contraband out the back of his pharmacy. He had layers.

"I can find you someone," Orchid said. "What can you pay?"

"Ten grand. But it has to look like an accident."

"Let me ask around."

And then Star, with her tiny body, her courageous heart, stepped forward.

"I'll do it," she said.

39 THE SUSPECTS

WHEN I SEE Constable Kash's towering form heading for his office, I hustle toward him. I could call out, make him pause, but the hallway is full of students shuttling between classes, and I don't want to draw attention to this confab. The twelfth-grade counselor in private consultation with the school cop is fodder for the rumor mill. "Do you have a sec?" I ask, poking my head inside before Kash can close his door.

"Sure." He invites me into his tiny quarters, perhaps even smaller than mine. But Kash's space is furnished with a simple tabletop desk and two utilitarian chairs, making it feel more spacious. My large ergonomic chair and metal filing cabinet may have been a mistake. When we are seated facing each other across the table/desk, Kash asks, "What's up?"

I inhale deeply. Kash and I work well together; we have a rapport. I appreciate the way he handles the students—with firm kindness, strict compassion. I am hoping he can help me. He feels like my last hope.

"Someone is harassing me," I tell him in a shaky voice. "I called the police, but they say they can't help me."

"Harassing you how?" he asks.

I start small, telling him about the emails, the reviews, the phone calls, the flowers, and the pizza delivery.

"Those sound like pranks," he says. "You know most school staff have been targeted at one time or another: air let out of their tires, eggs thrown at their house, a fake Facebook account made of them...It's annoying but it's not dangerous."

"It's gone beyond that," I say, lowering my voice, though we are alone. I tell him about the disturbing images of the little girl, the death threats, the hacking of my computer to interfere in my friend's marriage.

"That doesn't sound like kids," he says. "That sounds like adult behavior. And it sounds personal."

"It is personal." My voice wobbles with emotion. "Someone who *knows me* is doing this. And I'm scared it's escalating. I have a daughter to protect."

"Any ideas who might be behind it?"

"I'm narrowing it down."

"If you have a viable suspect, I could pay them a visit." He sits up straighter, as if to highlight his size. "Sometimes, seeing me on the doorstep poking around is all it takes to get someone to stop."

"I appreciate that, Kash. I'll let you know."

He sighs, rubs a hand over his stubble. "I wish there was more we could do, but online abuse is tricky to investigate, and even trickier to prosecute. We'd like to set up a task force, but we just don't have the manpower."

I nod, feeling forlorn but also like an asshole. I know how bad things are in the city. I know there's been an increase in violence, in property crime, in substance abuse. My harassment pales in comparison.

"In the meantime, keep track of everything that's happening so that—"

I interrupt because I know the drill. "Thanks, I will." I get up to leave, and then pause. "Any news on the Abby Lester situation?"

"Nothing," he says. "No one's talking."

"Do you think there were other kids there that night?" I ask. "Or did Fiona, Lily, and Mysha make that up to protect themselves?"

"They probably made it up. If there were other kids there, then why wouldn't the girls turn them in? Unless these mystery kids are even more terrifying than Fiona and her crew."

"That's hard to imagine."

"Yeah," Kash says. "I thought Abby might open up now that she's left the school, but those girls did a number on her. She's still scared shitless."

"I hate that they're getting away scot-free," I say. "What's to stop them from doing something cruel and heartless to someone else?"

"I agree. If you hear anything..." But he trails off. Because I won't hear anything, not now that Abby's been driven out of this school. It's over.

"Sure. Thanks," I mumble, and head into the hallway.

After work, I take the bus downtown to meet Martha. Parking in the city is both a nightmare and a fortune, and taking transit allows me to have a few drinks. My nerves are taut and jangly from recent events; a drink or two will take the edge off. And some liquid courage will help me broach the subject of Rhea. The sense of betrayal has dissipated since I learned of their friendship. I doubt Rhea would bad-mouth me to my oldest and dearest friend, nor would Martha stand for it. What I want is Martha's insight. Because Rhea McMillan is now top of my suspect list.

Martha had texted me the evening after I'd turned up at Sophia's.

Sorry I missed you at the café. Want to come to Felix's next
gig with me?

I didn't really. I don't *hate* jazz like Theo does, but I wouldn't
say it's in my top seven musical genres. But I knew that this invitation was an olive branch, so I said yes and suggested we grab a bite
before the show. It would be difficult to talk with Felix freestyling
in our ears.

I step off the bus on the seedy Granville strip, home to most
of the city's nightclubs, and a burgeoning community of homeless young people. Head down, gait brisk, I move west toward the
Davie Village, the city's vibrant and funky gay district. Felix's trio
will play at a hole-in-the-wall bar later tonight, so Martha and I are
meeting at a cozy taverna for Greek food first.

She's there, looking bohemian and sexy with dangling earrings
and a peasant-style top. We order wine and a trio of dips to start,
and then I get down to business.

"I saw Rhea McMillan at the café. Felix said you're friends."

"We're *friendly*," Martha corrects me. "She comes into the café
to write sometimes. She lives in the neighborhood."

"Has my name ever come up?"

"Of course. When I realized she was a writer, I mentioned you.
Rhea said you used to be in the same writing group before you got
published."

"What else did she say about me?" Our server sets two glasses of
wine on the table. Martha picks hers up before responding.

"Not much. She said you're a great storyteller. We mostly make
small talk."

"But Felix said you took a class with her."

"It was a meditation class, Cam. Not a lot of chitchat."

I take a fortifying sip of wine. "Rhea sent links to my bad reviews to everyone in the writing group. She pretended to be concerned, but she loves that I'm being attacked online. She's reveling in it."

"Really?" Martha asks as the dips materialize. "That's so mean."

I grab a pita wedge, scoop up some tzatziki. "She didn't like a critique I gave her in class once. She's hated me ever since."

"I thought that was the point of writing groups?" Martha asks through a mouthful of hummus. "She's never said anything negative to me. Is she really that spiteful?"

"My friend Navid thinks so." I take a sip of wine. "Do you think she's capable of harassing me online?"

"Oh my god." Martha leans forward. "You think Rhea's behind all this?"

"She knows me, you, and Felix. She's jealous of my success. And I shared some very personal short stories in class. Rhea knows a lot about me."

"Wow…" Martha reaches for her wine. "Is she tech-savvy enough to hack you? When she comes into the café, she hand-writes in a notebook like Jane Austen."

"That's probably so she looks more literary and poetic." I roll my eyes. "It doesn't mean she doesn't know how to use a computer."

"I guess it's possible." But I read the doubt on Martha's face.

"The only other person I can think of who might do this is Tori."

"Adrian's Tori?" Martha's eyes are big with surprise. "I thought you were civil with each other."

"We are. We were. But I dropped by there the other night, and she was positively venomous."

My friend leans back in her chair, head clearly reeling, like mine has been for the past few weeks. Martha waves to our server for two more glasses of wine and then says, "There's something you should know."

The pita bread in my stomach turns to lead. "What?"

"Felix told me not to tell you, but I can't keep this from you."
She swallows audibly. "When you got your book deal, Theo was
not happy."

Not this again. "He was, Martha. He celebrated with me."

"He told Felix that he was already second to Liza and now he
was going to be third after *Burnt Orchid*."

Heat creeps into my face. I don't know what I'm feeling: confused, embarrassed, betrayed...but I'm not sure by whom.

Martha continues. "Felix cares about you. The comment landed
wrong with him. He felt that Theo was being childish. And
possessive."

"So you think my boyfriend has been trolling me? And scaring
the shit out of me?"

"That's not what I'm saying."

"You think Theo got into my computer and sent that email to
Felix? Felix beat him up! That doesn't make any sense!"

"Please, Cam." She reaches for my hand. "Don't shoot the mes-
senger. I just want you to have all the information."

I squeeze her hand back. "Okay. I got it."

A plate of moussaka lands before me then. I eat it, but I taste
nothing.

40 THE OVERTURE

FINALLY, THE WEEK is over, and Liza is coming home. I've respected her need for time and space, given her several heartfelt apologies to accept in her own due course. Now, as I wait for her arrival, I hope that she has forgiven me. I hope that we can regain our close relationship. Liza hasn't even told me when she's leaving for Australia, what her route will be, who is joining her other than her friend Sage. I'm out of the loop and it's making me feel panicky, like I'm losing control. I know my daughter is growing up, I know she is breaking away, but she is still my baby. She is still my world.

Tori's accusation flits through my mind.

"She rerouted her entire future while you were on Instagram."

Well, Liza has my full attention now. When I'm with her, I'm going to be present and engaged. All my stress, anxiety, and fear will be balled up and tucked away in a back corner of my brain to be dealt with at another time. This may not be the healthiest coping mechanism, but it must be done, because I need to reconnect with my daughter before she leaves the continent. To ensure that happens, I've bought her a gift.

When I hear her key in the lock, I jump up from the sofa. I'm anxious, excited, slightly nervous. I've never felt uneasy with my own kid before, but I've never had her cut me off like she did. A child seeking independence can sometimes do so through parental conflict; I know this from my studies. Liza and I have always been so tight, it's natural for her to push me away, to create space for her independence. But now I'm going to win her back.

"Hi, honey." My greeting is bright, perhaps a little too bubbly.

"Whoa," Liza mutters under her breath. "Calm down."

Still mad at me, then.

She kicks off her shoes, shuffles directly to her bedroom with her duffel bag without even a glance my way.

"Liza," I call. She doesn't answer. "Can you come out here please?"

A single word emanates from her bedroom. "Why?"

"I have something for you."

After a few moments, her head pops out of her doorway. "What?"

"Come see."

She slouches into the living room, arms crossed at her chest. Her body language is hostile, closed off, until she spots it. My gift is a large backpack from a prestigious outdoor company, an expensive, stylish, and ideal accoutrement for her travels. There is a physical softening in my daughter, a subdued delight. The present is perfect. I've nailed it.

"Do you like it?"

"It's great. Thank you."

"I told the girl at the store that you were backpacking around Australia. She said this was the perfect size and it's waterproof and durable."

"Nice." She's warming up.

"Should we get takeout tonight?" I ask hopefully. "Sushi maybe?"

"Sage is picking me up in twenty minutes. We're meeting some friends at the beach."

"Okay," I say, masking my disappointment. "Can I make you something quick? An omelet?"

"We're going to grab some food and eat there."

"Right. Well, I'm glad you like the backpack. And I'm glad you're home."

"Thanks, Mom." She comes over and kisses my cheek. It's a gesture of appreciation with little warmth in it, but it's a start.

After she leaves, I tidy the apartment, fuss around making a salad, feeling at loose ends. I know I need to talk to Theo, but I've been putting it off. Martha's confession about my boyfriend's jealous reaction to my book runs through my mind. It had sounded petulant and childish, even mean-spirited. But I'm also hearing this thirdhand and out of context. I need to give Theo a chance to explain.

Both Martha and Felix suspect Theo could be behind my harassment—some of it anyway—but I can't believe it. They don't know him like I do. Theo's not vindictive. And despite what he said to Felix, he's been loving and supportive. Mostly. His juvenile response to my trip to Miami revisits my memory. And it's been nearly a week since my meltdown at Adrian's, since Theo and I discovered the mortifying TikTok video, and my partner is still giving me the cold shoulder.

With a fire in my belly, I grab the phone. "Look," I say when I hear his dull greeting, "I know you're mad at me, but we need to talk."

"I'm not mad," he says. "I'm frustrated. Because you're being reckless and making stupid choices. You drove to Bellevue without even telling me. What if something had happened to you, Cam?"

"I know that was dumb. I know I should have told you. But you can't keep punishing me forever."

"I know."

"There's something else we need to discuss."

"Sure. I'll come over."

"You can't come here. Liza will be home later."

There's a nearly inaudible huff of annoyance, but I let it slide.

"I can come to your place," I suggest, though it's not ideal. Theo shares a run-down house with his twentysomething cousin, Liam, who spends most of his time lounging on the sofa, sucking on a bong, and watching *South Park*. "Or we can meet somewhere?"

"Come here," he says. "We can walk out to a bar."

"I'll be there in an hour."

I'm putting on some makeup when my phone pings. My stomach tightens, worried the sound signals another onslaught of threats and abuse, but I check it anyway. It's Liza.

Can you pick me up?

My spirits lift. Because I know this means my daughter has forgiven me. If she was still angry at me, she could have gotten a lift with a friend, called an Uber, or walked home along the seaside path. We'll be alone in the car; it's the perfect opportunity to talk. I glance at the time on my phone. It's barely eight o'clock.

Of course. Everything okay?

Just come, she replies.

*   *   *

Spanish Banks is the last in a series of beaches that run along the waters of English Bay, before the terrain turns rocky and inaccessible. It has a large parking lot that is always jam-packed on pleasant evenings such as this one. I don't expect to find a spot, but I'll pull over and text Liza with my location.

I'd canceled on Theo, obviously. My daughter sounded upset, and I've vowed to be more supportive and available to her. His text response was one word. Make that one letter: K.

He's probably annoyed, he may feel slighted, but if he can't understand that Liza must come first—particularly after the blowup he witnessed the other night—then our future is limited. I can tolerate Theo being petty and jealous of my book, but not of my child. He knew when he met me that I was a mom.

As predicted, a stream of vehicles enters and exits the lot, but I pull in anyway. I plan to double-park, but a car to my right begins to back out, allowing me to slide into its spot. I text my daughter that I'm in the parking lot, and then I climb out of the car for some seaside air. The sun is warm on my face, the breeze fresh and briny. I close my eyes, listen to the sounds of seagulls, laughter, and a boombox owned by someone arrogant enough to provide a soundtrack for the entire beach.

Liza hasn't responded to my text, but I'm not concerned. And I know enough not to approach her clique. Being picked up by your mom is highly uncool, so I'll be patient. Wandering onto the expansive grass field across from the water, I take in the view of the north shore mountains, the navy-blue Pacific, the shirtless boys playing Frisbee. I smell the scent of meat grilling on hibachis, watch some children eating sticky Popsicles, admire a sheepdog catching a ball in midair. It's all so idyllic, a world where nothing could be wrong. But pretty surfaces can conceal a lot.

As I look toward the water, I spot her. Liza is with a circle of kids sitting on the grass beneath a sprawling willow tree. She's half kneeling, saying goodbye to Sage and her school friends Astrid and Maggie. I see Wyatt, on the far side of the group, his eyes on my daughter. From this distance it's hard to read his expression, but he's clearly not happy. He is either sad or angry, and I wonder if they've had a tiff. Two boys I don't recognize flank Wyatt, and then there's a kid with dirty-blond hair who looks vaguely familiar. He resembles Wyatt a little, could be a taller, slimmer brother. I can't place this boy, but I know a lot of teenagers. I must have met him at Liza's school or maybe at Maple Heights. There's not much cross-socializing between the two high schools. The public school kids think the private school kids are snobs and jerks. The private school kids think the public school kids are stoners and losers.

Liza is walking toward me now, and I give her a subtle wave. As I wait for her to join me, my eyes flick back to her group of friends one more time. The blond boy is standing now, looking at something on his phone. He is tall and fit, likely an athlete of some sort. A sharp gasp of shock and recognition escapes me as his identity slots into my mind.

This is the boy I saw in Megan Prince's window. The one she said was her nephew. He is the one who filmed me. The one responsible for the denigrating TikTok video. What is he doing here in Vancouver? What is he doing hanging out with my daughter?

"Hey," Liza mutters as she approaches. She's clearly unhappy.

"You okay?"

"Not really." She doesn't want to talk about it. Not yet. We move to the car in silence. I'll give her some time to open up; I won't force the issue. But I need to find out how she knows that boy.

Once we're on the main road home, I force a casual tone. "Who was that tall blond boy with you? He was sitting one over from Wyatt."

"That's Hugo."

"Who is he?"

"I don't really know him. He plays on Wyatt's soccer team."

"Does he live here?"

"Of course he lives here. Why are you so obsessed with him?"

"I'm not." But I'm doing it again. I'm allowing my own issues to distract from my daughter's. "Did you and Wyatt have a fight or something?"

Liza sighs. "Remember when I told you that Wyatt wasn't possessive?"

"Yes."

"Well, he sort of is." Her words send a chill through me, as I visualize Wyatt sitting outside our apartment, running down the side of Adrian and Tori's house. I remember his texts: Where r u? Over and over again.

"Did he do something to you?" My voice is tight with fear and anger.

"No, Mom. Wyatt's not a psycho." She sounds annoyed, like the suggestion is ludicrous. "But he doesn't like some of the girls I'm going traveling with."

"He doesn't have to like them. As long as you do."

"That's what I said."

"I'd like to meet them," I add. "Before you go."

"Of course. We're not even leaving until September."

"Has your dad met them?"

"Tori invited them over with their parents," Liza volunteers. "So we could talk about plans and stuff."

A flash of guilt is quickly followed by relief. I should have done this, but at least Adrian has vetted these kids and their families. He's overseeing their plans.

Liza says, "But you'll meet them, too, Mom."

I smile over at her, and my chest fills with love and something else...a fierce protectiveness. Wyatt—and this Hugo kid—will not do any more damage to my family.

41 THE DISCOVERY

AS A COUNSELOR, I've seen teen relationships turn dark and obsessive. From the media, I know they can devolve into violence, suicide, and even murder. *Wyatt's not a psycho* loops through my mind like a panacea. Liza's assurance had sounded so confident, so certain. She's not afraid of her boyfriend. Adrian and Tori have seen no evidence of Wyatt's dark side. And yet something is not right here.

My research had informed me that trolls are usually young white men angry at the world. I'd been misled by Ingrid Wandry's name, by the women (Rhea and Tori) who have grudges against me. But Wyatt—and his friend Hugo—fit the profile. Could Wyatt be attacking me as a way to hurt or control Liza? What is Hugo's role in my harassment? Are they in this together? I need to find out more about the boy I saw in Bellevue.

It's nine o'clock Sunday morning and Liza is still asleep, but I close the door to my little office anyway. If my daughter caught me researching Wyatt and his friend, she might think I'm a pervert, that all the accusations against me are true. She might move in with Adrian full-time, or head to Australia as soon as school lets out. I can't be too careful.

My first Google search is for Hugo Prince. If he has the same last name as his aunt Megan, I'll be able to find him quickly. While I get a lot of hits (including an animated royal called Prince Hugo), none of them are the boy I saw at the beach. He must have a different last name, which complicates my mission. But I'm not giving up. There are other clues I can follow.

Liza told me that Hugo plays on Wyatt's soccer team, so I start there. I feel like a creep as I type my daughter's boyfriend's name into the search bar, add the word soccer. I feel even creepier as I peruse the soccer league's website, scouring the team photos, zooming in on these teenagers. But my unease is replaced with relief when I find him. Hugo Duncan is the goalie on Wyatt's team.

Now that I have a name, I go directly to social media. Hugo doesn't appear to have a Facebook page, and he probably uses some creative Instagram handle that I can't find. I check TikTok, thinking about his aunt's creative use of Hugo's footage of me, but if he's on there, I can't find him. When I google his full name, his school soccer team turns up. This kid attends the same high school as Tori's daughter, Savannah. Is this simply a coincidence? Or do Hugo and Savannah know each other? Has Tori's disdain of me spread to her daughter? Savannah has always been perfectly pleasant toward me, but who knows what poison Tori has been feeding her.

I press my fingers into my temples, brain aching with the effort of trying to piece together this puzzle. If the vet technician from Bellevue is Hugo's aunt, that means she's a sibling of his mother or father. So who are Hugo's parents? Do they know me and resent me? Googling Hugo Duncan, mother and father offers no results. And Duncan is a relatively common surname, as well as a first name, so not helpful on its own.

Clicking back to the soccer team's website, I check their game schedule. They play today, starting in about an hour. I know what I have to do; there's no other way. But first, I need to check on Liza.

With a cup of coffee in hand, I tap tentatively at her door. I take her muffled "yeah?" as an invitation.

"I brought you a coffee," I say, slipping into her room. It's a mess as always, but the backpack I gifted her has pride of place at the foot of her bed.

My daughter rolls over and stretches, slowly sits up. I pass her the mug. "Thanks." She takes a grateful sip as I perch beside her.

"What's up today?"

"Studying," she says. "I've got two more exams."

"Need any study fuel? Snacks or anything?"

"I'm good."

"I've got to run some errands," I say breezily, telling myself it's not a lie. "And I'll get groceries. Any dinner requests?"

"Mac and cheese," she suggests. This is her go-to comfort food, her *breakup, bad grade, fight with a friend* meal.

"Of course," I say. I place a comforting hand on her leg. "Do you want to talk about Wyatt?"

"It's fine, Mom. I think we just need a little space."

"Good idea. You've both got a lot going on right now. You should focus on your own needs."

"I will."

"Australia is a big country. You don't have to see him there if you don't want to."

"I know."

"What about prom? Will you still go with him?"

"I don't know…" She sets the cup on the side table, lies back down. I've pushed it too far and she's closing off. With a squeeze of her shin under the blankets, I slip out of the room.

Hugo and Wyatt's team plays on one of the expansive soccer fields at the University of British Columbia. I park on the far side of the pitch, across the street from a cluster of campus housing. The team is several yards away, but I stay concealed in my car, slouched down in my seat. If I've estimated the length of a soccer game correctly, the game should be wrapping up soon.

Hugo is easy to spot standing in goal. I look for Wyatt but he's harder to find in the scrum of athletic teens midfield. An opposing player bursts out of the pack and descends on Hugo, but his kick falters and Hugo stops it easily. A couple of minutes later, a whistle signals the end of the match. Both teams rush in to hug and pat each other, making it impossible to know who won and who is being consoled.

I spy Wyatt as the teams drift to the sidelines to drink water, stretch their calves, listen to lectures from their coaches. There are a handful of adults loitering nearby, but I don't recognize anyone. I don't know Wyatt's mom and dad, though our children have dated for a year and a half. His mom runs a daycare, and his dad drives a delivery truck. Liza says they're always busy, but that may have been an excuse not to arrange a meet-and-greet.

Suddenly, Hugo breaks free from the group and jogs toward me. I shrink farther into my seat, dread knotting my insides. Could he have spotted me from this distance? Is he coming to confront me? My brain scrambles to concoct a story: I thought Liza was here. I came to pick her up. But Hugo veers away from me, and I realize his car is parked just two cars ahead of mine. He beeps his fob and climbs inside. The car shoots off and I recognize it. Hugo drives a silver Volkswagen Golf, like the one I saw sitting outside my apartment that night. Was it Hugo, not Wyatt, watching Liza? Or was he watching me? Had Hugo followed me home from his aunt's Bellevue home after that ugly confrontation? Has he known where I live this whole time?

Jaw tight with determination, I turn on the ignition and follow him as he turns onto the thoroughfare that cuts through Pacific

Spirit Park, leads back toward town. Hugo drives fast, like any teenage boy in a zippy little car, but I keep him in my sights. I hang back, though. If he has been watching me, if he is the one out to get me, it's imperative that he doesn't spot me tailing him.

We turn left, travel downhill, headed toward the water and my neighborhood. I don't know where Hugo lives, but his high school is southeast of here. Where is he going? I trail him past the turnoff to my apartment, allowing a small sigh of relief as he scoots into the parking lot of the Dairy Queen. He's a boy and he wants ice cream. It feels so innocent, so benign, that for a moment I consider going home. But as the tall boy hurries inside, I park in the lot, facing the building.

From here, I watch Hugo move through the restaurant, slide into a booth across from a girl. Her face is hidden from view by a poster featuring a trio of new Blizzard flavors, but I can see her lightly tanned arms, a cuff of bracelets, her long acrylic nails. It's standard-issue teen attire and provides no clue to her identity. I need to know who she is. This girl could link Hugo to me.

I should stay in my car, keep my distance, but I'm anxious and impatient. Why can't I go inside and grab a dipped cone? Why should I hide from a couple of teenagers? I'm a grown woman, strong and confident and capable. Climbing out of the car, I march inside, head held high.

But my back is sweaty and when I hit the air-conditioning, it sends a chill through me. I go straight to the counter, wait for the young couple ahead of me to order, keep my eyes on the menu boards above. Only after I've ordered a chocolate-dipped cone do I turn, casually, toward the table.

The girl's eyes bore into mine, so wide, so innocent. Her smile is pink, glossy, and malicious. Hugo is sitting with Fiona Carmichael.

I'm fucked.

42 ACCUSATIONS

As soon as I enter the school on Tuesday morning, I can feel it: a nasty energy permeating the hallways, a pervasive sense of hostility. Fiona Carmichael is behind it. When we locked eyes in that Dairy Queen, I knew I was doomed. I don't know how she will do it, when, or even why, but she's going to bring me down. It's only a matter of time.

I'd barely slept, hypothesizing about Fiona's role in my harassment. If Fiona is friends with Hugo Duncan, she might know his aunt Megan. And if Fiona follows Megan's private Instagram account, she could have stolen Megan's photos to create Ingrid Wandry's profile. Fake-Ingrid's brutal email and terrible review had been mature, articulate, and convincing. I'd assumed that my abuser was an adult. But Fiona is a bright senior, a coercive leader. She could have been behind this all along. She and Hugo Duncan.

With a cup of staff room coffee in hand, I go to Constable Kash's office. "Do you have a sec?"

He invites me in, and I close the door behind me, take a seat. "You okay?" he asks, brow furrowed with concern.

I'm wearing my stress and lack of sleep on my face. And lately, I've been neglecting household chores, like laundry. This morning, I'd grabbed a rumpled shirt out of my laundry basket, not noticing the grease stain on the chest. "Hectic morning," I say with a rueful grin. "But I have a solid suspect in my stalking case. I'd like you to talk to him."

"Okay." He reaches for a pen. "Who is it?"

"His name is Hugo Duncan." I give him the only details I know: his school and his soccer team.

Kash's brow furrows. "You think a teenage boy's been leaving you nasty book reviews? Didn't we decide the harassment seemed adult and personal?"

"This kid's been lurking outside my apartment. And outside my ex's place. And I saw him at the Dairy Queen with Fiona Carmichael."

"You think Fiona has something to do with this?"

"I don't know." I sigh, overwhelmed by the possibilities. "She's a horrible kid. She's a monster."

"She's just a kid, though, Camryn."

I see concern and judgment in his dark eyes, and I realize I've crossed a line. Guilt twists my stomach. "I didn't mean that," I say, shaking my head. "I'm just so tired of it all." My voice cracks with emotion, and I worry I'm about to fall apart. Quickly, I get up. "Please, Kash. Talk to Hugo Duncan. I need this to stop."

I hurry into the hall.

I've barely returned to my desk when I'm summoned to Monica Carruthers's office. "Be right there," I say obediently into the phone. I have no idea what this meeting is about, but I feel a sense of foreboding. Moving through the barren hallways, I mutter under my breath, "What have you done, Fiona?"

Once I'm seated across from Monica, she gets down to business. "We've received a flurry of complaints about you through the online snitch portal."

Well played.

Monica continues. "I wanted to give you the opportunity to address some of these accusations."

I cross my arms, defensive. "Let's hear them."

The vice principal reads off her computer screen. "I told Ms. Lane that my mom's boyfriend touched me and then she put it in her book."

I roll my eyes. "I'd have an obligation to go to the authorities if a student told me that. You know that, Monica."

She nods slightly—giving me a pass on that one—and then continues reading. "I used to live on the streets of the Downtown Eastside. Ms. Lane asked me all about it. I thought she cared but it was just research for *Burnt Orchid*."

"I'd have to be a complete sociopath to do that," I retort. "And if any of our students had been homeless, social services would have surely let us know."

"True." She reads another one. "Ms. Lane messaged me on Instagram. She invited me over to her apartment to get high."

An incredulous laugh escapes me. "You're not seriously entertaining these comments?"

"You know we have to look into them."

"Why would I invite a student to my apartment? Am I insane?" My voice is escalating. "I don't even get high, Monica. Plus my daughter lives with me so that would be a little awkward."

"She only lives with you part-time, right?"

"Right," I snap. "On the weeks she lives with her dad, I invite all the high school kids over to get stoned and have orgies."

"Calm down, Camryn."

"This is all ridiculous." I take a labored breath through the tightness in my chest. "This is all Fiona Carmichael's doing."

"Fiona? How do you know?"

But what can I tell her? That I found the teen boy who took a humiliating video of me? That I went to his soccer game, watched him from my car before tailing him to the Dairy Queen where he met Fiona? It sounds unprofessional. It sounds creepy and crazy.

Monica sighs, clasps her hands on the desk in front of her. "I know Fiona is a mean girl, but do you really think she's behind all of this?"

"She hates me."

"She's a popular teenager about to graduate high school. You might be overestimating your importance in her life."

Maybe. But Monica doesn't know Fiona like I do. "Are we done, Monica? I have work to do."

"I'll need to talk to Nancy about this," she says, referring to our warmhearted principal. "But you can go." Gratefully, I lurch from my chair and out of the room.

Back in my office, I bring up Fiona's timetable on my computer. This is the last week of regular classes before exams and my nemesis is currently in French class. I call the teacher and have her sent to my office. About five minutes later, there's a tentative knock at my door.

"You wanted to see me, Ms. Lane?"

"Yes, Fiona. Come in and close the door."

The girl slips inside, shuffles the chair to shut the door, and sits. She looks at me expectantly, her façade of naivete so convincing. But I'm not fooled.

"What's your beef with me?" I ask.

"Umm...pardon?"

"You clearly hate me, Fiona. Why? Because I want to hold you accountable for your actions? Because I think you should pay for what you did to Abby Lester?"

"All I did was share the video," she says, eyes narrowing. "I know I shouldn't have done that, but I'm not the one who gave her the Molly. I'm not the one who recorded her."

"But you're protecting the kids who did. Can't you see that that's wrong?"

"Don't you remember what it's like, Ms. Lane? I'd be destroyed if I snitched on the other kids."

I doubt that anyone could destroy this powerful girl, but I continue. "Who is Hugo Duncan?"

"He's a guy I've been seeing."

"Has Hugo been watching my apartment? Or lurking outside my ex-husband's house?"

"Why would he do that?"

"That's what I'd like to know. Do you know his aunt Megan? In Bellevue?"

"Hugo goes to a soccer camp in Bellevue," she says, brow furrowed. "But we've only been dating a few weeks. I haven't met his family."

"Do you follow Megan Prince on Instagram?"

"Ms. Lane, I honestly don't know what you're talking about. And all these questions are making me uncomfortable."

Her stress is real, and palpable. She's just a kid. I'm scaring her. "Go back to class," I mumble, and the girl practically flies out of her seat. But as she fumbles her way out the door, I catch it. The faintest flicker of amusement dances across her lips. At least I think I saw it.

And then she's gone.

43 GOING VIRAL

WHEN I GET home that night, Liza is in her room, likely studying. I can hear her moving around, turning pages, the rustle of a box of crackers. I need to pull myself together, be a mother. I have to make dinner or at least order some takeout. My daughter needs me to be supportive and present—she has her own issues going on—but I'm a mess. The accusations through the school portal could threaten my livelihood, destroy my reputation. The thought makes panic flutter in my chest.

My phone rings, and I wonder if it's Theo. We haven't spoken since I ditched him to pick up Liza. We need to, but he had another tour and I've been highly distracted. Snatching my phone off the counter, I see Janine Kang's name on the display.

"Turn on the news. Channel 104," she says, without a greeting. It's the news station she works at.

"Why?" I ask, but I'm already clicking the remote.

"I'm so sorry. I tried to stop it, but I was outvoted."

Oh god.

Hanging up, I stand in front of the TV. The anchor is another familiar face. The blandly handsome white man has a friendly, folksy delivery. He's midway through introducing the next clip.

".. . bad reviews are part of the deal, right? Well, this local author did not agree, and she drove three hours to confront her reviewer in person. The video of author Camryn Lane has gone viral on social media..."

I've seen footage of people losing their shit. Usually they're fighting in a parking lot, refusing to give up their place in line, or attacking a flight attendant. Even in a world gone mad, outrageous behavior is still deemed worthy of our attention. And now my tirade is the latest showcase of a person breaking the social mores, disrupting the peace, cracking open.

The anchor disappears as the video fills the screen. There I am, screaming with rage at an innocent woman, gesturing violently at the teenager in the window. The caption beneath the scene reads: Author attacks reader over bad review.

They're oversimplifying it. They've got it wrong. But there's nothing I can do but watch in horror.

"Oh my god! Is that *you*?"

I whirl around. My daughter is behind me, staring at the TV, her face contorted in anguish.

"I...I'm sorry," I stammer.

"What did you do?" Her eyes, trained on my image, are brimming.

"I messed up, Liza. I know I did. I never thought..."

But she turns and runs back to her room as the anchor comes back on-screen. He's composed, but amusement sparkles in his eyes. He moves on to the next story, and I turn off the TV.

My phone on the counter starts to ring, but I ignore it. I need to talk to Liza, to beg her forgiveness. But when I enter her room, she's already throwing clothes into her duffel bag. Her face is pink and streaked with tears, but her expression is pure anger.

"I'm going back to Dad's," she mutters without looking up.

"I understand. And I'm so sorry."

"It's gone viral on TikTok, too," Liza informs me. "I've already had a bunch of messages from friends. Soon every girl at school will have watched it."

"I know this is horrible, but I promise you it will all die down." My voice is weak, pleading. "People will get bored and move on."

"I'll be gone in three months." She zips her bag closed and finally looks up. "You couldn't have waited to act like a psychotic stalker until after I left?"

She pushes past me and heads to the door. I watch, helpless, impotent, as she steps into her shoes and leaves.

Alone in the apartment, my phone buzzes continually. I have missed calls from Jody, Theo, and Navid. There are a number of texts, too, and I scan the messages. Theo wants me to call him. Navid tries to console me. Martha asks if she should come over with wine. And Jody tells me to check social media.

> #stayinyourLane is trending

Fuck.

With a glass of wine in hand, I head into my office and log onto Twitter. I haven't been on social media for several days, and I have a number of notifications. But I ignore them and type the hashtag into the search bar. And then I scroll through the tweets.

> This is actual footage of an author attacking a woman for giving her a bad review. #stayinyourLane #boycottBurntOrchid

My meltdown has become a gif, a loop of me screaming *"My book has been bombarded with bad reviews!"* on Megan Prince's front lawn. Humiliation makes me feel sick and sweaty, almost dizzy. But I sip the cold wine and continue to scroll. Most of the tweets contain the gif and the same hashtags.

> This is not the first author to attack a reviewer. If you can't handle the criticism, don't read it. Or don't publish.

> A male author physically assaulted a teenage girl over a bad review. A female author doxed a reviewer over a mediocre rating. And now this. When will publishers hold this behavior to account?

My publisher is tagged in the comment, and my face burns with shame, deep and ugly. Another feeling is stirring inside of me. Resentment, even blame. My publishing team had told me to stay off social media, not to engage or defend myself, but that's only made things worse. Theo's sage words drift into my memory.

No one cares about your career as much as you do.

I knew all along what was right, but I'd been too compliant, too eager to please. I should have spoken from my heart, apologized right out of the gate, admitted my mistakes, and promised to learn from them instead of sharing some canned, generic apology. I should have tried to explain.

I take a fortifying breath, my fingers hovering over the keyboard. I know a response could inflame the situation. I know that trolls live for a reaction. But if I choose my words carefully, I can make people understand. I can show them that I'm a decent person who did nothing wrong. I can fix this...

Or am I a little drunk?

Finally, I type a comment under the last tweet.

> I should never have gone to this woman's house, and I
> apologize for any fear or stress I caused her. I can and do
> accept criticism of my work, but I won't stand for unfair
> accusations made about me as a high school counselor. I
> would never exploit the children I work with.

No sooner have I hit reply than a barrage of responses fly at me:

> A reader does not need an author's permission to have an
> unfavorable opinion. #stayinyourLane #boycottBurntOrchid

> You think you can control if a reader likes your book? You're a
> grade A narcissist. #stayinyourLane #boycottBurntOrchid

> You need help. You're abusive. #stayinyourLane
> #boycottCamrynLane

> Privileged Bitch. #killCamrynLane

Another image pops up, a photo from the school yearbook. I'm standing in the foyer, next to the trophy case. My arm is draped around the shoulders of Monique Whitford, a student who graduated a couple of years ago. I remember the moment. Monique had just won a city track meet. I'd been helping her cope with her performance anxiety. My face beams with pride. It's a wholesome scene, impossible to be misconstrued as anything but. The Twitterverse disagrees.

> Camryn Lane has been using and manipulating kids for years.

The look on her face is lecherous. Disgusting.

This poor kid. Camryn Lane needs to be stopped.

The narrative has shifted, darkened, worsened. I'm not only an unhinged author, now I'm a predator and pedophile. My denials are rapid but ineffective. My explanations land on deaf ears. The mob has turned me into the ultimate villain; they're enjoying tearing me apart. No one defends me, and I can't blame them. I only have about three hundred followers, and no one is brave enough to take on an angry mob. Besides, most of them barely know me. They might think I'm the deranged narcissist people say I am.

For the first time, I notice that I have eight DMs. I'm sure they're not anything good, but I open the first one.

Kill yourself you disgusting animal! Save me the trouble of finding out where you live!

Bile rises in my throat. Clearly there's no need to read the rest.

I go back to the main page and watch the vitriol roll in. I feel sick to my stomach, but I don't stop. I'm like a masochist, addicted to the abuse, though each insult is like a blow. And then I see a tweet that sends a chill through my body, into my bones. None of the Twitter handles have been familiar, until now. My breath catches in my chest as I read.

IngridWanders

This author abuses children and consumes child porn. She's sick. Who wants me to dox this bitch so someone can shut her up for good?

Affirmative responses are coming in furiously, but I don't read them. Instead, I click on the name. The profile picture is the Instagram photo of Megan Prince. The cover image is the gray cat.

1   0
Following   Followers

It's her. Or him. Or them.

A guttural sob escapes me. I slam the laptop closed and hurry out of my office.

44 THE BREAK

When my alarm goes off at 7:00 a.m., I've barely slept. My nervous system is too wired, too alert to the possibility of danger to let me rest. My address has likely been shared to the Twittersphere...though I haven't confirmed it. I should go online and report the abuse, but I can't bear to see the threats of violence and rape and torture. It will only take one outraged individual with shaky mental health to come to my building, wait outside my doors, and make me pay for what I've done. Anyone within driving distance. Anyone who can afford a plane ticket. Just like Chloe Winston, I've been doxed. I'm no longer safe.

I can't go into work today. I'm too distracted, too jumpy, and I don't want to put the students and staff in jeopardy if someone is coming for me. In my head, I try to calculate my sick days, but I've lost track. It's too many; I'm almost sure of it. But no one will expect me to show up. My humiliation has gone viral. I can't bear the mockery of the students, the pity or disdain of my colleagues.

As I'm dragging myself out of bed, my phone buzzes. It's Nancy Costella, the school principal, calling me from her personal number. She has been my boss for almost seven years. She is a supportive, understanding, and compassionate person, but she can be tough when she needs to be. I remember how excited she was when *Burnt Orchid* came out, how she'd announced it to the whole school. But now that book may have destroyed my career as a counselor. I'm about to find out.

"Hi, Camryn." She's seen me on the news or online. It's obvious in her tone. "We need to talk."

"I can't come in today, Nancy. I'm sorry."

"I think that's for the best. Why don't we meet for coffee? Somewhere near you."

"Or you could come here?" I suggest. I can't admit that I'm afraid to leave the apartment, but she will understand my shame.

"Sure. I'll pick up a couple of lattes. See you soon."

While I wait, I scroll through the barrage of messages and missed calls on my phone. Virtually everyone I know has seen the mortifying video of my meltdown. Most of my friends are concerned, asking if there's anything they can do, offering a meal like I'm sick or grieving. Adrian asks me to call him, and I worry about Liza. Did she go to school today? Or is she too ashamed? I shoot him a text asking after our daughter and tell him I'll call him later. My ex is righteously upset, but I can't deal with it right before my meeting with Nancy.

Even Rhea McMillan has sent me an email.

Hi Camryn,

I saw the video and felt I had to reach out. The pressure of putting your heart's work out into the world and having it attacked is a vulnerability not many can understand, but I do. If you need to talk, I'm here. Remember that you are talented enough to get a publishing deal, which is an enormous feat in and of itself.

Warmly,
Rhea

It sounds sincere, but is it? I'd been so suspicious of her, wondering if she could be the ringleader of the online vitriol, but I decide to take her message at face value. I respond with a quick note of gratitude.

Theo's numerous calls and texts must be addressed. He is losing patience with me, and I can't blame him. Last night, after the doxing threat, I'd felt terrified and alone. I'd picked up the phone to call my boyfriend, but something gave me pause. Was it Felix's suggestion that Theo was jealous of my book? Even if he was, Theo wouldn't hurt me, he wouldn't scare me. And yet I didn't want his comfort or his presence. I didn't reach out to him in my time of need.

As if he can hear my thoughts, Theo texts again.

CALL ME FFS

His obvious anger sends a chill through me. It's not what I need right now, not moments before my boss shows up to scold me, if not fire me. But his frustration is understandable because he cares about me. And I've been keeping him at arm's length. I ask if he can come over later, after Nancy leaves, and he agrees.

Conspicuously absent are any missives from my publishing team or my agent. They saw the video, but do they know it's now reached the mainstream masses? Are they aware of my Twitter meltdown? My publisher was tagged in numerous outraged tweets. They know. Their silence is ominous. I wonder if there's some sort of damage control I can do before they reach out to me. But there's no time to think about that now. The principal is at my front door. I can only try to save one job at a time.

Nancy is in her late fifties, a compact woman with a pleasant face and a commanding presence. She bustles inside with two coffees in a cardboard tray. I've managed to wash my face, apply a little makeup, throw on a pair of jeans and a clean top, but I know how I look: drawn, tired, terrified. As we sit on the sofa, I take in the principal's expression. She is concerned for me, but she has a job to do.

"I'm sorry you're going through this, Camryn. I really am." I nod, too emotional to respond. "But I've had several emails from concerned parents who saw that video. They don't feel like you're emotionally stable enough to be counseling their kids. Not right now."

"Understood," I mumble.

"The school year is almost done, but I think you should finish now."

"But what about the kids who need help submitting their final grades for college? Or the ones who still need to take summer courses to graduate?"

"Ramona will help, and I'll pick up some of the slack."

"Are you firing me?" I'm in a union; I know it's not that simple. But I need to know what Nancy's intentions are. If she wants me gone, she can make it happen. She can transfer me to another school, even another district. Or she can make a convincing case for my dismissal.

"No..." But the word is open-ended, far from definitive. "I just think you should take some time off right now. You've been through the emotional wringer. Use your vacation time. Or apply for stress leave. But you need to stay away from Maple Heights."

It's a command, not up for debate. "Okay."

Nancy sips her coffee, eyes appraising me over the cup. "Kash said you asked him to interrogate a teenage boy from another school."

"I didn't say *interrogate*." I set my paper cup on the low table. "Kash said if I had a viable suspect, he'd question them for me. I've seen this kid, Hugo Duncan, lurking outside my apartment, Nancy. I caught him running down the side of my ex's house. He's the one who took that awful video of me. And"—I face her, shoulders squared—"he's dating Fiona Carmichael."

Nancy inhales calmly, drinks more coffee. "Monica says you're fixated on Fiona."

"I'm not *fixated*," I clap back, annoyed that Monica has painted me this way. "Fiona is very charming and popular, but she's manipulative, and she's cruel."

"So you think Fiona has orchestrated a plot to bring down your writing career?"

"No. But she's definitely behind all the false accusations that came through the school portal. I wouldn't be surprised if she's stickhandled some of the other abuse, too."

"She might have sent the accusations through the portal. But why would she go beyond that? Fiona's about to embark on the next chapter of her life. She's smart and beautiful and the world's her oyster. Do you really think she'd jeopardize all that to hurt her high school guidance counselor?"

I realize how insane it sounds, but still...I do. It's clear that Nancy does not. And I'm not helping my case by insisting. "It doesn't matter anyway," I try. "Fiona will be off to Queen's University in the fall. If she's behind this, it will end when she gets wrapped up in classes and new friends and parties."

"Apparently Fiona has deferred her acceptance." Nancy sips her latte. "She's decided to take a gap year."

My chest constricts. "What? Why don't I know about this?"

"Fiona felt more comfortable discussing it with Ramona."

"Is Fiona staying in town? What are her plans?"

"I don't know." Nancy sits forward, preparing to leave. "But I highly doubt she'd divert her entire future just to pester you, Camryn."

Pester me? It's so diminishing as to be condescending. But I say nothing. I just walk Nancy to the door, thank her for the coffee, and promise to abide by her decree. Then I deadbolt the door and head back to the sofa.

BURNT ORCHID

1998

Why can't I do it?" Star demanded, her bottom lip protruding slightly. She looked like a child—she *was* a child—and Orchid felt a swell of protectiveness that was almost maternal.

"You're too young. You're too new," Orchid said, lifting the hair off the back of her neck. It was sweltering in the small apartment—too many bodies, too little air-conditioning. "If you fucked it up, there would be real consequences."

"I wouldn't fuck it up," Star pleaded. "It's easy. And we could use the money to get a bigger place. A little house maybe."

"I said no." Orchid brought the bottle to her lips, sipped the tepid beer. The money was tempting, the thought of more space a definite draw. Four of them slept in this noisy studio, two mattresses on the floor and a broken-down sofa serving for beds. Ten grand would set them up somewhere decent, adjacent but a bit removed from the chaos.

"It's not even dangerous," Star said, lowering herself to the floor in front of Orchid's armchair. There was something worshipful in their positioning, and Orchid felt a swell of power. And responsibility. The three girls in this apartment were her court, her commune, her children. They would not survive without her, not for long anyway.

"It's not even murder," Star said.

But it was. And if Orchid allowed Star to do it, the girl would never make it off the streets, would never have a chance to live a normal life. Star would have crossed a line that changed who she was, made her a killer. It would twist her, calcify her, shrivel her soul. Orchid tried to protect the girls' psyches as much as their physical beings.

Allan had explained what he wanted. A grease fire in the kitchen that would lick the curtains, light up the whole house. His wife was a drunk, he told them. She'd be passed out in her bedroom by 4:00 p.m. The assassin's job was simple: set a pan alight in the kitchen and then leave. No one would think twice about a housewife full of wine passing out with a pan on the stove, succumbing to the smoke before she could call 9-1-1. Allan would collect the insurance and be rid of his wife. And someone would collect ten thousand dollars. But not Star.

Lucy lay on the sofa, a lazy smile on her features. She was drinking too much lately, and Orchid would soon need to intervene. The girl sat up, movements languid, serpentine. When she spoke, her words were slightly slurred. "I can do it."

She could have. Lucy, like Orchid, had been forced to do unthinkable things to survive. These acts of desperation would have crushed most people, but Lucy had become callous, impervious. She'd left that filthy trailer a damaged girl and morphed into something new: hard exterior, sharp edges, an internal force for survival. Lucy was a machine. Still, Orchid wanted to protect her from the worst.

Orchid glanced at Tracey, sitting in the corner, picking at her cuticles. Her hair was lank and greasy, eyes black, mouth sunken. Orchid had rescued this girl from a garbage-filled tent, folded her into the coven, but Tracey had suffered too much. She was using, numbing herself, disappearing. It was only a matter of time...Orchid was simply sheltering her until the end came.

Orchid turned to Star. "I'll talk to Mal. He'll get it done for eight. We'll take a two grand cut, and we won't need to get our hands dirty."

"Why settle for two grand?" the girl whined. "I told you I don't mind getting my hands dirty."

"And I said no." Orchid glowered down at her. "Stay out of it, Star, or you're out. Do you understand me?"

"Got it." The girl got up, moved toward the bathroom. But Orchid didn't trust her. She'd have to watch Star carefully.

45 THE MEN

WHY DIDN'T YOU accept my calls? Why didn't you respond to my texts?" Theo is sitting in Nancy's spot on the couch, possibly still warm from her visit. When I texted him, he had raced over on his road bike, faster than crawling through traffic. He's a little sweaty and his hair is mussed from his helmet, which makes him look adorable, even younger than he is. But his expression is grave, verging on angry. "I was worried sick about you," he finishes.

"I'm sorry." The apology is genuine. "I was overwhelmed and ashamed. I didn't talk to anyone."

"You don't have to be ashamed with me, Cam. I should be your safe place."

"I know. And you are," I say, though I'm not sure it's true, not the way Theo wants it to be, anyway. I sigh, press my fingers into my temples. "I went down a Twitter rabbit hole." I tell him about the trending hashtag, the gif, the accusations. "I took your advice and I apologized from my heart. But it backfired."

"I didn't tell you to take on a Twitter mob," Theo retorts, leaning forward, elbows on his knees.

"But you told me that no one cares about my book as much as I do. And you're right. My PR team told me to stay off social media, but everything got worse. I thought maybe if I'd apologized in the first place, this could have been averted."

"Yeah but wading in at this stage was stupid. There's a viral video of you losing your shit on network TV. You're a punch line, Cam. You're a cautionary tale."

"I know." Emotion wells up in me, but I swallow it down. "I'm pretty sure I've been doxed but I'm too scared to go back on Twitter to check."

"Jesus Christ." Theo gets up, paces in front of me. "You're in danger here. Pack up some stuff. You can stay at my place."

"I'll be fine," I tell him. "The building is secure. And you already have a roommate."

"Liam can crash with a friend if it's too crowded. I'm not leaving you here when a bunch of lunatics have your address."

He has a point, but I can't stay at Theo's house. It's a bachelor pad. It's filthy. And even if Liza is staying with Adrian, I need to be accessible to her. "I appreciate the offer, but no."

"It's not up for debate. Get packing."

My hackles rise with his controlling tone. "Theo, I said no."

He stops pacing, turns to me with narrowed eyes. And then he laughs darkly. "Do I mean anything to you?"

"Of course you do."

"You don't reach out to me when all hell's breaking loose. You don't even take my calls. And now you won't let me keep you safe."

"This isn't about you," I retort, but Theo is making it so. It's become a pattern with him. My first (and only) writers' festival had been a supposed slight against him when I wanted to go alone. He'd pouted because I hadn't told him about my (admittedly stupid) plan to drive to Bellevue. And now he's miffed that he won't get to save me from the bogeymen outside my building.

"Nothing ever is," he mutters, heading to the door, his so-called protector role forgotten in his anger.

241

I trail after him, my ire up. "When I got my book deal, did you tell Felix that you were going to be third in my life—after Liza and *Burnt Orchid*?"

"Oh my god." He whirls around. "It was a throwaway comment over a couple of beers. I didn't mean anything by it."

"Felix thought you did."

"You're going to listen to the guy who thought I was sleeping with his wife? The guy who punched me in the fucking face?"

Again, Theo is the focus. Theo is the victim. "Answer me," I continue. "Are you jealous of *Burnt Orchid*?"

"I'm not jealous of your stupid book," he snaps. "And I'm not some fucking teenager who can't control his emotions. But was our relationship a lot better before you published *Burnt Orchid*? Yeah, it was."

I look at his attractive face turned ugly with anger. I see the cold disdain in his eyes. I'd told Jody I didn't know anyone who loathed me enough to harass me this way, had thought Rhea was the only one who would revel in the death of my writing career. But Theo...

When I open my mouth, my voice sticks in my throat. These words, when uttered aloud, will change everything. They will destroy us, no matter the response. But I have to ask.

"Did you pretend to be Ingrid Wandry and send me that horrible email?"

Theo takes a step back, like I've slapped him, like I've spat in his face. He shakes his head as if his ears can't be trusted. "You didn't just ask me that."

"Just tell me," I croak.

"If you really think I could do something like that to you, then this relationship is over."

Tears well in my eyes, and my throat is thick. "Answer me," I say.

"Fuck you, Cam." Grabbing his bike, he wrenches it over to

the door. I watch him struggle into the hallway, disappear without looking back. It's over. I've lost him. And my heart breaks.

But still... Theo never denied sending that horrible message.

Heading to my bedroom, I turn off my phone and collapse onto the bed. I'm still tense and on edge, but I'm also despondent, unmoored, and exhausted. I haven't slept and now my system is overloaded; it's shutting down. I pass out for two hours, maybe a little more, until the buzz of my phone wakes me. I'd set it on Do Not Disturb, so that only my emergency contacts can get through. That means this call is from my mom or my sister in Toronto, Liza, Adrian, or Theo. I want it to be him, calling to tell me that he didn't do it. To assure me that he still loves me, and that we can get through this. But it's Adrian's name on the call display. I answer.

"Hey. How's Liza?"

"She's angry. And embarrassed."

"I fucked up. I'm so sorry."

"We need to talk about how we're going to handle this going forward. Your address was shared on Twitter."

Fuck. Now it's confirmed.

"I've reported the tweets," Adrian says, "but it's not safe for Liza to be there right now."

"I know."

"She can stay here, of course, but Tori and I are taking Savannah to the UK next month. We'd like to talk to you about a plan for while we're away."

"I don't want to talk to Tori."

"What do you mean? Tori is Liza's parent t—"

"No, she's not." There's no point telling him about our pizza interaction, about Tori's bitterness toward Adrian's mother, my daughter, and me. "*We're* Liza's parents, Adrian. I only want to talk to you."

"Fine," he mutters, lowering his voice. He's clearly afraid Tori will overhear. "Then let's meet somewhere. Grab a beer?"

I look at the bedside clock. It's already four twenty-five. I haven't left the apartment all day, and while I'm still nervous, I can't remain on house arrest forever. My car is in the secure garage. I can drive out and survey the scene, look for any dangerous characters while safely ensconced in my vehicle. "Give me half an hour," I tell him.

Despite my mental assurances, I'm uneasy as I ride the elevator to the basement. I know the gate is locked, that this building is secure, but I also know bikes have been stolen from the underground lockup, that determined thieves have managed to gain access. When the doors slide open, my pulse is thudding in my neck and my mouth feels dry and papery. But I walk briskly to my Mazda. I am almost there when I see it.

White spray paint is splattered across the hood of my car in letters large but illegible from this angle. I hurry to the front of the vehicle and read the word stretched across the blue surface:

PEDOPHILE

My face burns with embarrassment, and I glance around for any witnesses. I touch the paint, and it's tacky, slightly wet. My stomach plummets. Despite the locks and the key fob entry, someone got in here. That means they could get into the building, too.

It means that even behind locked doors, I'm not safe.

46 THE PLAN

ADRIAN COMES OVER with a bucket and some kind of graffiti-removing soap he picked up at the hardware store. As we erase the horrible accusation from the hood of the Mazda, I can tell he's not happy to be playing this role again: my rescuer, my support system, basically, my husband. Tori must be furious. Adrian is probably wondering why Theo isn't helping me do this, but he doesn't ask.

When the job is done, we stow the supplies in Adrian's SUV and walk down the street to a dank bar, a mainstay despite its incongruity with the rest of the neighborhood. We are both alert for suspects, any unusual or dangerous characters watching me, but there are a lot of unusual people in this city. None of them pay me any mind.

It's a beautiful, sunny evening so the rooftop deck is full, but the dark bar is sparsely populated. We choose a back corner table with maximum privacy and order two glasses of lager. We drink in silence for a few moments, and I note how comfortable we are together. It's muscle memory. Despite all that went wrong between us, our physical bodies are still content in each other's presence; we feel no pressure to force conversation.

Eventually, Adrian sets his pint glass on a coaster. "Liza came home from school early today. She said everyone saw your video and they were all whispering about her."

The beer in my stomach turns acidic, and I feel sick at the thought of my daughter suffering because of my actions.

"She's pissed at you, Cam. She doesn't want you to come to her graduation ceremony."

The words pierce my heart like a blade. "She doesn't mean it."

"She says it will be too distracting if you're there. That everyone will be looking at you, and talking about you, and it will ruin her big day."

Tears well in my eyes, because she's not wrong. If I go to her graduation, I'll be the sideshow attraction. Instead of a bearded woman or a fetus in a jar, I'll be the deranged author who attacked an innocent woman over a critical email. The parents will whisper and judge; the kids will stare and snicker. And Liza will hate me even more. Because of my own stupid choices, I'm going to have to miss my only child's graduation. Grabbing a rumpled tissue from my pocket, I dab at my eyes.

"Maybe things will have died down by then?" Adrian says kindly.

"I doubt it. It's only a couple of weeks away."

"Sorry."

I lean my head on his shoulder: strong, solid, familiar. Adrian strokes my hair, as was his habit when we were together. There are no romantic remnants between us, but if anyone saw us, they'd think we were a couple. If Tori saw us, she'd be livid. If Theo rode by and looked in here, he'd be even angrier than he already is. I sit up and compose myself, blow my nose into the tissue. "I'll be okay."

"Good." Adrian reaches for his beer. "Liza wants to stay alone at our place when Tori and I take Savannah to the UK. But given all that's going on, I told her I'm not comfortable with that."

"Me neither," I say. "There are no images of Liza on my socials, but I might have mentioned her in an interview or something. It's too risky."

"She wants to stay at Sage's house," my ex continues. "Apparently it's fine with Derek and Amber."

"She can stay with me," I say, feeling territorial. "I know I screwed up but I'm still her parent."

"Your place isn't safe. Someone got into your secure garage. Who's to say they won't get into your building? Why don't you move to an Airbnb for a while?"

Because I can't afford to pay two rents, I want to snap. *Because I don't have rich parents to bankroll such indulgences.* But instead, I make a suggestion. "I could stay at your place while you're away. Take care of Liza and the garden."

"I thought of that, too, but Tori's not comfortable with it."

I roll my eyes, but Adrian lets it go. "Okay, I'll rent an Airbnb," I say, though I will struggle to afford it. "A secure apartment that nobody knows about. I'll keep Liza safe. I promise."

Adrian's nod is infinitesimal, but he's in agreement. He knows I love our daughter fiercely, that I would bow out if I was worried about her safety. My ex changes the subject.

"I met the girls she's traveling with," he says, sipping his beer. "They seem nice. Tori invited their parents over for dinner."

"I heard," I say, and I'm grateful. Even if I wasn't a pariah, it would have been awkward for me to host this get-together. Most of the parents at Liza's private school live in massive single-family dwellings, not cozy apartments. They have professionally decorated interiors, not pieces cobbled together after a divorce. Tori is a far better cook, a far better hostess. And Liza is not ashamed of her.

"You need to look at this trip as a reset," Adrian says. "Let Liza go and have her fun. When she comes back, everything will be water under the bridge. And she'll have missed you so much, it won't matter anyway."

I nod, lips pressed together to hold my emotions in check. "I don't want her to leave here hating me."

"She doesn't hate you," he assures me. "She's just mad." He drains the rest of his pint. "You're her mom and she loves you. She'll come back to you."

I wish I had his confidence.

Adrian escorts me back to my building and up to my apartment, even coming inside to ensure that it's vacant with a quick tour. "Thanks for your support," I say. "Sorry about all this."

"We're still family," he says. "We'll always be Liza's parents."

I smile. "I hope this doesn't cause any problems with Tori."

"It'll be fine," he says, effectively shutting the conversation down. "I've got to go. Lock the doors. Call if you need anything."

"Thanks, Adrian." A quick hug, and then I'm alone.

The draft beer is leaden in my belly and my brain feels fuzzy. Despite the afternoon nap, I'm groggy and tired. I should pounce on this feeling, catch a few hours' sleep while I can. Because I know the anxiety is still there, under the fugue of alcohol and exhaustion. Someone got into my parking garage. They can probably get into the building. I need to be alert.

I make a piece of toast and eat it standing at the counter. Then I put the plate in the dishwasher and bumble into my bedroom. Digging through the drawers, I find a comfortable pair of sweats and a baggy T-shirt and put them on. I move to the attached bathroom to wash my face. But when I flick on the light, I pull up short.

Gelatinous blobs of a milky substance are splattered on the mirror, covering the tiles, oozing into the sink. It looks bodily, sexual, but there's so much of it. It's everywhere. I shrink back in disgust and my back foot slides out from under me. I hadn't noticed, but the slippery stuff is coating the floor, too.

With a shriek into the emptiness, I fall hard into the revolting puddle.

47 THE MESS

MY HIP AND elbow are bruised and throbbing, but I scramble to get up, get away from this disgusting slime. The stuff is on my clothes, my hands, and my stomach rolls over in revulsion. And then the scent hits me: lavender, clover, a touch of sweet pea. It's a familiar aroma, and realization lands on me then. Someone has squirted my pricey salon shampoo all over my bathroom.

"What the fuck...?" I say as I grab a towel and wipe the soap from my hands. Someone was here, in my private bathroom. Someone who wanted to scare and upset me. It's so creepy, so invasive and unnerving. Who did this?

Dropping the towel on the counter, I hurry to the front door to check for signs of forced entry that Adrian and I might have missed. But the lock is secure and intact. There's no evidence of any tampering with the door or frame. Next, I check all the windows. I live on the third floor. It would be nearly impossible to climb the abutting trees and get in this way—*nearly* impossible. But the windows are all closed, locked, undamaged.

Grabbing my phone, I start to dial the police, but I stop. Would they deem *spilled shampoo* a crime worthy of their attention? There are no signs of a break-in. Nothing else seems to be amiss. When

I'd contacted them about the online harassment, the officer was dismissive. And I've already called in one false alarm. Do they have some sort of file on me now?

I need to get out of here. Moving back to the bedroom, I rummage in my closet for an overnight bag. I'll go to Martha's. Even if things have been weird between us lately, she is my best friend. She'll let me crash on the basement sofa bed. I'll be safe if not exactly comfortable. I've thrown a couple T-shirts into the bag when I pause. I'm still covered in sticky shampoo. And I should clean up this mess before I go.

As I wipe up the shampoo with a rag, rinse the suds down the drain, I run through the possible culprits. Liza probably knew I was out with her dad, so she could have come home. My daughter is furious with me, but would she do this? It's so juvenile, and so nasty. Dropping the cloth, I grab my phone and take a photo. I send it to Liza with these words:

If you did this, I won't be mad, but I need to know.

But the message doesn't deliver. My daughter has blocked me.

I resume my task, mind spinning. Theo still has a key to my apartment. He's hurt and angry, but he wouldn't come into my private bathroom and vandalize it with shampoo. Would he? Adrian has a key for emergencies, and anyone in his household could access it. Could Tori have taken his key and done this? It's too weird, too childish. Would her daughter, Savannah? But why? I barely know the girl. And our interactions have always been pleasant.

Someone could have stolen Liza's key and come in here. Wyatt immediately springs to mind. He knows I'm against Liza shelving her college plans to go to Australia, that I'm concerned about his possessiveness. I recall Liza's accusation: *"I know you don't like him, Mom."* It wasn't even true then. But Wyatt probably thought it was.

Liza's friends could have found her key, but they're all quality girls, from good families, with bright futures. But I know that's no guarantee of kindness or decency. Rinsing the rag, I run through the list of her pals for anyone who might dislike me, hold a grudge against me for some reason. My rules are stricter than most parents', including my ex-husband and *cool mom* Tori, but I've always welcomed these girls into my home, driven them to the movies or the mall, made popcorn on movie nights. Why would they hate me?

The book...

I think about Abby Lester, about Fiona Carmichael and her friend Lily. Maybe my troll was right. I shouldn't have written about teenage girls when I'm so immersed in their real-life worlds. Of course, I would never exploit them, never use them, but they are young, addicted to drama, prone to histrionics. They might *think* I did.

With the sink, counter, and floor clean, I change into fresh clothes and return to my overnight bag. But my packing soon peters out. I don't want to show up on Martha's doorstep asking for lodging. It will mean explaining that someone got into my apartment and defaced my bathroom, that my car was vandalized with the word PEDOPHILE, that I melted down on Twitter and got myself doxed. I'm embarrassed and I'm ashamed. I've handled everything so badly, turned so many people against me. Martha and Felix will think I'm pathetic, quite possibly insane.

Returning my clothes to their drawers, I toss the bag back into the closet and head out to the living area. I drag a dining chair over to the door and prop it under the handle. Then I grab my laptop and move to the couch. I'll research short-term rentals, see if there's an Airbnb anywhere in this city that I can afford. I turn on the TV for background noise, toss a blanket over my lap. There's no point trying to sleep tonight because someone was in here.

Someone who hates me.

48 THE UPSHOT

THE CALL FROM my agent, Holly, comes in at 8:00 a.m. Her silence has been conspicuous, but I know what it means: Discussions with my publishing team have been happening behind the scenes; decisions about my future are being made. It also means that Holly has been at a loss to console me over the viral video, the ensuing Twitter tirade. What can she say in the face of such stupidity? There are no words.

I'm awake but exhausted, still on the sofa in the sweats I dozed in last night. But I sit up straight, answer brightly, professionally. "Hi, Holly."

"How are you holding up?" she asks.

"Not great," I admit, but I decide to leave out the attacks in my building and home. Holly can't help me with that. And her focus is my career. "I'm sorry I went on Twitter," I say. "I really thought I could explain."

"Yeah, well..." She doesn't admonish me, but she doesn't need to. "I got a call yesterday," she continues. "Are you familiar with the talk show *The Upshot*?"

"I am." It's a slick Hollywood production in the popular format of several opinionated women sitting around a table arguing about the news of the day.

"A producer reached out to me. Megan Prince is going to be a guest on their show next Monday."

"Shit."

"They'd like to give you an opportunity to share your side of the story. And hopefully, to make peace with Megan."

"Really?" A bubble of hope wells up inside me. Could this be a chance to fix things? To explain that authors are human beings with feelings that can be hurt, and hearts that can be broken? "What do you think?"

"It's not without risk. They could spin the narrative against you. You know some of the hosts are aggressive and confrontational."

"But if they're inviting me on the show, they must at least be interested in my side of things?"

"They are. And I think they'd give you a fair shot."

"Would they fly me to LA?" I ask. A trip south would be a relief. Whoever vandalized my car and squirted my shampoo is not going to follow me there.

"Megan will be in studio, so they'd like to Zoom you in on-screen. She feels more comfortable that way."

The fact that Megan is still afraid of me makes my face warm with shame. "But she's open to talking to me? To hearing an apology?"

"Apparently it took some convincing, but yes."

For the first time in weeks, I feel a sense of hope. "I can do this, Holly. I'll beg Megan's forgiveness. I won't be defensive. I won't try to justify what I did. I'll fix it. And then I'll go dark. I promise."

"It could work."

"And this will be publicity for the book," I continue buoyantly. "If people see that I'm human, they might stop the boycott. And even if they hate me, they might want to read *Burnt Orchid* out of curiosity."

"I think it's worth a try. But let me talk to Nadine first."

"Of course," I say. And there is someone I need to talk to, as well. Because I can't do this without my daughter's permission.

Liza has blocked my calls, so I have no option but a surprise visit. I don't have her exam schedule, so she could be at school, or studying at a café or in the library, but I'll start at her dad's house. I spray some dry shampoo into my hair and apply a little blush and concealer. Tori works from home so unless she's out staging someone's mansion, I'll probably bump into her. That woman always depletes my confidence, and after our recent run-in, it's bound to be worse. I throw on my most flattering jeans and a clean T-shirt. Tori doesn't need to know I've barely put on a bra in the past few days.

Since I was vandalized, I've taken to parking on the street. Surveying my surroundings, I hurry to my car, lock the doors once I'm safely inside. But my stomach churns as I drive toward the house. Tori had hidden her resentment of both my daughter and me so deep that it had rotted and festered inside her, finally surfacing like an infected boil. Now that I know the anger she feels toward Liza, and the distaste she feels for me, it's safe to assume she won't be thrilled to see me on her doorstep at 8:35 a.m.

I ring the bell and wait, hoping against hope that Adrian will answer. But he's always been a night owl and regularly sleeps in even on weekdays. (Thanks to his understanding boss/mom, this has never been an issue.) Ideally, Liza will answer and not run screaming at the sight of me. Even Savannah would be preferable. But it is Tori, looking sleek and put together despite the hour, who greets me.

"Liza doesn't want to talk to you."

Good morning to you, too.

"And Adrian's asleep, if you wanted to see him *again*."

I knew she'd hate that Adrian came to my rescue yesterday, that I insisted we meet one-on-one. I can't really blame her.

"What's happened to your little friend Theo?" Tori asks, like he's a toddler I babysit and not my boyfriend. Ex-boyfriend, I guess. "Did you two have a tiff, so he can't help you clean up your messes?"

"I need to see Liza," I state. "I know she's angry, but this is really important."

"She's in her room, sleeping or studying. I'm not going to interrupt her."

"Then let me in, Tori. I'll go talk to her."

"You're not welcome in this house, Camryn. Your daughter is staying here to avoid you."

"Can you just get Adrian, please."

I see my request pierce her insides, reddening her face, twisting her features. She hates that Adrian and I are still a team, that he might align with me in any way.

"Everyone in this house thinks you're a lunatic, including your daughter," Tori says through gritted teeth. "Go home."

She's about to close the door in my face, but I reach out a hand to block it.

"Did you..." But I can't accuse this woman in her linen pants and silk tank top of letting herself into my apartment and squirting shampoo all over my bathroom. Can I?

"Did I what?"

"Did you use Adrian's key and go into my apartment last night?"

"Wow." She steps back, like my paranoia is contagious. "You're delusional."

She's deflecting not denying. "Just answer me then."

"And why would I want to go into your apartment?"

Even as I'm speaking the words, I know it sounds ridiculous. "Someone squirted shampoo all over my bathroom last night."

Tori laughs, shrill and high-pitched. "Are you fucking serious? You think I vandalized your bathroom with shampoo?"

"There's a key to my apartment in this house," I press. "You or someone who lives here could have gotten in while I was out."

"If it was someone in this house, it was Liza. She despises you, and I can't blame her."

"Liza doesn't need to vandalize my bathroom. She speaks her true feelings. She doesn't bury them under a façade of perfection."

"You need help, Camryn. You have a victim complex."

Savannah suddenly materializes in the entryway. "Jesus, Mom. Let her in. You two are making a scene."

Tori glances around, notes the neighbor watering her garden, the couple walking a dog across the street. It's obvious they've heard us in the way their eyes dart to the porch and then away. She steps back to let me in and slams the door behind me.

"Go talk to Liza and then leave," Tori says. "I won't dignify your ludicrous accusations with a response." She storms off toward the kitchen.

My pulse beats in my throat as I make my way down the stairs to Liza's basement bedroom. It's a cozy, fully finished space tucked behind the washer and dryer. My daughter probably likes the privacy, but I can't ignore the symbolism of the location. It's so distant, so separate from the rest of the house. And the rest of the family.

No noise emanates from the room, but I can sense Liza's presence. I knock softly and wait for her to answer. "Yeah?" she says.

I enter without announcing myself. I can't risk her refusing to let me in. She's wearing sweats, sitting cross-legged on her bed, her laptop in front of her. There's a small study desk in the corner, but she always prefers to do her homework semi-prone, propped up on pillows.

"Hey," I say, and watch her face fall when she sees me.

"What are you doing here? You know I don't want to talk to you."

"I completely understand why you're mad at me. But there's something I need to ask you."

"You're not coming to my grad, Mom. I'm not changing my mind."

It stings like a slap...likely her intention. "That's not what this is about."

"What then?" Her eyes are cold and angry, but there's a glimmer of curiosity.

I won't ask about the shampoo incident. She'd only attack me for accusing her. Instead I stand at the end of her bed and make my pitch. I tell her about the talk-show invitation. I assure her that a public apology and a carefully orchestrated explanation are the quickest ways to make this all go away. If I handle this right—and I will—everyone will forgive and forget. There's even a chance that I can salvage my career as an author. That I can be seen as more than that screaming woman on Megan Prince's lawn.

Liza listens, her body language hostile but attentive. When I'm done, she inhales deeply. "You think going on TV in front of millions of people to talk about what happened will help?"

"I do. My agent thinks so, too."

"Then you should do it," she says, and a swell of relief bubbles up in me like a sob. "But if you do, I will never forgive you."

"Liza..."

"I mean it. If you add to my humiliation to save your career, then..." Tears well in her eyes, and she swipes at them. "I don't even know, Mom."

The choice is laid bare. But there is never a choice when it comes to my daughter. I will give up anything for her, even my soul's great passion. For Liza, I will stop being an author. I'll be satisfied with my life in the public school system, content to write short stories that no one will read. I can't hurt her more than I already have.

"I won't do it," I say, moving to her on the bed. "I promise." She lets me put my arms around her, lets me stroke her hair while she cries. She doesn't hug me back, her posture is still stiff, but it's a start.

After a few moments, she says, "I need to study."

"Okay." I take my cue and leave, hurrying up the stairs and slipping out of the house unseen.

I'm in my car when my phone rings. I pull over and answer. It's Holly.

"I talked to Nadine," she says, and I hear it in her voice.

My career as an author is over. It's done. She doesn't need to say the words.

49 THE END

Dear Camryn,

This is a very difficult email for me to write. I've been a passionate fan of your work since I read the manuscript for *Burnt Orchid*. Your insight into two disparate worlds—one of politics and privilege, the other of poverty and desperation—was so authentic and visceral that I devoured your pages in one sitting. Your voice is compelling, and your writing is fluid and accessible. But as you are well aware the release of your novel has been met with significant controversy.

Our publicity department has worked tirelessly to try to address the issues that have hindered the sales of *Burnt Orchid*, but to no avail. In fact, the negativity surrounding the book seems only to build. We, as a team, are not confident that another release from you would not be met with similar vitriol. While the outline you sent me was quite powerful, and I have no doubt you could turn it into another heart-rending, thought-provoking novel, we will not be able to publish it.

We wish you the best of luck placing it elsewhere. I'm

confident that your talent as a writer will see you through these current travails, and you will have a long and successful career.

Warmly,
Nadine Sommers

The sun is sinking through the trees, the remnants of light dappling my living room. I'm on the sofa, watching the day drift away, preparing for a night of lying awake, wondering how it all went so wrong. My writing career is over, my dream dead after one book. Of course, I was going to let it go anyway—for Liza's sake. But Nadine's email, so official, so final, has still hit me hard.

I reach for the bourbon-and-Coke sweating on the coffee table and take a drink. Yuck. I thought a strong highball might make me feel better. Perhaps I just needed something to fulfill the ritual of the disillusioned writer, drowning their sorrows in whiskey. But I don't like the taste. And I'm not Hemingway or Parker or Joyce. There is nothing romantic about my situation. It's simply depressing.

Holly hasn't mentioned dropping me, but I assume it's just a matter of time. We are friends, but she's an agent. Her job is to represent clients who can create work she can sell. Even if I were to write the most brilliant novel of the decade, no publisher will take a chance on me. Maybe I could write under a pseudonym? But eventually my editor would find out who I really was, and they'd back out. I'm a loose cannon, a liability.

Swirling the ice in my glass, I see that it's half empty. Or is it half full? I try to look at my status through an optimistic lens. In the fall, I will apply at a different school, have a fresh start. I'll work full-time again. The structure will be comforting; the pace will leave me too exhausted to need a creative outlet. My daughter will be happier with her mom out of the public eye. And the abuse will stop. Whoever was trying to ruin me has done it. They've destroyed my writing career, ended my romantic relationship, and my daughter hates me. "Well done," I mutter, setting the glass down and pushing it away.

I try not to think about the summer stretching long and lonely before me. Without Liza, Theo, and my writing, I will have nothing but time on my hands. Time to find out who did this to me. It's not about retribution—not really, anyway—it's about knowledge. Because my troll could still be in my life. They could be a jealous acquaintance or even someone I love and trust. There is a simple way to find out, but it'll cost me. It will mean maxing out credit cards, perhaps taking out a small loan, but it'll be worth every penny. Because I have to know who did this to me.

Reaching for my phone, I dial.

"Camryn, how are you?" Janine doesn't wait for me to respond. "I'm sorry I haven't checked in. It's just with grad and everything, I've been swamped."

I should be busy with prom plans and grad festivities, but I'm not. I push away the hurt, get down to business. "I need the number of that cyber detective you know."

"Sure," she says. "I'll send you his contact details."

"Thanks."

"I'll see you at the grad ceremony?" she says, a question in her voice.

I don't want to get into it, not now. "Yep," I say, and then I hang up.

Shane Miller is sitting at a wrought-iron table in front of a quirky independent coffee shop, a black coffee in front of him. I'm not sure who I was expecting (someone out of *The Girl with the Dragon*

Tattoo maybe?), but he's not it. He's a heavyset guy in his late twenties, balding, with cool glasses and groomed facial hair. When I'd called him yesterday, he'd suggested we meet at this café on Commercial Drive, close to his home office. He told me to bring my laptop.

"So," he says, when I've grabbed a cup of coffee and joined him, "I looked at your social media last night. It's pretty ugly."

I nod, feeling foolish. "I know not to feed the trolls. But ignoring them wasn't working, either. I thought it was worth a try."

"Apparently not."

There's a flicker of amusement in his eyes, and my temper flares. Shane Miller probably thinks I'm some Luddite boomer too unsophisticated to deal with the modern world. He's wrong...I'm a Luddite Gen X'er. I dunk my lips in my coffee to keep from commenting. I can't afford to piss this guy off.

"I can't do anything about the haters," Shane says, audibly slurping from his cup. "But I can identify who sent you the emails. Can you show me?"

Opening my laptop, I select the message from Ingrid Wandry and pass the computer to Shane.

"Fuck. Proton Mail."

"Is that a problem?"

"It's encrypted data sent to private servers. It complicates things. A lot."

"Can you still do it?" My voice is tight with dread.

"I can do anything. For the right price."

"How much?"

"I can't give you a figure until I dig into this."

"I'll pay," I say, even though I don't know how I'll get the money. I will sell my car, even my apartment, to know who is out to get me. "Just do it."

He closes the laptop. "I'll need to keep this for a few days."

"That's fine," I say glumly. "I won't be needing it."

"When I have a name and address, I'll contact you," Shane continues. He leans back in his chair. "You need to emotionally prepare yourself. You might not like what I find out."

"I'll be fine."

"I've seen things go bad," Shane says with a sigh. "I've seen friendships blow up and families come apart. Sometimes it's better not to know."

The thought makes the coffee churn in my belly, but I can't back out. No matter who is behind my abuse, I'd rather know.

No matter how it may destroy me.

50 THE WALK

And so I wait for the information that will protect me and possibly crush me. Alone in the apartment, I clean, I putter, and I watch cooking shows on TV while my mind spins with possibilities. No one I care about would do this to me, I assure myself. My tormentor is a virtual stranger—a former student, a high school rival, an envious writer I met at a course. But Shane Miller has planted a seed that is sprouting into dark thoughts and disturbing possibilities. If someone I love is behind my abuse, how much would I be willing to forgive?

When my phone rings out in the silent space, I jump out of my skin. Most of those close to me aren't speaking to me right now, and I worry it's another prank call. But it's my friend Jody inviting me to meet her downtown for a walk.

"You need to get outside, get back into real life," she says cheerfully. Almost *too* cheerfully. Jody doesn't know all that's happened. I tell her about the graffiti on my car, about the shampoo squirted all over my bathroom.

"Someone has access to the building," I say. "Someone has been inside my apartment."

"All the more reason to get out of there then."

She has a point.

Jody continues her pitch. "Fresh air, exercise, and a good gossip session will make you feel better. I promise. And I'll buy you an iced coffee after."

"Okay," I agree. "See you in an hour."

I always take the bus downtown and I decide it will be safe. I'll be surrounded by people, and there's a bus stop just down the street. I don't want to stand there like a sitting duck, so I check the schedule. If I time it right, I can basically walk onto the number 2 bus headed downtown.

As I'd hoped, the ride is uneventful, the other passengers glued to their phones. I begin to relax as we fly over the scenic Burrard Street Bridge, drawing closer to my destination. There are several stops on the route, and I watch as passengers get on and off, calling thanks to the driver as they depart. (This city, for all its problems, has good manners.) And then a girl I recognize gets on, taps her card, and moves toward me.

Her name is Eva and she's one of my twelfth-grade students. I'd helped her with her college applications, even written her a letter of reference for a scholarship application. She's one of the kids who came to congratulate me when my book came out. But Eva will hate me now, like they all do. I turn my face away and stare out the window.

"Ms. Lane?" Eva's words are tentative.

I turn back and look up at her. "Oh, hi, Eva." I feign surprise.

I expect her to move on. To hurry to a seat and text her friends that she's on the bus with Maple Heights High's very own Cersei Lannister, but she hovers. "My friends and I don't believe what everyone's saying about you at school," she says, leaning down to keep her voice low. "You've always been helpful and nice. We've never seen you act weird or creepy at all."

"Thank you." I blink back my emotions. They're the nicest words I could hear right now.

"Take care," she says, and moves toward the back of the bus.

*   *   *

I get off at a stop in front of a Gothic Revival cathedral, incongruous with the glass high-rises looming around it. I move with the crowd, just another anonymous person in the sea of tourists, shoppers, and businesspeople. Eva's kind words have lifted my spirits. For a moment, I almost feel normal.

My friend Jody is there, on the allotted corner, looking fresh and breezy in her tights and T-shirt. She's texting someone, a smile playing on her lips. But when she looks up and sees me, she shoves her phone into her pocket, rearranges her features into a suitably somber expression.

"How are you doing?" She gives me a hug, rubs my back consolingly.

"I've been better," I admit.

We move out of the business district, heading north toward the waters of Coal Harbor. As we get up to pace, I open up about my editor's letter, about my breakup with Theo, and about Liza's estrangement.

"God, Cam." Jody stops walking on the seaside path. I halt, too. "That's so awful."

My throat closes, so I respond with a nod. If I speak, I'll start to cry.

"It's too much all at once. You must be totally overwhelmed."

A jogger rushes past us, buffeting us in his wake. The seawall is not a place to stand still. Jody takes me by the elbow and leads me to a bench in a small grassy park. We sit, side by side, my friend angled attentively toward me.

"I'm so sorry you're going through all this. It will get better. I promise."

"Thanks," I manage to mumble.

"Have you talked to anyone?"

My brow furrows. "Anyone like who?"

"Like a therapist? Or a Reiki healer?" Jody is into alternative medicine. "Your adrenals must be totally shot right now. It's a lot to process."

"I haven't," I say with a sigh. "I'll look into my medical coverage. Maybe I can see a therapist."

"It would be good to clear away the negative energy and get some emotional support."

It's not a bad idea, but the thought of rehashing it all makes me feel weak. "Yeah, maybe."

She reaches out and squeezes my hand. "I don't want to lay any more on you, but there's something you need to know."

The hair at the nape of my neck prickles, but I feel oddly numb. There is literally nothing else that could go wrong. Is there? "Tell me."

Jody takes a breath. "There's a theory going around in some online writing communities that you did this to yourself."

"Did what to myself?"

"The online harassment. A few people think that you faked it for the publicity."

It's ludicrous. I can't help but laugh. "How would I even do that?"

"It wouldn't be hard. You'd just have to set up a fake email account and fake social media accounts."

"I'm not that technically sophisticated."

"It's really very simple to do."

Something in her tone makes me bristle. "Who's been saying this about me?"

"I don't want to name names. I just wanted you to know."

"Where are these groups? On Facebook? I'll check for myself."

"They're private groups," she says quickly. "You have to request membership, and no one's going to approve you."

269

"Do *you* think I did this to myself, Jody?" My voice has risen. "Do you think I destroyed my relationship with my daughter for fucking publicity?"

"Of course not," she says. "I've been defending you. But people are saying you had no way of knowing it would go so wrong. That when you did this—*if* you did this—you didn't expect it to affect your personal life."

Jody was the one to alert me to the TikTok video, to notify me about the Twitter abuse. And now she knows about a cruel theory circling in private literary groups. Is my friend just really tapped into social media? Or is there more to it? Is she stoking the fires of vitriol against me? Or worse...could she have started these rumors?

I stand up. "I'm going to go."

"Don't go, Cam. Let's walk." She stands, reaches for my hand. "I'm sorry I brought it up. I just wanted you to be aware."

"Yeah, thanks." I pull my hand away. "I just really need to go home."

I feel Jody's eyes on me as I scurry away, but she doesn't chase after me.

I move through the streets, my vision blurred with tears. So the writing community thinks I'm desperate, and manipulative, and crazy...and maybe I am. But I didn't send those emails to myself. I didn't create a maelstrom of attention for my book. I would never do that...no matter what those other writers think of me.

When I've put some distance between Jody and me, I stop to call an Uber. I'm on the verge of falling apart, and I'd prefer not to do that on public transit. As I wait on the corner for the white Corolla, I take deep breaths, try to calm myself. It doesn't matter what the writing community thinks of me, because I'm out. I'm done. I'm not a writer anymore. But this line of thought is not at all comforting.

The white car pulls up and I climb into the privacy of the back seat. As we move through afternoon congestion, a few tears trickle down my cheeks, but I swipe them away. The visit with Jody has made one thing clear: Hiring the cyber detective was the right move.

I'm more determined than ever to identify my troll.

51 THE MARTINIS

I'M ON THE sofa with a bowl of ice cream smothered in micro-wavable hot fudge when my phone ding-dongs. The alert sends a chill through me. Now that my address has been published online, it could be anyone at my front door: a prankster, a duped delivery person, or someone here to hurt me. I don't respond and wait, chest tight, hoping they'll go away. But the doorbell rings again. And then again. I pick up my phone to call for help, but who would come? Not Theo. Not Adrian, or the police. Thankfully, whoever is out there gives up.

The silence settles, but my nerves won't. The ice cream melts in my lap, my appetite extinguished by anxiety. I get up to take the bowl to the sink when my phone rings. I see Martha's name on the display.

"I'm out front," she says. "Let me in."

Relief washes over me, almost annexing the annoyance over an uninvited guest. I've told my friend, repeatedly, that I wasn't up for company, that I needed some time alone to process everything that's gone wrong and grieve all that I have lost. The need for solitude was validated after my disastrous walk with Jody. But at least it's not a murderer. And Martha has traveled across town to see me, so I can't turn her away. "Come in," I acquiesce, pressing the button to release the door.

Moments later Martha bustles into my apartment with two canvas grocery bags, glass bottles audibly clinking. "I know you said you wanted to be alone, but Felix and I don't think that's healthy." She drops the canvas sacks on the kitchen counter with a *thunk*. "So we're going to make cocktails."

"Much healthier than being alone."

"Vesper martinis," she announces, removing bottles of gin, vodka, and Lillet from her bag. "Have you had one before?"

"No."

"They're my new favorite. Do you have a cocktail shaker?"

I dig a shaker out of the cupboard over my fridge, and fish some ice out of the freezer as Martha plays bartender. She's also brought an array of cheese and crackers, and a bag of chips, which I appreciate since my dinner of ice cream has now melted. When our drinks are poured, and the food is set out on plates, we move back to the living room.

"Cheers," Martha says, holding up her glass. "To new chapters and new beginnings."

I understand she's trying to bolster my spirits, but my losses are too recent and too many. How can I look forward to a new beginning without Liza? Or Theo? Or my writing? Halfheartedly, I lift my glass and take a sip of the concoction. It's strong but floral and delicious.

"I know you've been through a lot," Martha continues, softening her tone. "But you're so resilient, Camryn. You got through a divorce, and that's harder than this is."

"In some ways, yes," I explain. "It was definitely more disruptive. But Adrian and I were unhappy for so long. My writing career had just started."

"You don't have to quit *writing*," Martha says. "Maybe you could write for magazines? Or for TV?"

Like that's so easy.

"Or you could teach classes. You're a published author. It's a huge accomplishment."

One day, these options might be appealing, but right now they're little consolation. "I wanted to write another book," I say glumly.

Martha leans forward, fixes herself a cracker with blue cheese and fig jam. "I was a little worried about your next book, actually."

"Worried?"

"The plot sounded a bit *familiar*." She sits back, pops the cracker into her mouth, and chews. "You were going to write about a couple whose marriage is shaken up by a platonic girlfriend from the husband's past."

"Yeah...?" Did I share this idea with Martha? I don't recall.

"It sounded a lot like Felix and his friend Ellen."

Ellen. I grapple to place the name in my memory, and then I remember. When Martha and Felix first started dating, Ellen was his best friend. He assured Martha they were nothing more than pals, that Ellen was happy with her partner, Omar, and Felix loved only Martha. But Martha never believed him. She always worried that if Ellen and Omar split, Felix would want to be with her. Eventually, the friendship gave out under the strain.

"I'd forgotten all about her," I say.

"You must have remembered her on some level, or you wouldn't have written about that scenario."

"Did Ellen's partner die?" My brow furrows. "That was really the crux of my plot."

"No, Omar's fine and they're still together. I just meant that the friendship between Ellen and Felix was the jumping-off point for you. And that would have been hard for me."

I set my glass down. "I don't think you're the only person who's felt jealous of a partner's platonic friendship."

"I'm not." There's an edge to her tone. "But I might be the only one whose best friend was going to write a novel about it."

This conversation is making me uncomfortable. I feel muddled and defensive. I need more clarity. "When did I tell you the plot of my next novel?"

Martha reaches for a handful of chips, but her casual façade is slipping. "Rhea and I were talking about some of the work you guys did in writing class. She mentioned a short story you wrote and said you were going to pitch it as your next novel."

"How did *she* know I was turning that story into a novel?"

"I have no idea."

But I do. Navid must have told her. Was he my ally in all this mess or was he dishing behind my back with Rhea?

"Rhea sent me a note," I mumble, almost to myself. "She said she understood what I'm going through."

"She does. She feels awful for you."

"I thought you two were barely acquaintances?"

"We've gotten closer lately. Because we're both concerned about you."

"Does Rhea think I did this to myself?" I ask, eyes narrowing. "Is she part of the online group making those ridiculous accusations?"

"Rhea doesn't know what to think," Martha says, which means yes. "It's all so confusing."

I reach for my drink and swallow the rest of it. It burns in my chest, but I want to numb myself. Martha's visit has made me feel more alone than ever. When I speak, my tone is pointed. "I guess you're pretty relieved that I won't be publishing another book."

"I am." Martha picks up her glass, too. "But only because

publishing was decimating you, Cam. I hated watching you suffer. At what point is it not worth it anymore?"

I look at my friend and try to gauge her sincerity. Is she really here to support me? Or is there something exultant in her manner? The people I'd trusted the most—Theo, Jody, and now Martha—all have reasons to revel in the demise of my career. Until I get definitive news from the cyber detective, I don't know who I can trust.

"I'm tired," I say, which isn't a lie. "I'd like to be alone."

"Don't be like that."

"Like what?" I ask, and my eyes are moist with emotion. "I'm exhausted. And drinking myself into oblivion probably isn't the healthiest way to cope with all the stress."

"Okay." She holds her hands up like I've got a gun on her. "I'm sorry. I'll leave you alone."

In tense silence, we pack up the snacks and bottles, and I stand by as she calls Felix to pick her up on the way to his gig.

"I'll meet him out front," she says, forcing a conciliatory smile. But I don't return it. I just close and lock the door behind her.

I've just settled into bed when my phone buzzes with a text. Picking it up, I see that it's from Theo.

I think I left a set of office keys there. Can I get them?

I haven't seen a set of keys lying around, but it's possible they're here. It's also possible this is just an excuse to talk to me. My heart melts a little. Because I want to talk to Theo, too. I miss his comforting presence, the way he supported me. Even if it's too late for us romantically, I hate the way we ended things.

I haven't seen them, I write back, but I can look for them.

Thnx. It sounds abrupt. If you find them, let me know. I can swing by on Monday.

Or we could meet for coffee?

The ellipsis shimmers as he composes a response. I wait, wondering if he's going to tell me he just wants his fucking keys, that he doesn't want to talk to me, and he can't forgive my accusations. Whatever he was going to say, he must have reconsidered, because a single letter comes through.

K

BURNT ORCHID

1998

Orchid stared at the suburban sprawl through the scratched bus window. Someone had etched the word *balls* into the plastic glazing, and it skewed and refracted her view. But the streets were brightening, the human and material refuse thinning. Allan's neighborhood was not upscale, but it was clean and pleasant, something wholesome about the dated single-family homes. On the surface at least.

Fucking Star. The girl had been told not to come here, threatened even. Orchid had grown complacent, used to the blind trust and loyalty of Lucy, the lack of agency of Tracey. Star was a different breed: a rebel, a firecracker, a problem. But she was not a killer. Not yet.

The bus stopped and Orchid got off in front of a convenience store. Allan's address was on a piece of paper, crumpled in her front pocket. She had kept it away from Star, but the girl was resourceful. She could have found it while Orchid slept or gone to the pharmacy and gotten it from Allan directly. There was no guarantee Star had come here, but Orchid had to check.

She walked calmly through the suburban streets, quiet but for light birdsong and distant traffic. The neighborhood was well kept but deserted, its residents off at their middle-management jobs. A cab would have gotten her here quicker, but Orchid didn't want a record of this trip. There was no way of knowing what would happen next, but she had a strong sense that it would be better if she was never here.

Allan's home was like all the others on the street: a split-level, seventies design with a manicured front lawn, watered to a deep green despite the arid conditions. The pharmacist had assured them that his wife—her name was Carol—would be passed out in her room. He'd added a sedative to her bottle of wine, but Carol regularly drank herself into a stupor by four o'clock each day. But Orchid knew a lot of drunks, and she knew they were highly unreliable. There were still plenty of ways this mission could go horribly wrong, and Star was not prepared for any of them.

Orchid slipped stealthily down the side of the house, to the backyard. The lawn was patchy and yellow back here, with a small, wilting flower garden. It was easy to find the lone decorative gnome that concealed the spare key. Tipping it over, Orchid saw only soggy grass, dirt, a couple of worried centipedes. The lack of a key meant that Star was already inside.

On silent feet, Orchid climbed the back steps up onto a sunbleached deck. Sliding along the length of the house, she passed two windows with their blinds drawn tight. The third window had yellow gingham curtains tied back to reveal a sunny kitchen. Orchid scanned the room. From the glass bowl of fruit to the cactus on the windowsill, nothing appeared to be wrong. Except for the wisp of a girl standing before the gas stove, a pot of oil beginning to smoke before her.

Orchid moved around to the kitchen door and slipped inside.

"Fuck!" Star said, jumping back from the stove. "You scared me."

Without a word, Orchid crossed the room and smacked her, not hard, but enough to rattle her, wake her up to the mistake she was about to make. And yet it had no effect.

"It's almost done," Star snarled, her teeth gritted with determination. "Get out. Let me do this."

Orchid glanced at the smoke curling from the pot. Soon it would burst into flames. "Turn off the gas. Let's go."

"No."

"You do this, and we're done. Do you understand me?"

"I'm doing this for us," Star hissed, voice low. "And you're not going to walk away from me when I have twenty thousand dollars in my pocket."

Orchid was about to lecture this girl on trust and loyalty, how the means didn't always justify the ends, when a female voice called out from another room.

"Who's there?"

Allan had promised that Carol would be comatose, that she wouldn't hear a thing. But the woman was awake. She knew they were there. She could enter the room at any second and see them. She could be calling the cops right now.

"Let's go," Orchid whispered, and Star nodded, her face pale with fear. Orchid didn't see the cup of water that was sitting on the counter until it was too late, until Star was already tossing it onto the small flicker licking out of the pot.

"Don't!" Orchid screamed, but her voice was drowned out by the roar of the flame shooting into the sky like lava, spraying an arc of fire across the room. Star screamed, stumbled, held up an arm to protect herself, and then she disappeared, enveloped in the hot orange glow.

Fifteen-year-old Star was on fire.

52 THE PERFORMANCE

THE VERSION OF Megan Prince on my TV screen is somewhere between the filtered version I saw on TikTok and the real-life version I confronted on her front lawn. She's clearly had her hair and makeup professionally done and she looks pretty and polished in a sunny yellow dress. Despite being on national TV, Megan seems composed and comfortable. She looks honest and trustworthy.

The segment opened with "the viral video that shook the book world." And now it's time for Megan's interview.

"Tell us how this happened," one of the show's hosts asks. I can't remember her name, but she's a stunningly beautiful former attorney who now writes children's books.

"First of all," Megan begins, "I had never even heard of *Burnt Orchid* before that day."

"That makes two of us," another host quips. She's the former comedian, an older woman with a bombastic manner.

Megan chuckles and then continues. "Someone using my image and a fake name set up accounts to troll Camryn Lane's book with bad reviews. A lot of people were upset because Camryn is a high school counselor, and her book is about troubled teens."

"That's not appropriate," the gorgeous lawyer says.

"That's reductive," I mumble into the silence.

Megan continues. "Camryn Lane was so upset, she decided to find out who was behind the criticism. Through my photos, she managed to find out where I work, and she showed up there."

"So she stalked you?" another host asks.

"It was terrifying," Megan says, her voice wobbling for effect.

"Wait a second," the comedian interjects. "Aren't bad reviews part of the deal when you publish a book? I mean, when I was doing stand-up, I expected hecklers. It was the cost of doing business."

"Another snowflake," a coiffed blond host says. I think she's new, but I can tell by her style that she offers the conservative viewpoint.

Megan continues, explaining how she drove home after a long day of work, excited to see her cat, Gervais, to put her feet up and have a glass of wine, when a screaming, spitting lunatic accosted her on the front lawn. Luckily, her nephew was visiting and captured the verbal assault on video.

I should turn this off. It's overly dramatic and inaccurate. But though I feel feverish and queasy, I'm transfixed.

The youngest host, a dancer I think, asks, "Do you have any idea who used your photos to attack *Burnt Orchid*?"

"No idea," Megan says, wide-eyed and innocent. She doesn't mention that it has to be one of the 207 people she has allowed to follow her private account. That she could find out who's been attacking me if she wanted to. But she doesn't care. She's too busy enjoying her fifteen minutes of fame.

The lawyer speaks next. "Have you taken any legal action against Camryn Lane?"

"No." Megan's features contort with pity. "I just want her to get the help she needs."

"She needs a rubber room," the unfunny comedian says, and I remember why I don't watch this show.

"We're so sorry for all you've been through," the young dancer says before turning to face the camera. "We invited Camryn Lane to share her side of the story via video link, but she declined our offer."

I turn the TV off.

In a cap and sunglasses, I walk up a side street to meet Theo. We've chosen a shitty chain coffee shop about half a mile from the apartment. I'm unlikely to run into any of my caffeine connoisseur acquaintances there. Now that I've made my daytime TV debut, I'm officially a pariah. The doxing made me fear for my personal safety. Now I also fear the disapproval and disdain of my community.

But I couldn't invite Theo over to my place. After all that went down between us, it doesn't feel right. I need to set boundaries and protect my personal space. And while I miss him, I can't forget how angry he was. Or how he played the victim, twisting situations until they were all about him. Once I know for sure that he is not my harasser, can I forgive his self-centeredness? Can I tolerate his immaturity?

I'm so lost in thought that I almost don't notice the car trailing behind me. It's an electric vehicle, nearly silent, still several feet away. But it's inching along, clearly following me. When I turn to look, it speeds up, racing forward. The passenger window is open, and as the vehicle moves past, something flies at me. I turn away, duck, and the object whizzes by me, but the accusation hits its target.

"Fucking pedo!"

I'm frozen for a moment, watching the car move away from me, blood rushing through my ears. And then I start to run. I want to go home but I'm too far away. The coffee shop is just around the corner, and I sprint toward it. I want to be inside, safe, in Theo's arms. Traffic is sparse so I fly across the street, too shaken to wait for the light. Panting, I burst into the chain restaurant.

There are a number of customers, mostly men in workwear, sipping coffees and snacking on donuts. Theo is at an unwiped table with two cups of coffee on it. He looks up when he hears me enter, and his face pales at the sight of me. It's only then that I realize my face is wet with tears, that I'm quivering like a Chihuahua.

Theo jumps up, hurries to me. "What happened?"

"A car followed me from my apartment," I mumble through terrified sobs. "They threw something at me."

"Jesus, Cam." He wraps his arms around me, and I sink into him. "What did they throw?"

"I don't know," I cry into his neck. "I think it was a burger or something. They missed."

"Take a deep breath," he says, holding me at arm's length. "Let's sit down."

"Can you please take me home?" I sniffle.

"Of course. My car's in the back lot."

Thank God he didn't ride his bike for once.

Theo's arm around my waist is both comfortable and comforting as we approach my building. He scans the area like a bodyguard, and I feel small, helpless, but protected as we slip into the lobby. In the elevator, he holds me to him and strokes my hair. It would be so easy to slip back into this relationship. To forget all his anger and selfishness. And maybe I will. Because I know, in my heart, that Theo is not my tormentor, and soon the hacker will confirm it. Then maybe I'll suggest couples therapy. Our issues are nothing insurmountable.

When we're inside, I go to the bathroom to wash my face while Theo makes tea. I'd put on some makeup to look pretty for my ex, and now it runs in streaks down my pale cheeks. Wiping away the remnants, I return to the sofa, where Theo joins me moments later with two mugs of chamomile.

"I looked for your keys," I say, bringing the steaming cup to my lips. "I couldn't find them."

"It's fine." He smiles. "It was an excuse to see you."

I smile back, grateful he admitted it, grateful we're not playing games. "I wanted to see you, too. I'm sorry about the last time you were here. That was ugly."

"I'm sorry, too. I lost my temper."

"I should never have accused you, though. It was a horrible thing to do."

"You're under a lot of stress. Everyone's worried about you."

I cock my head. "Everyone?"

"Your friends," he says, without meeting my eye. "Martha and Jody."

"Did you talk to them?"

"Martha called me. She and Jody connected. They're worried this is all too much for you. They think maybe you should get away for a while."

"Get away where?"

"They're looking into some options."

"Narrow it down for me," I snap, because suddenly, I feel like Frances Farmer, about to be committed and lobotomized against my will.

"Calm down," Theo says. "They meant like a yoga retreat. Some sort of healing center where you can get away from social media and all the craziness."

That's got Jody's name written all over it.

"Somewhere with healthy food and no alcohol." He softens his delivery. "You've been drinking a lot lately."

My jaw clenches, but my response is measured. "I'm fine," I tell him. "I'm not going to be sent away. My daughter is here. She's about to graduate."

"But she doesn't want you there," he says gently.

I've told no one that. It's too painful to articulate. But somehow, Theo knows. "Have you been talking to Adrian?"

"Tori called," he says, and he sees me recoil. "We all care about you. We all want you to get through this. And get back to being your old self."

The realization lands like a piano on a cartoon cat. Theo didn't want to see me today because he loves me. He's been sent on a mission by my so-called friends. I've become a project. They're worried about me. They probably have a group chat called Camryn Is Losing Her Mind.

"Who else is on this? Navid? Rhea McMillan?"

"No..." But I can't tell if he's lying or not.

"I need you to leave, Theo."

"I don't think you should be alone right now."

"What do you think I'm going to do? Throw myself off the balcony? Drink a bottle of bleach?"

"Jesus, Cam." He's annoyed by my histrionics. "If someone really threw something at you, they might still be out there."

" 'If'?"

He blanches, caught out. Theo doesn't believe me. He thinks I made up the drive-by assault. Jody must have told him about the online speculation that I've orchestrated the attacks myself, for publicity, attention, and sympathy. I can almost hear my friends' gleeful gossip. *The poor thing couldn't handle the pressure of her book not selling. She thought turning herself into a victim would help.*

"Go." It comes out a rasp, but Theo hears the steel in my words.

"Fine," he says as he stands up. "Stay inside, Cam. Eat something." At the door, he pauses. "I'll call you later. Please answer."

But I won't. And he knows that.

Because I can't trust Theo or anyone close to me.

53 THE MEET

I'S 11:17 P.M. when Shane Miller calls, jarring me from a melatonin-induced sleep. It's a rude and ridiculous time to phone, but I guess cyber-security experts don't keep regular office hours. Luckily, I've added him to my emergency contacts, so the call rings through.

"I've got a name and a home address," Shane says.

My groggy mind struggles to process the enormity of his words, and for a moment I float in that liminal space. Shane knows the identity of my troll. He holds the information that will change my life. But until he shares it with me, I still don't know who I can trust. Is this a Schrödinger's cat scenario? (I've never understood quantum mechanics.)

"I can meet tomorrow morning," Shane continues. "How's eleven?"

"That works," I say quickly. "Can you tell me anything now? Even a first name?"

"No money, no name."

"Initials even?"

"This isn't a game." He shuts me down. "What I did for you was not simple or technically aboveboard."

"Sorry."

"Let's meet at the same café. I prefer to be paid in cash."

"Sure. How much?"

He tells me and the amount is staggering. Shane Miller must be loaded, but Janine said he lives in a dingy basement suite. What does he spend his money on? Collectible action figures and Uber Eats? But I need this information. And I've figured out a way to get the money. Before Shane hangs up, I have one last question.

"And you're sure you've got the right person?"

"I've got the right household," he says. "If multiple people live there, I can't pinpoint who's been harassing you."

It's enough. I hang up and try to get back to sleep. But I won't. The truth is too close now. And it could change everything.

Early the next morning, I sit with a cup of coffee and my phone. I know what I need to do, but I'm shaky and nervous as hell. As predicted, I barely slept, and my brains feels fuzzy. But I have to find out who is trying to ruin my life, so I can bring my daughter back home. And that means I need money to pay Shane Miller. Swallowing my fear, I place a call to Adrian's mother.

The request I'm about to make may be presumptuous to the point of delusion. Marion Fogler might shut me down, scold me, even berate me. But I pray she will understand my panic and my plight. And as the mother of her granddaughter, I hope she still considers me family. As the phone rings in my ear, I clear my throat and prepare my pitch.

"Camryn," she says, her tone cool and superior, but it always is. "This is a surprise."

"Could we meet for coffee?" I ask, voice tremulous. "I need to talk to you. It's urgent."

There's a beat of silence. "Come to the house," she says, and it's evident that Marion Fogler knows about my public meltdown. She's ashamed to be seen with me. And who can blame her?

"I'll be right over."

Adrian's parents live in Shaughnessy, a tony residential neighborhood in the center of the city. Most of the homes here are sprawling heritage mansions with well-tended gardens, circular driveways, and guesthouses. The residents of these exorbitantly priced abodes are not wealthy, they're rich: the multi-home, yacht-vacation, hire-your-son-to-do-nothing type of rich. As I drive through the streets lined with ancient elm and oak trees, it's quiet to the point of being eerie.

I find Marion seated by her pool with a teapot and two china cups set on a small table. She doesn't get up, doesn't hug me, but she points to the chair opposite her, and I sit. "What can I do for you?" she asks, filling the cups with black tea.

There's no time for charm or small talk. I'm meeting Shane Miller in just over two hours. "I need a loan, Marion. It's a lot of money, but I promise I'll pay you back."

"How much?" She doesn't flinch when I tell her; it's nothing to her. She picks up her delicate cup. "And what's it for?"

I reach for my tea, but the cup rattles when I touch it. I'm trembling with nerves, so I sit back and press on. "I hired a cyber-security expert to identify the person who's been harassing me online."

"Adrian told me about that," she says, after a sip of tea. "But some of my friends at the club think you've made it all up. They think it's an excuse for you to act like an angry toddler because you can't handle criticism."

Ouch.

"My masseuse thinks you should be in jail," she continues. "She says you stalked and attacked an innocent person."

I've humiliated her and she's angry. But I can't back down. I need the money. I will beg if I have to.

"I know I made some bad choices." I ignore her snort of affirmation. "But I'm not a liar, Marion. Someone has been harassing me—online and in real life. I need to find out who so I can make it stop. I need to protect Liza."

Her delicate cup clinks as she sets it on the matching saucer. "And this cyber hacker knows who's behind the attacks?"

"He knows the household, yes. I can figure it out from there."

She sighs and for a moment, I worry she's going to turn me down flat. But Marion Fogler is a mother and a grandmother. She may be haughty, condescending, and parsimonious with her approval and affection, but she loves her family. "I'll do this for Liza," she says, leaning forward in her chair. "Let me get my checkbook."

At the bank, I slide the check to the teller and ask for fifties and hundreds. If the young man wonders why I need such a large sum of cash, he doesn't show it. Does he often get customers who are paying white-hat hackers? Drug dealers? Or ransom for their children? It's not like I need a suitcase to carry the money, but the two thick envelopes weigh heavy in my purse.

I drive to the Commercial Drive coffee shop, arriving about five minutes early. Last time I was here, I barely noticed the décor, but this time I take in the hexagonal subway tiles and dark wood. At the counter, I order a decaf coffee; I'm already jittery, and caffeine might put me over the edge. I'd get a coffee for Shane, too, but I can't remember what he was drinking last time. And with the sum I'm about to hand over, he can afford his own drink. I sit inside this time, at a small table near the front door. And I wait.

I'm both desperate and terrified to know the identity of my

harasser. Speculation is pointless when the truth is moments away, but my mind still runs through the possibilities, the best- and worst-case scenarios. I'm preparing myself, hoping the information won't be too devastating. But one thought makes me want to get up, to run out of here before Shane Miller arrives. The culprit could be someone I care about.

Even someone I love.

54 THE MISS

WHEN SHANE MILLER is half an hour late, I text him.

I'm at the café. Are you running behind?

Just as I hit send, the door opens, and I startle in my seat. But it's not Shane who enters. It's a young couple, pierced and tattooed, engaged in a lively conversation about a drag show they recently attended. I settle into my chair and check my phone. There's no response from Shane. A flutter of panic travels from belly to chest, but I inhale deeply to calm myself. Given the hour that Shane called last night, he probably considers this early morning. He's slept in, that's all it is. I'll wait.

Fifteen more minutes pass. And then another fifteen. I begin to wonder if I got the day wrong. Or the meeting time. I touch my cup of cold coffee and realize I've been here a full hour. I decide to call him. Panic clutches my throat when I hear Shane's curt voice-mail greeting. Where the hell is he? Not only does he have the information I so desperately need, but he also has my laptop. Even if my writing career is dead in the water, I still want my computer back.

Next, I dial Janine. She recommended Shane. She can tell me

if this flaky behavior is to be expected. Did he have some sort of hacker emergency? Is that even a thing? Is it possible I've been scammed? But Janine doesn't answer, either. She's probably too busy prom-dress shopping with Grace or getting mother-daughter pedicures before the festivities. I hang up without leaving a message.

I stay for another hour because I don't know what else to do. If I knew where Shane lived, I would go there and confront him, but of course he hadn't divulged that information. I google him on my phone but, not surprisingly, nothing comes up for this specific Shane Miller. Feeling guilty for hogging the table, I buy an enormous muffin and pick at it though my stomach feels even worse than when I arrived. I call and text him again and again. Finally, at one o'clock, I give up.

As I walk back to my car, my head spins. Was Shane Miller playing me all along? Was this all an elaborate ruse to get my laptop? But if he was a scammer, wouldn't he have asked for the money up front? And Janine had recommended him. It's not like I found him in an Instagram ad promoting his hacking skills. But now I recall that Janine didn't use Shane to find her troll. She said that the police found her tormentor after he threatened her daughter. Janine had done a story on Shane when he was a teen. Maybe now he's gone to the dark side?

There's a quaint Italian grocery store near my parking spot, and I duck inside. If I've been scammed, at least I can stuff myself with cheese and pasta to dull the pain. Since Liza moved in with Adrian, I've existed on peanut butter toast and takeout, and my nutrition is suffering. I should stock up on some real food.

I grab a plastic basket and wander the aisles. There's an excellent selection of olive oils, exotic vinegars, and decadent pasta sauces. My stomach rumbles. Despite my lack of appetite, my body is craving sustenance. I grab a jar of tomato sauce, some marinated olives, and move around the corner to the pasta aisle. The narrow passage is partially blocked by a stock boy and a rolling cart full of boxes of orecchiette. As I approach, the young man turns toward me. It's Liza's boyfriend.

I'd forgotten that Wyatt lives in this area, commutes across town to his posh boys' school. While most of the pupils there probably have generous allowances, Wyatt's family is blue collar. He knows the value of hard work. We are alone on the aisle, practically face-to-face. Avoidance is not an option.

"Hi, Wyatt."

"Uh...hi, Camryn." He's clearly uncomfortable. "What are you doing over here?"

"I was meeting someone for coffee," I explain. I feel forced to make small talk before I can hurry on my way. "So...are you done your exams?"

"I have one more on Friday."

"You must be excited to graduate."

"Yeah."

Wyatt must know that I've been banned from my daughter's grad festivities, but it feels odd not to comment. "I'm sure you and Liza will have fun at prom next week," I say, wrapping up this awkward exchange.

"Liza and I broke up."

I tilt back on my heels, shocked. "What? When?"

"Last week," he says, eyes drifting to the pasta cart.

I can't believe Liza didn't tell me. It must have happened after the viral video that drove Liza out of my home and made her stop talking to me.

"I'm sorry, Wyatt." And I'm sincere. "I'm sure that's sad for both of you."

He shrugs but his face darkens. "I guess. But Liza's changed a lot."

"How has she changed?"

"She's got a bunch of new friends. She's different around them."

Liza had said Wyatt was controlling. That he didn't like the girls she was going to travel with. "Who Liza chooses to spend her time with is really none of your concern," I say tartly. "I'd advise you not to try to control your next girlfriend's personal relationships."

Wyatt's eyes widen slightly at the attack, but he composes himself. "You wouldn't say that if you knew these girls."

"What does that mean?"

"Nothing. Forget it."

"Tell me, Wyatt. What do you mean?"

"I have to work," he says.

He turns back to his pasta boxes, and I am dismissed.

55 THE NEWS

BY THE TIME I get home, I'm almost positive Shane Miller has scammed me for my laptop. I don't know what my recourse is, but I need to report him. Predators like him luring desperate single moms and naive seniors need to be stopped. As I unpack my groceries, I call the police non-emergency line (again). An automated voice asks me questions to ensure I'm not in any present danger, and then asks how it can help. But how do I explain this situation to a robot? Do I say that I hired a hacker who stole my laptop? I suddenly wonder if Shane Miller's tactics were legal. I hadn't cared at the time, but could I be in trouble for contracting him? It's not a chance I want to take. I hang up and dial Kash Gill.

I'm not sure how Kash feels about me now. The entire staff of Maple Heights Secondary likely considers me stark raving mad. But Kash knows me on a different level. We've worked on some very difficult student cases together. He's seen the lengths I'll go to for these kids, how much I really care about them. He knows I'm not a monster.

When he answers, his voice is cool and professional. "Hi, Camryn."

"Hi, Kash. Thanks for taking my call."

"Look," he says, and I hear him sigh. "I didn't go see that Hugo kid. I'm sorry but it didn't feel—"

"I understand," I say quickly. "That's not why I'm calling."

"What's going on?"

I tell him everything, trusting that he won't judge or accuse me. "I know I shouldn't have handed over my laptop, but a friend recommended this guy," I say. "And I was desperate to know who was behind these attacks." My voice thickens. "I need to know who is trying to destroy my life."

"That's understandable," Kash says gently. "I'm going to need some details on this hacker."

I share everything I know about Shane Miller, which is not a lot. Kash promises to look into him for me. "But it could be a while before you get your computer back, if at all," he adds. "Hopefully your work is on the cloud."

"It is," I mutter. This was my personal computer, used for my writing. None of my work matters. Not anymore.

"We can file a police report so you can claim it on insurance," Kash adds. "But let me see what I can find out about this guy first."

After I hang up, I address the next issue weighing on my mind: my daughter's breakup. Moving to the sofa, I call Liza but find I'm still blocked. I hang up and dial Adrian. As it rings, I wonder if his mom told him she loaned me money to pay for a hacker. It's likely a moot point now anyway. If Shane Miller is a fraud, I'll be able to give Marion her money back immediately.

"Hey, Cam." Adrian's greeting is monotone. I've become a problem, a nuisance.

"I bumped into Wyatt," I say quickly. "He told me he and Liza broke up. Is she okay?"

"She was upset at first, but her friends have been rallying around her. She seems fine now."

"Which friends?" I ask.

"I don't know..." He sounds flustered. Adrian loves his daughter, but every other teenage girl looks the same to him. "Sage and some other girls," he tries. "A Mindy maybe? Or a Molly?"

"Why did Liza and Wyatt break up?" I ask. "Were they fighting? Do you know what it was about?"

"I didn't ask. I respect Liza's privacy. You might want to try it sometime."

My ex is being influenced by his new wife, but I bite my tongue. "Can I talk to her?"

"It's not long since you publicly humiliated her, Camryn. She's still angry."

"I just want to make sure she's okay."

"I told you, she's fine," he barks, but his next words are softer. "Liza will come around, but she needs more time."

"Just let me tell her that I love her. And that I'm here if she needs to talk about the breakup or anything else. Please, Adrian."

"She's not home. She left about half an hour ago to write an exam. But I'll tell her you called." He hangs up.

And I scramble for my car keys.

I'm at the front door of the building when I reconsider my plan to drive to Liza's school. Showing up at her final exam unannounced would not be appreciated. And trying to console her about her breakup in front of her classmates would be ill advised. Liza would be even more humiliated, even more enraged. She would cut me out of her life: for weeks, months, even years. And lurking outside the school would prove Adrian's point about not respecting our daughter's privacy, while also feeding into the crazy stalker narrative that's been dogging me. Fighting my maternal instinct to go to her, I ride the elevator back up to my apartment.

As I make a cup of tea, I reflect on my encounter with Wyatt.

I know young love can be fickle and ephemeral, but something doesn't feel right. Not long ago, Liza was ditching college to meet Wyatt in Australia. And suddenly, it's over. It feels too abrupt. Something must have happened—an argument, an incident, or something worse. Adrian had assured me that Liza was *fine*, but he's not exactly tuned in to the emotions of a teen girl. He can barely tell her friends apart. I need to talk to my daughter. But how?

Tears brim in my eyes, and I swipe them away. Regret and self-pity are not going to help me get my daughter back, but the emotions come hard and fast. Next week, Liza will toss her mortarboard into the air, pop some sneaky champagne with her girlfriends, and take celebratory photos with Adrian and Tori. In a couple of months, Liza will leave, embark on the next chapter of her life, leaving me alone. I'd consoled myself that this was time for me to focus on my writing career, to develop my true passion, but now that's all gone, too. I feel desolate and abandoned.

With my cup of tea, I move to the sofa and sink into the cushions. I'm about to indulge in a pillow-pounding cry when my cell phone rings on the kitchen counter. Blowing my nose into a tissue, I hurry to answer it. I'm hoping it will be Shane Miller calling to tell me that he had a family emergency, a terrible flu, a brutal hangover, but he has the information I need. When I look at the number, it's blocked, just like Shane's was.

"Hello?" I am almost breathless.

"It's Kash." I forgot that police officers also use private numbers. "Is this a good time to talk?"

"Sure."

"Are you alone?" His tone is odd.

"Uh, yeah."

"You might want to have someone with you," he says. "Why don't you call a friend and then call me back?"

My heart is pounding, throat tight. "It's fine, Kash. What is it?"

"I have some upsetting news." His exhale is audible down the line. "About Shane Miller."

I've been scammed, dammit. I knew it. "Just tell me."

"Shane Miller is dead."

BURNT ORCHID

1998

As time froze, as the girl burned, these thoughts ran through Orchid's head:

Never throw water on a grease fire.

Star was too young, too stupid, too naive to know it.

Orchid had been right all along.

Her pondering took less than a second, but even that was too long to waste. Orchid clicked into rescue mode, sprang into action. There was a tea towel beside the sink, and she ran to it, covered her hands. She grabbed for Star, pushed her from the burning room, swatting at the flames that continued to lick up her body. Outside, she shoved the girl off the deck onto the crisp lawn, where Star rolled and writhed in anguish and terror. Orchid dove on top of her, smothering the flames with her body. Orchid wore jeans, a flannel shirt over a T-shirt. Only the exposed skin at her neck and ankles smarted and singed, but she stayed there until Star stopped moving.

Climbing off her, Orchid saw the damage. The girl was charred and blackened, but she couldn't be sure what was soot and what was burned skin. Star was beginning to tremble with shock, the pain too much to handle. Orchid knew she needed help, and fast.

"You'll be okay," she told Star, though it may have been a lie. "I'm going to find a phone and call for help."

Star's words were muffled, barely audible. Her throat was probably burned. "Don't let me die." Her eyes, white against her skin, bore into Orchid's, pleaded with her.

"You're not going to die." Orchid sounded confident to the point of annoyance. But this girl needed an ambulance fast, or she *would* die. Orchid replayed her route here, the quiet streets, the vacant homes, the convenience store several blocks away. Running for help would take too long. There was a phone inside Allan's house. Turning toward it, she saw that the flames were still contained in the kitchen. But not for long.

Even as she ran back onto the porch, kicked in a living room window, and watched the glass splinter, she knew this was risky, probably stupid. She knew she could succumb to the smoke before she found the phone, that she could collapse and die while Star expired on the back lawn. But she was already climbing through the broken pane, already finding herself in an outdated living room, the smoke hovering near the ceiling still. Orchid peered around the room at the ornate furniture, the silk flower arrangements, the linoleum flooring. Where was the fucking phone?

"Help!"

It was Carol. In Orchid's panic, she had forgotten about Allan's wife, the person Star had come to kill. The woman's voice was thin and distant, down a hallway, in a bedroom probably. But why wasn't she coming out? Even if she was drunk, she was conscious. Surely, she could stagger out of the room to save herself.

"Please!" The voice came again. "Someone help me!"

Life had hardened Orchid, but she was not without a soul. She could not walk away and let this woman burn to death. Not while she called out for help, begged and pleaded for her life. Orchid ran toward the sound of her voice.

Carol was in the last bedroom on the right. At first, Orchid thought the room was empty, but then she saw her, lying on the floor next to a single bed. Several feet away, pushed into a corner, was a wheel-chair. Allan's wife wasn't an alcoholic: She was a paraplegic. He had wanted his disabled wife to burn to death.

"Who are you?" the woman asked through a voice hoarse from screaming.

Orchid didn't answer. She searched the room for a phone and found it on the dresser, unplugged from the wall. Allan had thought of everything...except for the fact that Orchid still had a kernel of compassion in her. She hurried to the phone, plugged it in, and dialed 9-1-1. When she'd given them the address from the crumpled piece of paper in her pocket, she moved to the woman's bed.

Carol coughed weakly. Orchid lifted her body, so wizened, so shriveled, but still heavy in Orchid's arms, and placed her in the wheel-chair. Then she pushed her down the hall, into the living room now misty with smoke, and up to that broken window. With great effort, Orchid hoisted the older woman through the gap and climbed out after her. She half carried, half dragged Carol out into the yard, dropping her next to Star's blackened body, though the woman shrank away in horror.

Orchid took off her flannel shirt and draped it over her prone friend. "You're okay, Star. They're almost here."

"Don't leave me," the girl whispered, but she was drifting in and out of consciousness.

"I'll be right here," Orchid assured her as she watched Star fade away. Her chest still moved, slowly, imperceptibly. She was alive. But for how much longer?

Carol coughed out a word, "Why?"

"Your husband wants you dead," Orchid said. "*He* did this."

The sirens were drawing closer, and Orchid knew she couldn't stay, couldn't explain what she and Star were doing here, how it had all gone so wrong. So she ran. She left the two women in the grass, injured but alive, and she sprinted away. Star might die. Carol might never be the same, but Orchid had to go.

Her damaged lungs screamed, her throat was parched and sore, but she ran through the neighborhood, still eerily quiet despite the tragedy playing out nearby. She moved away from the emergency vehicles, back the way she came, until she reached the convenience store. At the bus stop, she collapsed onto the seat, prayed her ride would come quickly.

As her breathing slowed, as her rabbiting heartbeat calmed, Orchid looked at her hands. The tea towel had provided minimal protection as she'd batted at the flames engulfing Star, and they were badly burned. Though she felt nothing, her palms were smooth and red, her fingertips already blistering. Orchid looked at the skin stretched thin, smoothing the whorls and ridges unique to her. The skin would die, fall away, and with it, her identity.

The bus to take her home was approaching, and Orchid stood. She could get on it, go back to her single room, to hardened Lucy and damaged Tracey. She could return to a life of dealing, grifting, and scamming. Of helping a man burn his paraplegic wife to death. Or she could seize this opportunity. In the distance, the sirens had silenced. Help had arrived.

Orchid crossed the street and hailed a cab.

56 THE QUESTIONS

I HAVE NEVER BEEN in a police interrogation room before, but I pay little attention to my utilitarian surroundings. My head is too full of questions: What the hell happened to Shane Miller? Was it a car accident? A drug overdose? An underlying condition? He was young, he seemed healthy, though his lifestyle was probably quite sedentary. And why do the police want to talk to *me* about him? After Kash told me the horrifying news, he'd suggested I meet him at the Cambie Street police station.

"You might know something that could help the investigation," he'd said.

"What investigation? What happened?" But Kash insisted he tell me in person.

Now Kash and I sit at a laminate table facing Inspector Nadia Trigg. The detective is about my age, petite but solid in a blazer and jeans. She's said nothing to make me think I'm in trouble, but something in her manner makes me feel guilty. Obviously, I've done nothing wrong, so I agree to let her record our interview. Her hazel eyes watch me intently as she begins.

"How did you know Shane Miller?"

"I hired him to find out who's been trolling me and my book," I tell her. "He called me last night and said he had a name for me. I was supposed to meet him this morning."

The two cops exchange a look that I can't read. Kash asks, "Did you find out who's been harassing you?"

"No." Kash knows this, but I assume it's for the record. "Shane never showed up to the meeting. And he still has my laptop." I shift in my seat as I correct myself. "He *had* my laptop."

"Who knew you'd hired Shane Miller?" Trigg asks.

"A few people. I'd have to think…" I clear my throat. "Can you please tell me what happened to him?"

The inspector's voice is measured. "Shane Miller was killed in a house fire."

"Oh my god!" It's worse than anything I'd imagined. "That's awful. Poor Shane."

"The fire investigation concluded that it started as a grease fire in the kitchen," she continues. "But our arson team is looking into it now."

"You think it was arson?" I gasp. "You think someone set the fire deliberately?"

"Miller's body was found in his bedroom," Trigg continues. "It's possible he left a pan on the burner and went to bed, but that's more common with the elderly or substance abusers."

"Are they doing a tox screen on the body?" Kash asks her.

"Of course." She looks back at me. "But given Miller's line of work, we can't rule out homicide."

My mind spins and my breath comes in shallow, panicky gulps. The inspector thinks Shane Miller was *murdered*. I feel unmoored and out of my element. My harassment has been scary and unnerving, but this is on another level. But who knows what kind of entanglements a hacker could get into? Clearly this has nothing to do with me. Except…

"In my novel..." I start, but I trail off. The grease fire in *Burnt Orchid* is nothing more than a coincidence.

"In your novel *what*?" Kash presses.

I clear my throat. "A young woman sets a grease fire in the kitchen," I admit. "She pours water on it, and it burns the house down. It's a murder-for-hire scenario."

Trigg's face darkens. "Tell me more about the harassment you got over your book."

And so, I do. Kash knows most of it, except the word PEDOPHILE painted on my car, and the shampoo sprayed around my bathroom.

"Someone broke into your home, and you didn't call the police?" Inspector Trigg sounds incredulous.

"There was no forced entry, so I assumed it was someone I knew. Maybe even my daughter." My tone turns arch. "And I'd already gone to the police. The officer told me there was nothing they could do to help me. She was rude and dismissive."

Trigg is watching me, her hazel eyes cold. She thinks I'm an idiot. Or does she think I'm a suspect? Suddenly I feel vulnerable. I turn to Kash. "Do I need a lawyer?"

"You're not in any trouble, Cam." Kash's voice is reassuring, but I don't like the way his eyes dart to Trigg's. And I don't like the weight of her gaze on me.

"I'd like to leave." I'm suddenly desperate to get out of this stifling room, to get away from all these questions. I'm afraid that I'm somehow culpable in Shane Miller's death, and I'm terrified that Trigg thinks I may have done it. Kash nods and I stand up...but there's one more thing.

"Shane Miller had my laptop..."

"It was likely destroyed in the fire," Trigg says, making me feel shallow for asking when a man is dead. "If it wasn't, it will be evidence."

"Right."

Without another word, I hurry out of the station.

*　　*　　*

As soon as I let myself into the apartment, I can tell I'm not alone. With all that's going on, I should be unnerved, but the banging of drawers and the soft giggling can only mean one thing: Liza is home. Emotion wells up in my chest. After the tragic news of Shane Miller's death, her presence is a panacea, a much-needed comfort.

"Liza?" I call, moving into the kitchen.

My words are met with abrupt silence. Dropping my purse and keys on the counter, I walk toward her room, but my daughter emerges and meets me halfway there.

"I thought you weren't home," she says. "I just came to get some of my makeup and stuff."

"Can we talk?" I say gently. "Please?"

"I've got a friend here," she says, motioning toward her bedroom. "We're going to the beach."

"I'm sure Sage won't mind giving us a few minutes alone."

"I'm not ready, Mom." I see her chin wobble. "I'm still upset."

"I understand, Liza, I do. But you're my baby." Tears slip from my eyes. "I need you."

And Liza needs me, too, I know she does. Despite how I've humiliated her, this is a pivotal time in her life and her mother's love and support is requisite. She softens, just a little, and I can sense her receptiveness. I take a tentative step toward her, about to draw her into my arms, when Liza whirls around. Her friend has joined us. But it's not Sage.

It's Fiona Carmichael. In my home. With my daughter.

Liza turns back to me, her expression conflicted. "You know Fiona, right?"

Yes, I know Fiona.

"Hi, Ms. Lane." The girl's smile is saccharine. "Sorry to

interrupt, but everyone's going to be waiting for us at the beach, Liza."

"I have to go," my daughter says.

"No." It's my stern mother voice, my school counselor tone. The gravitas of my tenor belies the thudding of my heart, the racing of my pulse.

"Mom..." Liza begins, but I don't let her finish.

"We need to talk. You can meet your friends later."

I watch the girls exchange a look, fear fluttering in my belly. I've lost all authority in recent weeks. They could turn on me. Fiona could lead my daughter out of here and poison her against me. But Fiona reaches out, touches Liza's shoulder.

"I'll walk down to Jericho. Come as soon as you can, 'kay?"

Liza nods and looks at me. My shoulders sag with relief. I've won. This battle anyway.

But as Fiona heads to the door, she calls out, "Nice to see you, Ms. Lane."

And somehow, it sounds like a threat.

57 SECRETS

"LET'S SIT," I say when Liza and I are alone.

"Why?" she snaps, returning to hostile mode. "This isn't going to take long."

I don't push it; I need Liza to stay, to talk to me. So we remain standing where we are. "How long have you been hanging out with Fiona Carmichael?"

"A few months."

"Why didn't you tell me?" The words sound desperate and pleading.

"We thought it would be awkward since you were her guidance counselor."

We. Like they are a unit, a team. It sends a chill through me.

"Did Fiona ask you not to tell me?" I press.

"No, we decided together." But uncertainty flits across Liza's features, and I know the subterfuge was Fiona's idea.

"Is she going on this Australia trip with you?"

"Yeah, she is." My daughter folds her arms. "So?"

I feel panicky, but I steady my voice. "Do you know what Fiona did to Abby Lester?"

My daughter rolls her eyes. "She didn't do anything, Mom."

"She did. She uploaded a video to Snapchat of that poor girl overdosing. She's admitted it."

"Abby's not the innocent angel you think she is." Liza's face is twisted and cruel. "She took Molly and went after Hugo Duncan, even though she knew Fiona liked him."

"What are you saying?" My mouth tastes sick and sour. "You think Abby's to blame for what happened? You think it's her own fault?"

"Kinda."

My voice trembles. "Jesus Christ, Liza."

"Abby was a party monster that night! She *wanted* to get messed up. She was so desperate to fit in."

We stare at each other wordlessly. My mind is scrambling through every course I took on counseling teens, every parenting book I've ever read, but I'm at a loss. What do I say? Do I even know my daughter anymore? I've been so absorbed by the publishing process, so immersed in the trolling drama, that I took my eye off the ball. And now Liza has morphed into an entirely different person, someone cold and cruel and without compassion.

On rubbery legs, I move to the couch before I collapse. Thankfully, Liza doesn't bolt for the door, but follows me, sitting at the opposite end of the sofa. She breaks the silence.

"No one forced Abby to take those pills, Mom. She *wanted* to take them."

"Even if she did, those kids stood by and watched her take a deadly dose of MDMA. And when she went into medical distress, no one called for help. They stood by and they laughed."

"It wasn't like that." There's something so assured in her tone, so certain.

"How do you know?" My throat closes, but I force my voice to come. "Were you *there*?"

312

Her cheeks flush with guilt, and she swallows thickly. "For a bit."

My heart sinks into the pit of my stomach, but I press on. "Did you...did you see what happened to Abby?"

Liza's face crumples with emotion, and she looks like my little girl again. "I was staying over at Sage's that night. Wyatt picked us up later. We got there after Abby had already taken the pills. Fiona said that Abby took so many to get attention. Everyone said she was desperate to get in with the cool kids. And then Abby started twitching and freaking out."

"She could have died, Liza. Do you know how serious that was?"

"I wanted to wake up her parents, Mom. I really did." The tears spill over. "Wyatt almost did, but then...he...he couldn't."

"Why not?"

"We would have been attacked. We would have been called narcs and everyone would have turned against us."

She's probably right. But I want to believe that I raised a girl with a stronger moral compass, one who would put another child's safety above her personal reputation. Wyatt's words loop through my mind.

She's got a bunch of new friends. She's different around them.

"Who brought the drugs to the party?" I ask.

"I'm not sure."

"Tell me, Liza."

"I honestly don't know. I think it might have been Hugo. He sneaked in before we got there."

"Fiona's boyfriend," I state. "I know that girl, Liza. Fiona Carmichael is not a good person."

"She's nice to me," my daughter says sulkily. "And she's popular. Everyone wants to hang out with her. She has tons of followers on social."

"You're smart and curious and amazing. Since when is looking cool on social media so important to you?"

"You're one to talk," Liza snaps back.

"What do you mean?" But my face burns with guilt.

"You've spent the past year and a half on your phone, posting selfies in Miami like some influencer. It's gross, Mom. It's embarrassing."

"It's my responsibility to promote my book," I try, but it sounds feeble.

"You think the girls at school don't talk about *Burnt Orchid*?" she continues. "They've all read it, you know. And they all bug me about it. They ask me if I was molested by your boyfriend. They ask me if I went to juvie or if we were ever homeless. They send me gifs and memes of you screaming on that woman's lawn. I hate it!"

She's so angry, and I can't blame her. For the briefest moment I consider the possibility that my own daughter is behind my online and in-person harassment, but she would never do that to me. She wouldn't terrify me. She wouldn't send me child pornography. She is still my baby. Under her anger, she still loves me.

"I'm sorry," I say through my own tears. "I didn't know it would be like this."

"You never thought about me at all," Liza says, getting up off the couch. "You just wanted your dream of becoming a famous author. You didn't care what it did to the rest of us."

"Where are you going?" I get up, too, and trail her toward the door.

"Back to Dad's."

"You're not going to the beach?"

Her eyes, red with tears, harden. "Suddenly, I'm not in the mood for a party."

She storms out, slamming the door behind her.

Moving back to the living room, I sit on the sofa and drop my head into my hands. I've failed as a mother. I let my daughter down and she's made toxic friendships, terrible decisions. I'm filled with regret, self-loathing, and guilt. So much fucking guilt. I'm overwhelmed and I'm exhausted. But I know what I must do.

I reach for my phone and make the hardest call of my life.

58 COMING CLEAN

I HAVEN'T SEEN ABBY Lester's mother since my disastrous visit to their home, but now she sits across from me, hands on a pottery mug full of tea. We're at a homey coffee shop on neutral territory, away from the school, several blocks from the Lesters' charming duplex.

"Abby doesn't know I'm here," Rebecca says, sipping her rooibos. "She wouldn't want me talking to you."

"I understand." My eyes feel damp, so I blink rapidly. Rebecca notices.

"Don't take it personally," she says. "Abby has blacklisted a lot of people since the incident, including most of the students and staff at Maple Heights."

My voice is hoarse. "I think there's more to it than that."

"Like what?" Rebecca's brows knit together.

"There's something you need to know about that night." I swallow thickly, emotion and dread coating my throat. "My daughter, Liza, was at Abby's party."

"What?" Rebecca leans forward, hands pressing on the table. "Why didn't you tell us that before?"

"I just found out," I say quickly. "Liza told me everything last night."

Confusion and distress pinch Rebecca's features. "But we checked on the girls around midnight. Only the four of them were there."

"My daughter sneaked into the party later, with her friend Sage and a boy called Wyatt Tillman. He was Liza's boyfriend at the time. Another boy called Hugo Duncan was already there."

"So there *were* other kids at the party." Rebecca shakes her head. "We thought Fiona, Lily, and Mysha were just covering their own asses."

"We all did."

"I've never even heard of those kids. Why did they come to Abby's party?"

"From what I can gather, Abby had a crush on Hugo. But Fiona Carmichael liked him, too. Hugo plays on Wyatt's soccer team."

Rebecca sighs, leans back in her chair. "Will your daughter tell us what happened that night?"

"She says Abby had already taken the Molly when she got there."

"And you believe her?"

"I do," I say. "Liza was really upset. She said she wanted to wake you and Craig. Wyatt did, too. But they were scared of the other kids."

"So they put their popularity over my daughter's life?" Rebecca snorts. "That's nice."

She's angry. She has every right to be.

"I'm sorry. I'm so disappointed, in Liza and in myself." My voice wobbles. "I thought I'd raised her better than that. But Liza's been going through some stuff of her own."

Rebecca's eyes blaze. "What's she been going through that justifies standing by and watching my daughter overdose?"

"Nothing. Nothing justifies what those kids did to Abby."

"I really don't know what to say, Camryn. This is upsetting, to say the least."

"If I had known Liza was at the party, I never would have tried to counsel Abby. In fact, my attempts may have retraumatized her."

"For Christ's sake." Rebecca pushes a hand into her auburn curls. "What am I supposed to do with this information?"

"You'll need to tell her therapist," I say, and Rebecca nods slightly, but she's gone inward, consumed with worry and concern. I watch her in silence; there really are no words. And then something catches my eye outside the plate-glass window: a girl, tall, pale, and furtive. Her right arm hangs at her side, wrapped in white bandages from wrist to elbow. Within a blink, she is gone, but not before I saw her. She looked like Abby Lester.

"Does Abby have a cast on her arm?" I ask Rebecca.

"It's a bandage."

"What happened?"

Rebecca comes to, picks up her tea. "She burned it."

A frisson runs up my spine, tickling my scalp. "How?"

"She went to a party at the beach. They had a bonfire and she stumbled. Her shirt caught fire and her arm was quite badly burned."

"Abby went to a party at the beach?" I confirm. "I thought she wasn't socializing?"

"We were surprised, too. But she's met some new kids. When she asked to go out that night, we were thrilled."

"What night was that?"

"A couple of nights ago," Rebecca says, lips on her cup. "Why do you ask?"

"Just...wondering."

"It was Monday." She sets the tea down. "I remember because it seemed a weird night for a party, but school's not in regular session."

Monday, two nights ago, was when Shane Miller's suite caught fire. The night he died. My pulse is thudding in my throat, the hairs on my arms prickling with electricity. My body knows something isn't right, even as my brain struggles to put this together. Abby Lester's arm is burned. It has to be a coincidence. Abby could not be responsible for the fire at Shane Miller's basement apartment. Unless...

"How did you know about Abby's bandage?" Rebecca asks. "When did you see her?"

"I...I think I just saw her outside the window," I stammer.

"Oh no." Rebecca collects her purse from the back of her chair. "Abby must have overheard our phone call and followed me here. I should go." She stands abruptly, her legs banging against the table. Her mug of tea tips over, the remains of the milky liquid pooling on the surface, cascading over the edge.

"Shit," she mutters. "I'll get a towel."

As she hurries to the counter, I seize my chance.

Grabbing my purse, I hustle outside.

59 ABBY

No ONE IS lurking around the perimeter of the café and for a moment, I wonder if I imagined Abby's presence. But how could I conjure up an injury I knew nothing about? It had to be Abby peering in the window at her mother and me. And I have to talk to her.

I hurry down the side of the building and turn into the back alley. At the end, a delivery truck backs up to a grocery store, beeping its warning. Otherwise, the passage appears deserted. But I move forward on stealthy feet. There are a dozen places to hide: between parked cars, in loading bays, or behind dumpsters. As I pass behind a framing store, I sense more than hear her presence. I move closer and spot her. Abby Lester is crouched between an SUV and a small sedan. She is hiding from me.

It's possible, even likely, that Abby will scream and run away. She loathes me, and now I know it's justified. But I approach, slowly and carefully, like she's a skittish foal, a beaten dog, a cornered animal.

"Abby," I say gently. "Can we talk?"

Slowly she rises, her lithe form unfurling. "I have nothing to say to you."

"I just want to tell you that I'm sorry."

"Sorry for what?" she snaps. "Pretending to care about me?"

"I *do* care about you."

"No, you don't," she says bitterly. "You were supposed to help me, but you just wanted to protect your daughter."

"I didn't know Liza was at your party." My voice is pleading. "I just found out."

"She wasn't just *at* my party." Abby's pitch and volume rise. She takes a step toward me. "Liza gave me those pills. She told me they were a low dosage. That I could take five or six of them and just get a buzz."

I choke on a gasp, or maybe it's a sob. Did Liza lie to me? I feel sick to my stomach, but I need more clarity. "Liza said she wasn't there when you took the drugs. She said she came later with Wyatt and Sage."

"I don't know who came when," Abby snaps. "I just know that your daughter poisoned me."

The words are a gut punch, and I feel sick to my stomach. But something still isn't sitting right with me. Abby had told her parents, the police, and the school that she didn't remember what happened that night. Blacking out from drug use is not uncommon; neither is blocking out a traumatic event. So did Abby remember after all? Had she been lying about that?

I clear my throat. "So you remember Liza giving you the pills?"

"Yeah, of course I do." But she doesn't. It's obvious in the way she shakes her head slightly, the way her eyes flicker around the alleyway. I have enough experience to know when a teenager is lying.

"Are you sure?" I ask. "Or did someone tell you what happened?"

"I remember," she mutters. "But Fiona filled in the blanks. She's the only one who checks in with me."

A picture begins to form in my head. Fiona Carmichael threw Liza under the bus to protect herself. She's been telling Abby that Liza is to blame while simultaneously pretending to be Liza's friend to ensure she doesn't come forward. The girl is Machiavellian.

"I think Fiona is lying to you," I say gently. "To protect herself."

"No, she's not. *You're* lying to protect Liza."

"I think Hugo brought the drugs. And Fiona convinced you to take so many because she was mad that you liked him. And maybe he liked you, too. Fiona couldn't handle that."

I can see the doubt creeping in, but Abby pushes it away. "Fuck you. That's just what Liza told you."

She hates my daughter. And she hates me.

"Did you send me the emails about my book?"

"What if I did? I have a right to an opinion."

It's as good as an admission. "Of course you do." I recall Abby excelling in her programming classes, getting a scholarship to the best computer science program in the country. She had the technical skills to hack me. And the insider knowledge—supplied by Fiona, who has befriended my daughter—to hurt me and destroy my relationships. This broken girl was twisted and manipulated into hating Liza, into hating me, and she lashed out online while keeping her identity private.

I have to ask, "What happened to your arm?"

"I burned it. At a party."

"Where was the party?"

She pushes past me, moves down the alley. "I don't want to talk to you anymore."

I follow her. "Did you...did you set fire to Shane Miller's kitchen?"

Her shoulders tense, but she doesn't stop. She quickens her pace. I have no choice but to call out.

"He's dead, Abby!"

She stops and whirls around to face me. "No," she says, her eyes full of tears, and terror. "He's not dead."

"He is," I say, closing the distance between us. "Shane Miller died in the house fire."

"Why didn't he wake up?" she screams, like it's my fault. "Why didn't he get out?"

"I don't know," I say. "Maybe he was high or drunk. Or maybe he took a sleeping pill."

"I...I only wanted to destroy your laptop," she says through sobs. "So Shane couldn't prove that it was me."

I am trained for this. I nod, emanate understanding, let her fill the silence. And she does.

"I followed you to your meeting then followed him home. I was going to steal the laptop, but he kept it with him, and I had to go home. So I went back after the weekend, and I saw it through his kitchen window. When he went to bed, I got inside. I thought I'd do what Star did in your book. I put the laptop next to the stove and I lit a pan on fire. But it got out of control. I...I burned my arm. I had to run away." Her face is pale and haunted. "He was supposed to wake up."

"I know," I say gently. "It was an accident. And you've been through a lot, Abby. The police will understand that."

"You can't call the police on me! *You* made me do this! You and Liza! What happened to me is all your fault!"

She nearly collapses then, and I rush forward, catch her in my arms before she hits the pavement. Abby's having a panic attack, an emotional breakdown. She's been through so much that her nervous system is shutting down, overwhelmed by the flood of emotions. How can I call the cops on her when she's a victim in this whole mess, too?

And then I see Rebecca, moving slowly up behind her daughter. She is close, within earshot. She's heard the whole encounter. I notice the phone in her hand, the screen alight. Tears stream down Rebecca's face, but her voice is steady and strong when she speaks.

"I need the police, please."

BURNT ORCHID

1999

When Orchid first arrived in Chicago, she stayed at a shelter. For the first two weeks, her morning routine was the same. She walked to a church down the block that handed out day-old pastries donated by a bakery that couldn't serve them to paying customers. And then she went to the newsstand around the corner and bought the *LA Times*. She walked two blocks south to a small park, where she sat at a picnic table, spread out her paper, and ate her stale breakfast. She looked like any other person enjoying their morning. No one could tell what Orchid was searching for in that paper.

She needed to know if Star was dead. And if she'd survived, had she been arrested for attempting to murder Carol? When Orchid had told the disabled woman that her husband wanted her killed, had it sunk in? Carol was likely in shock, perhaps unable to process the fact that her mild-mannered husband wanted her to burn to death in her bed. But if Carol had understood, had told the police, then Star would pay, too. If she was alive.

But Orchid never found any news about the fire. Nor were there any articles on the arrest of a badly burned woman, or a shady pharmacist. Carol had either blocked out the information or chosen to stay silent, to protect the man who would have killed her in the cruelest way. And people like Star weren't worth the ink. No one cared if she lived or died. No one but Orchid.

For weeks Orchid fretted about the girls she'd left behind. But there was no way to contact them: no phone in the single-room apartment, and a letter might have given away her location. Their days in the apartment were likely numbered. Without Orchid, they wouldn't be able to make rent; they'd end up back on the sidewalk. She'd abandoned them to their sure demise. But even if she'd stayed, the girls were slipping away. Lucy and Tracey were both using. And Star, if she'd survived, if she wasn't in constant pain or badly disfigured, was a loose cannon, incapable of making smart life choices. Eventually, Orchid stopped buying the newspaper.

She got a job at a seedy bar owned by a woman with a deeply creased face, a bad back, and a soft heart. She let Orchid sleep in a storage room until she saved up enough for a deposit on a small apartment. Orchid worked the bar at night, and during the day she went back to the shelter. She volunteered at their drop-in center, serving meals, washing dishes, and listening. Because she knew what drove people to the streets. And she knew what it took to get off them.

A pastor ran the center, a Mexican American man with an easy smile and the patience of Job. He made Orchid feel valued and appreciated. She assumed it was just his Christian duty, but one day he made a suggestion.

"Have you considered getting a degree in social work?"

No, she hadn't. She'd gotten her GED in juvenile detention, but further education had never seemed like an option.

"We have some funding," he said. "We could sponsor you. You could work here while you studied part-time."

"Why would you do that for me?"

"You have a gift. You connect with these people. They open up to you more than they do anyone."

Life on the streets had taught Orchid to seize opportunities when they presented themselves. So she accepted the pastor's offer and went to college. It was exhausting but fulfilling. And sometimes it was even fun. Orchid began to let her guard down. She made social connections that could even be called friendships. The warm environment smoothed away her sharp edges, blunted her feelings of suspicion and mistrust. Orchid could almost pass for a normal co-ed.

One day, when Orchid was in the last year of her degree, a young man in a suit came into the shelter. He was rushed and frazzled, but his good looks and charisma shone through his rumpled exterior. "Who's that?" Orchid whispered to her colleague Nell.

"Legal aid," Nell said. "Apparently, he's a rich kid with a heart of gold. Wants to change the world and all that."

"Impressive."

"And adorable, don't you think?" Nell winked at her. "Let me introduce you."

They waited until the handsome man had finished chatting to a client, then they approached. "There's someone I'd like you to meet," Nell said to him, proffering Orchid like a prize.

"I'm Michael Carder," he said, taking her hand. She loved the way his hair fell across his forehead, the lines around his mouth. "And you are?"

"I'm Orchid Chambers." Their eyes connected then, and Orchid saw warmth, comfort, and promise. In a breath, she saw a future with this man, one she had never dared dream of: love, family, purpose . . . For the second time in her life, Orchid reinvented herself and became a new person.

But the people she'd abandoned on the streets had not forgotten her. And they would not stay silent. As Michael's political profile grew, as Orchid stood demurely by his side as First Lady of Chicago, the ghosts of her past—Lucy, Mal, even Star—would return. And once again, Orchid would be driven to desperate lengths to survive.

60 THE AFTERMATH

FIONA CARMICHAEL'S HOUSE of cards came tumbling down after that. A man was dead. A seventeen-year-old girl had been charged with criminally negligent homicide. It had all gone too far. And the kids involved were about to graduate, to leave home in most cases. Protecting a high school queen bee didn't seem that important anymore. Liza, Sage, and Wyatt told the cops everything they knew. But as my daughter had claimed, they'd arrived late. By the time they'd sneaked in through the Lesters' basement door, the devastation was already in progress.

But Lily Mathers had been there for all of it. She'd watched Fiona let Hugo in with his little bag of pills, stood by as Fiona cajoled a naive Abby into taking more and more. Lily had witnessed the overdose, saw Fiona urge the sick girl out of her clothes and stand by while Hugo laughingly recorded her. She was there when Fiona gleefully uploaded the video to Snapchat. Lily had wanted to come forward straightaway, but it would have been social suicide. Fiona could and *would* ruin her friend's senior year. So Lily had submitted the video to the school portal, hoping that the administration would find out who was behind it. But we never did.

Lily told the police everything that happened that night, and Mysha Naz backed her up. But Fiona and Hugo stuck to their story, professing ignorance over who brought the drugs and blaming Abby for taking more pills than she could handle. Sadly, they had plausible deniability. There was no physical evidence against them. There were no recordings of Hugo bringing the pills, or Fiona pushing them on Abby. It was their word against Lily's and Mysha's.

The police weren't interested in a spat between teenagers. They were too focused on solving Shane Miller's death. And these kids were no longer students, so the school had no power to mete out punishment. But what Fiona and Hugo did that night was monstrous, unforgivable, and their peer group would not let them get away with it. Their social isolation was complete and total. Even Fiona's most devoted sycophants turned against her, while all the kids she'd been unkind to delighted in her downfall. Hugo and Fiona became pariahs. They were harassed mercilessly online. I almost felt sorry for them . . . but not quite.

Fiona's parents shut down her social media accounts and took away her devices. They booked her into a six-month wilderness camp meant to build character (and hopefully perform exorcisms). Last I heard, Hugo had decided to join the military.

But before the girl left, I was granted a sit-down with her. I needed to know Fiona's role in the attacks on me, for my own peace of mind. Nancy agreed to reach out to the Carmichaels, and somewhat surprisingly, they allowed their daughter to talk with me. I'd expected them to accompany her to the school, and I'd booked a conference room that would accommodate us all. But Fiona showed up alone. Apparently, her parents felt comfortable letting us talk one-on-one due to our long-standing relationship. Or maybe they just couldn't bear to hear any more of her evil deeds.

The girl who sat across from me at the conference table was not the pretty, confident teen who had ruled Maple Heights. Fiona wore no makeup, and her blond hair was flat and unwashed. A smattering of pimples dotted her jawline, from stress likely. She was thinner, too, and those eyes—wide, innocent, with a hint of mischief—were dull and dead. It should have made me happy, but all I saw was another child destroyed.

"Abby did all the online stuff to you," she told me as soon as I closed the door. "She hated Liza, and she thought the best way to get to her was through you. That way, she wouldn't risk getting Liza's private school crew after her."

I didn't bother to point out that Abby only hated Liza because of Fiona's lies and manipulation. I wouldn't scold. I needed information.

"Abby's super tech-savvy," Fiona continued. "She's practically a hacker. And she knows a lot about books and all that stuff."

"How did Abby get the photos of Megan Prince to set up the fake accounts?" I asked. "She didn't know Megan. And Megan's account was private."

"I sent her those from Hugo's phone." Fiona looked down at her hands in her lap so I couldn't see her expression. "I never thought you'd be able to connect them back to us. Megan doesn't even live in this country."

Lingering shame reddened my cheeks at the memory of my trip south, but I pressed on. "You were spending time with Liza. Pretending to be her friend. Why?"

She looked up then, and I saw a glimmer of the cruel girl she had been. "So I could keep track of you and feed info to Abby."

Info like my friendship with Martha and Felix. Like the names of my boyfriend and my ex-husband.

"You were supposed to be my counselor, Ms. Lane. But you were being such a bitch to me."

Because I knew you were lying about what happened at Abby's party. But I clenched my jaw to silence my words. "Did you squirt the shampoo all over my bathroom?"

"It was a prank," she snapped. "Liza brought me home with her when you were out. She was packing some stuff, so I went into your bathroom." Her eyes met mine, fearless, even amused. "Hugo and I sent you the pizzas. And the flowers. He sneaked into your garage and tagged your car. Got a friend to throw that burrito at you. And I called you a couple times." She smiled that innocent smile. "We're just kids. It was just fun."

The girl was a psychopath.

"What about that nasty woman in the audience in Miami?" I asked.

Fiona looked bemused for a moment and then she shrugged. "I don't know. I guess some people hated your book for real."

A muscle in my temple throbbed, but I pressed on. "Why was Hugo watching my building?"

"When you showed up at his aunt's place, he raced home to tell me about it. I was hanging out with Liza, so he came to get me. I ran down the fire stairs when you turned up. When Hugo saw you staring at him, he took off."

It all made sense, but I had another question. "Was Hugo creeping around outside Liza's dad's house, too?"

"That was probably Wyatt." Fiona smiled. "He hated that Liza was hanging out with me. He was always trying to tell her that I was just using her, but she was too stupid to listen."

I remember the string of Wyatt's texts to Liza, asking where she was. He had been looking out for my daughter all along, and I'd suspected him. But I'd been right about Fiona. She was still cruel and horrible under the façade of contrition. My face was hot, and my voice trembled with anger.

"That's all I need to know. You can go."

Fiona stood, took a few steps toward the door, and then turned back. "Will you be writing another book soon, Ms. Lane?" Her eyes danced with humor.

"Have fun at your wilderness camp," I snapped. "Hopefully they can turn you into a human being."

Her mouth twitched, and I thought she was going to tell me to go fuck myself or worse, but she didn't. Her features rearranged into their somber affect. And then she shuffled out of the room, returning to her façade of remorse.

I believed Fiona that Abby had done the worst of it: hacked into my email, fomented online hatred, and doxed me. She even found the disgusting image of that exploited little girl to send to me. Her actions damaged my personal life and destroyed my writing career, but I couldn't be angry at a girl so abused and manipulated. Unlike Fiona, Abby had been punished enough.

Abigail June Lester consented to a Not Criminally Responsible on Account of a Mental Disorder verdict in Shane Miller's death. A court-ordered psychiatrist had diagnosed her with severe PTSD, and, thanks to her November birthday, she was still a child in the eyes of the court. But a man had died due to her actions, and Abby was given a brief custodial sentence at a forensic psychiatric facility. I knew from my research on *Burnt Orchid* that juvenile incarceration does not often lead to positive outcomes, but Abby will receive various therapies there. And I hope her stay will be brief enough not to have long-lasting effects.

Rebecca and Craig Lester moved away. No one knows where they went, which was likely their intention. When Abby is released, they can heal, start over without judgment. I hope one day, Abby Lester will get back the life she once had, the life she deserves. I hope the same for Liza. I hope the same for me.

My relationships have all been damaged: Jody and Martha didn't believe or trust me. Navid shared confidences with Rhea. Tori has finally shown me her true feelings. But none are beyond repair except one. Theo and I were already over, but we make it official over a beer and a final conversation.

"I'm sorry you had to go through all that mess with me," I tell him, toying with my coaster. "But I think it showed us that we're not meant to be together."

"Yeah, I think I need someone a little less…complicated," he agrees, but I hear the sadness in his voice. "I know I acted like a controlling jerk sometimes, but I loved you, Cam."

"Me too." I smile, a wistful lump in my throat. "But Liza needs all of me right now."

We say our goodbyes then, our keep in touches, let's stay friends, but we won't. We're too different. We want different things.

For now, all I want is to help my daughter deal with all she's been through. She feels incredibly guilty. About what happened to Abby and Shane Miller. And about what happened to me.

"It was never about your book, Mom," she sobbed in my arms. "It was about what I did. And now your career is ruined."

"It's okay, Liza." I shushed her. "I still have my job as a counselor. I'll be fine."

"But you loved writing. It was your dream."

I held her at arm's length, stared into her tear-filled eyes. "All I care about is that you're okay."

It's the truth. After everything that's happened—the hate, the abuse, the tragedy—my career aspirations feel inconsequential. Being a published author feels too vulnerable, too exposed. And I can't afford to drift away to a made-up world now. I need to stay present, to focus on healing Liza and our relationship.

And on healing myself.

EPILOGUE

MY NEW OFFICE is marginally more spacious than my last one, so the girl seated in my guest chair has some legroom. Her eyes, rimmed with long false lashes, roam over the new art I purchased to brighten the eggshell walls. The vivid abstract paintings are appealing, but Mikayla Shaw is not appreciating them. She's overtly ignoring me.

I wait patiently, surveying the thirteen-year-old who has been sent to talk with me. With her contoured makeup, glossy lips, and revealing top, she's working hard to look older than she is. But there's a childlike fullness to her face, and I sense the tension beneath her blasé façade. Mikayla is in big trouble, and she knows it.

Woodland High School is on the outskirts of the city, in a rapidly gentrifying neighborhood. (My daily commute has gone from twelve minutes to forty, but I often take the train so I can read.) The students here come from diverse backgrounds—socioeconomically and culturally. I've only been working here for about three weeks, but I've found most of the kids to be bright, open, and respectful. Still, every school has its troubled students, the ones who are damaged, angry, and rebellious. Mikayla Shaw is one of them.

"Do you want to tell me why you wrote the list?" I ask, keeping my voice gentle.

Mikayla meets my gaze, smirks. "No thanks."

"It's okay. I know why you did it."

She cocks an eyebrow at me, curious. "You do?"

"You ranked all the girls in your grade according to their looks to make yourself feel powerful."

"No," Mikayla mumbles, shifting in her seat.

"Putting other kids down made you feel better about yourself and your own insecurities."

"I don't have insecurities," she snaps.

"You wouldn't be human if you didn't, Mikayla."

"It wasn't about that," she says. "I just did it for fun."

I lean back in my chair. "Can you imagine if *your* name was on the bottom of that list?"

She snorts. "It wouldn't be."

She's right. Mikayla is physically very attractive, but I believe her cruelty is compensating for low self-esteem. Could she have learning difficulties? Are there tensions at home? Something is affecting this girl. I make a mental note to talk to her teachers and the vice principal about my concerns.

"Try to imagine it, though," I urge. "It would hurt. A lot." Thankfully, Mikayla had written a physical list on a piece of paper. It was intercepted by faculty before it was photographed and circulated online. If we've done our job right, the girls at the bottom will never know of its existence.

I see a shadow pass across Mikayla's features; it's guilt. She is capable of empathy. There is hope.

I continue. "There are other ways to have fun and feel good about yourself without putting other people down. The school has a lot of clubs," I suggest. "Or you could play on a sports team."

Mikayla rolls her eyes, armor slipping back into place. "Can I go?"

I've lost her, for now. But I'm not going to give up on her. I have five years to help Mikayla find her kindness and decency before she morphs into the next Fiona Carmichael. There won't be another victim like Abby Lester, not if I can help it.

"Okay," I acquiesce. "But I'm here to talk, Mikayla. Anytime."

"Got it," she grumbles, and bolts for the door.

Alone in my new office, I glance at the time on my computer screen. I have a meeting with vice principal Bruce Hooper in ten minutes, but I have time to make a quick call. Liza was asleep when I left for work this morning. She's on the night shift at the veggie burger shop, so she doesn't get up until ten-ish. I know today will be a tough one for her. This is the date she was supposed to leave for Australia.

The trip has been postponed indefinitely, her traveling companions scattering in the wake of their recent nightmare. Only Wyatt went ahead on a solo journey, and I'm glad for him. He was always a good kid, and I was wrong to suspect him. Liza has decided to stay home, to work, to save some money. She hopes to go to college next year, but her confidence is rattled. She's lost faith in her ability to judge people; she's wary of being manipulated again. She needs time.

"Hey, Mom." Her voice is bright, normal.

"I just wanted to check in," I say. "How are you?"

"I'm fine." She sighs then. "Sage texted to remind me of the date. We should be on a plane right now."

"I know. I wish things were different."

"Yeah." Her voice is wistful, but then it brightens. "I had an idea," Liza says, and I hear the sink running. She's likely cleaning up her breakfast dishes. "I'd like to go visit Auntie Kate in France. I haven't been since I was little. And I've saved up quite a bit of money over the summer."

"That's a great idea," I tell her, and my heart swells. Other than work, Liza has barely left the house for the past two months, preferring to stay curled up on the sofa watching TV with me. Now she's up for an adventure—albeit within the safety net of family. It's a big step forward. "Your aunt and uncle and cousins will be so excited."

"I'm excited, too." The sink turns off. "I've got to go get ready for work."

"I've got my watercolor class tonight with Martha. But let me know if you need a ride home."

"Okay. Love you."

It's a breezy, casual sign-off, but my eyes mist. "I love you too, Liza."

Grabbing a notebook and a file, I hurry toward Hooper's office. My shoes squelch on the floor, still shiny from its summer buff and polish. This is a new school to me, but I already feel at home here. There's a familiarity baked into the walls of these institutions; they all have the same hopeful energy. As I pass the library, the science lab, and then the trophy cases, there's a lightness in my step. I feel happy. Liza is moving forward. And so am I.

I've rediscovered the meaning in this job, remembered why I got into counseling in the first place. Most kids are good and decent at heart, but they can be easily led astray by various pressures. It's not an easy time to grow up. Maybe it never has been. I can make a difference. At least I can try.

But deep in my soul, I know I am still a writer. When Liza is older, healed, busy with her own life, I will try again. I'll use a pseudonym this time, stay offline like some nineties throwback. It may be hard to find a publisher willing to work with such a hands-off promotional approach, but I have a compelling story to tell. Names will be changed to protect the innocent—and the guilty—but one day, I will write another novel.

I think I'll call it *The Haters*.

THE END

ACKNOWLEDGMENTS

There are so many people to thank for bringing a book to life. I'd like to start with my wise and insightful editor, Karen Kosztolnyik, and the smart, passionate team at Grand Central, including: Lauren Bello, Theresa DeLucci, Staci Burt, Alli Rosenthal, Laura Jorstad, Carolyn Kurek, and Albert Tang. Huge thanks to Donna Nopper, Melanie Freedman, and the amazing team at Hachette Canada. And much gratitude to Anthea Baramais, Fleur Hamilton, and the fantastic team at Simon & Schuster Australia.

I am always grateful to my brilliant agent and friend, Joe Veltre, and his fabulous, enthusiastic assistant Hayley Nusbaum. I'm very lucky to be repped by Gersh.

Thank you to my early readers: Eileen Cook, Jo Rush, Daniel Kalla, and Roz Nay. I'm grateful for your time, insights, and friendship. Thank you to Ashley Kalagian Blunt for recommending I read *Troll Hunting* by Ginger Gorman. And to Toni Jones for information on Stymie, the anonymous online reporting tool used in Australian schools.

This business can be tough, and I don't think I could do it without the friendship and support of the crime writing community. To name but a few: Heather Gudenkauf, May Cobb, Clémence Michallon, Shari Lapena, Jennifer Hillier, Chevy Stevens, John

Marrs, Liz Nugent, Samantha Bailey, Hannah Mary McKinnon, Ashley Audrain, Marissa Stapley, Kaira Rouda, Lisa Barr, Mary Kubica, Amber Cowie, Sonya Lalli, Elaine Murphy, Wendy Walker, Samantha Downing, Christina McDonald, Laurie Elizabeth Flynn, Catherine McKenzie, Kimberly Bell... I know there are more and I'm grateful for all of you.

Thanks to all the incredible Bookstagrammers, Facebook groups, bloggers, and BookTokers who spread the word about the books they read. (An extra thank you to the ones who have come out to my live events and may have had pizza and wine with me!) Conversation about books, positive or negative, is always a good thing. Thank you to all the librarians and booksellers who bring books and readers together.

And, always, thank you to my husband, John... my brainstorming partner and my first (and least critical) reader.

A very special thanks to the "Anti-Haters" club. I really appreciate your support!

Kim Arsenault

Cydni Arterbury

Cheryl Baudin

Melanie Bronstein

Kelly Cano

Candice Cantin

Morgan Capodilupo

Melissa Carder

Yasmine A. Castañeda

Erin Catto

Allie Coffey

Frank DiLuzio

Angela Douglas

Angelica Engelken

Christina Faris (@books_by_the_bottle)

ACKNOWLEDGMENTS

Hailey "@fishgirllovesbooks" Fish
Joe Freeburn
Ceylan Goktalay
Susan Goldie
Christiana Gunn
Dustin Harris
Shemri Harris
Jessica Heatherly
Kristin Houle
Tosha Illingworth
Stephanie Jackman
Amanda Jourdan
Jen Jumba
Shannon Jump
Brittany Knapp
Kelly Kovalcik
Fiona Lamplugh
Amanda Latchford
Brandy Legros
Heather LiteratureChick
Nicole Mahar
Deseree Martinez
Sharon May
Kathy McKenzie
Tammy Moyer
Mindy Myint
DeeAnn Myres-Magboul
Liana Nermioff
John & Tisa Mae Nunez
Dana Orgnero
Stephanie Owens
Megan M. Pacheco

ACKNOWLEDGMENTS

Jennifer Quant
Gillian Rajsic
Becky Roy
Tanya Roy
Lauren Self
Carrie Shields
Stephanie Shockey
Kim Shwaluke
Anjelica Smith
Norma TheLiteraryLeprechaun
Rachel Thrush
Makenna Toffoli
Hanna Wren
Kayla Jo Wright
Pauline Yeo
Pamela Zinser

ABOUT THE AUTHOR

Robyn Harding is the bestselling author of *The Drowning Woman*, *The Perfect Family*, *The Swap*, *The Arrangement*, *Her Pretty Face*, and *The Party*. She has also written and executive produced an independent film. She lives in Vancouver, British Columbia, with her family and two cute but deadly rescue chihuahuas.

RobynHarding.com
Instagram @rhardingwriter
Facebook @AuthorRobynHarding